The NPR Curious Listener's Guide to

Popular Standards

MAX MORATH

A Grand Central Press Book
A Perigee Book

A Perigee Book
Published by The Berkley Publishing Group
A division of Penguin Putnam Inc.
375 Hudson Street
New York, New York 10014

PRODUCED BY GRAND CENTRAL PRESS
Paul Fargis, Director
Judy Pray, Executive Editor
Nick Viorst, Series Editor

NATIONAL PUBLIC RADIO
Murray Horwitz, Vice-President, Cultural Programming
Andy Trudeau, Executive Producer, Cultural Programming
Barbara A. Vierow, Project Manager, Business Development
Kate Elliott, Project Manager, Business Development

First edition: February 2002
Published simultaneously in Canada.

Visit our website at www.penguinputnam.com

Library of Congress Cataloging-in-Publication Data

Morath, Max.
The NPR curious listener's guide to popular standards / Max Morath.
        p.   cm.
Includes discography, bibliographical references, list of Web sites, and index.
ISBN 0–399–52744–3
1. Popular Music—United States—History and criticism.
I. National Public Radio (U.S.)   II. Title.

ML3477.M67   2002
781.64'0973—dc21
2001036848

Printed in the United States of America

10   9   8   7   6   5   4   3   2   1

Contents

Acknowledgments

I am deeply indebted to every author of every book listed in our "Resources for Curious Listeners," and to the diligent folks who construct and maintain the Websites on American music that are cited in that chapter. Of the authors, I stand quite literally in awe of the task Robert Lissauer set for himself in producing his monumental *Encyclopedia of Popular Music in America*; my copy is now affectionately dog-eared, highlighted, and coffee-stained in tribute. *American Popular Song*, the James T. Maher/Alec Wilder classic has also been close at hand. Robert Kimball's many works on the Popular Standards and their creators have been invaluable, especially the recent *Reading Lyrics* (with Robert Gottlieb). Bob Kimball has my additional gratitude for his personal support and advice. Thanks also to Mike Montgomery, Joan Morris, Michael Feinstein, Edward A. Berlin, Gene Jones, Murray Horwitz of NPR, Ellen Donaldson, Charles Sussman of Donaldson Publishing, Donald Kahn and Rosemarie Gawelko of Warner Bros. Publications.

My editor at Grand Central Press, Nick Viorst, deserves more than casual thanks for his professionalism and stamina. Nick plays Good Cop and Bad Cop with equal skill and experience, and has kept me from serious literary crimes such as woolgathering, outline evasion, and excessive adjective. Thanks are also due Judy Pray and Paul Fargis at Grand Central.

Best until last—my wife, Diane Fay Skomars. She occasionally read proof and checked grammar as spouses are expected to do, but was far more helpful (and candid) about content and clarity. I am happy to report, however, that whenever she found it necessary to say "I don't understand these two pages at all," she followed up with an offer of a cold beer or a back rub—sometimes both—a sure sign of a happy marriage and an underused spell checker. Thanks, Dolly.

Foreword

by Michael Feinstein

D o you ever listen to the songs that people hum or whistle in the street? I do. Psychologists say that a song appearing in our brain at any given moment is a clue about what is really going on in the subconscious mind. You can learn a great deal about people that way. For example, I'd avoid someone who sings "You Always Hurt The One You Love" and embrace the purveyor of "Love Is Here To Stay" instead. And that is the beauty of the American Popular Standard; a song exists for every conceivable emotion and mood, every nuance of possible behavior.

The greatest creators of this extraordinary body of work always searched for a way to newly express oft-expressed emotions, and my how they succeeded! To cite a few examples by some of my favorite writers: Jerome Kern crafted amazingly complex melodies that send the heart soaring with songs like "Long Ago And Far Away," "The Song Is You," "The Way You Look Tonight," and "Till The Clouds Roll By." George

Gershwin distilled the vitality and rhythmic swagger of 1920's New York with "Fascinating Rhythm," " 'Swonderful," and "I'll Build A Stairway To Paradise." As Gershwin matured in the thirties with "Of Thee I Sing" and "They Can't Take That Away From Me," other Depression-era writers made their contributions—like the unjustly neglected Harry Warren, who gave us "I Only Have Eyes For You," "Lullaby of Broadway," and "Remember Me." There are dozens of other great composers that could match Jerry, George, and Harry every step of the way; these just happen to be the melodists who spring to mind at this moment. It is no cliché to say that they were all good, because by today's standards, even the worst of them still hold up fine.

The wordsmiths who lyricized these extraordinary melodies were endlessly clever and poignant: Ira Gershwin with his playful lopping off of syllables; Oscar Hammerstein soaring to new heights with his proverbial "larks;" Dorothy Fields purveying the sarcastic perceptions of a sassy dame; Johnny Mercer, the chameleon who was at home as much with Harold Arlen and "Blues In The Night" as he was with Henry Mancini and "Moon River;" E. Y. Harburg with the cutting social commentary of "When The Idle Poor Become The Idle Rich" and the yearning of "Over the Rainbow." Then you get to the double geniuses like Irving Berlin, Frank Loesser, and Cole Porter, who supplied both music and lyrics with deceptive ease.

But what good is a song unless it is sung? I have a massive collection of vintage sheet music featuring photos of countless great and not-so-great performers who brought these works to life. They were the messengers without whom the songs would have laid silent. The lineage runs from Al Jolson to Louis Armstrong to Bing Crosby to Nat "King" Cole to Frank Sinatra to Bobby Darin to Harry Connick, Jr. Female vocalists more than held their own, from Sophie Tucker to Ruth Etting to Ethel Waters to Billie Holiday to Doris Day to Rosemary Clooney to Diana Krall—an oral tradition in the literal sense of the word. Many of the great songs have become inseparably linked with specific performers, thus ensuring their survival. It is not possible to think of "Over the Rainbow" without thinking of Judy Garland or "Puttin' on the Ritz" without Fred Astaire.

It all becomes overwhelming when you try to figure out where to start and what to listen to. Going to your local CD (or record) store is sure to promise a headache and more confusion. So, along comes Max Morath and this marvelous book to sort it all out and put it in clear-eyed perspective. He ably negotiates the waters by describing what a Popular Standard is and isn't, explaining its form and history, and suggesting who and what to listen to. My only regret is that you can't hear Max himself singing, playing, and illustrating all the songs. But that's why we have NPR. Happy listening!

Michael Feinstein is a Grammy-nominated performer, composer, and arranger, and one of the world's foremost musical scholars and archivists. Among other accomplishments, Feinstein has appeared on Broadway, toured the globe, played for presidents and royalty, and recorded twenty albums. His musical illumination of legends such as George and Ira Gershwin, Irving Berlin, Jerome Kern, Johnny Mercer, Duke Ellington, and Harry Warren have truly made him "America's Ambassador of Song."

Introduction

"Popular Standards" sounds like it might refer to a line of plumbing fixtures or a category at the public library rather than what it actually is: a distinct body of musical works, which collectively represent one of America's true cultural treasures. Popular Standards doesn't have the pizzazz of "jazz." It isn't grand, like opera, or brazen, almost onomatopoetic, like hard rock. But if the label is mundane, the songs to which it refers are anything but. Harold Arlen's "Over the Rainbow," the Gershwins' "Someone to Watch Over Me," Cole Porter's "What Is This Thing Called Love?," Bart Howard's "Fly Me to the Moon," Duke Ellington's "Sophisticated Lady"—these and hundreds of other works, all created during a few immensely fertile decades in the middle of the last century, exemplify popular songwriting at its best: vivid, literate lyrics set to haunting, elusive harmonies and gorgeous melodies. And they have come to hold an exalted place in American culture similar to that held by poetry in other times and in other cultures.

Most of the Popular Standards are love songs—love sought, unrequited, found, and lost again. In three- to four-minute dramas of poetic wit and wisdom, they sing of love as the powerful, mysterious thing we know it to be. They remind us of our own lives, of our trials in the bad times and our joy in the good times. They supply us, too, with a language for our hopes and dreams, and for our sorrows.

You Stepped Out of a Dream
Lover, Come Back to Me
My Heart Stood Still
Come Rain or Come Shine
Our Love Is Here to Stay

The words of these songs are not poetry as such, they are *lyrics*—superb specimens of a difficult craft demanding highly disciplined artistry. Their impact on our memory is double that of even the best-loved poetry because they are set to transcendent melodies that are irresistible, once heard. Why one melody endures and one hundred others fade away is a question no one—certainly not these songwriters—could have explained. It may be that the words and music of the Standards are so beautifully matched that one feeds the other, in a circle so perfect it makes the whole work unforgettable.

Of the Popular Standards, 99 percent were written for specific spots in shows, films, specialty acts, or revues. They were the product of professionals working at their craft, not self-indulgent, personal ruminations on love and loss. When the script called for the display of those moods or feelings, the songwriters obliged. Maybe that's the reason they continue to engender such a deep response. It's almost as if the songwriters are forever presenting their work anew, saying to us, "Here, put this song into the script of *your* life. We don't own it, never did. Go ahead and use it, make it work for you. Take possession of it, and let the words and music speak for you, and to you."

You'd be So Nice to Come Home To
If I Had My Way
I Would Do Anything for You
You're the Cream in My Coffee

In the hands of a singer like Billie Holiday, Frank Sinatra, or Linda Ronstadt—or a musician like Miles Davis or Wynton Marsalis—the Standards serve as a sort of musical thesaurus of the emotions, available to the rest of us, alone or with a loved one, to explore our memories, our hopes, our failures, and our dreams. They are easy to own. Enough years have passed since their origins in theater or film scores that we no longer know or care about their original setting. When we hear Jerome Kern's "The Touch of Your Hand" or Irving Berlin's "How Deep Is the Ocean?" or Rodgers and Hart's "You Are Too Beautiful," they conjure private emotion and memory. Each is a miniature scene from life; linked, they can caption a wide emotional journey.

What'll I Do?
If I Should Lose You
There Will Never Be Another You
You're My Everything

Every culture has had its folk music, doing the same job, providing words and music by some known or unknown bard, to give substance or expression to our sadness and our delight. The century-old stream of the American brand—the Popular Standard—is now free of any generational or nostalgic residue, unfailingly transcending time and place, and bringing its message of beauty year after year.

This book represents an effort to introduce readers unfamiliar with the Popular Standards to this magical chapter of the American songbook, and in the process help turn readers into listeners. For those who have already discovered the Standards, this book aims to further enhance appreciation of the music —the songs themselves and the songwriters and performers who brought them into being—and make many future years of listening all the more satisfying. Or as a few song titles themselves might put it:

Once in a While
Day In, Day Out
Through the Years
With a Song in My Heart
I Hear a Rhapsody

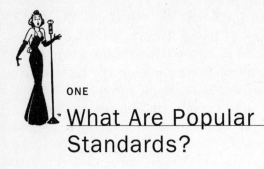

ONE

What Are Popular Standards?

The years from about 1920 to 1960 represented a unique period in the history of American popular music. It was a period that saw the advent of a new type of songwriting, utterly original in some respects, but grounded in the simple structures of the Tin Pan Alley era that had preceded it, and strongly influenced by the nascent musical form known as jazz (and by jazz's precursors, ragtime and blues). Mostly composed for Broadway shows and Hollywood musicals, picked up and performed by singers and musicians of every variety, recorded on disk and broadcast on radio, this songwriting style quickly won the favor of the mass listening audience.

Most of the vast catalogue of songs written in these decades, as in all ages, were instantly forgettable. Some, like "Yes We Have No Bananas" and "Mairzy Doats," were big moneymakers for a few months, on everybody's lips, but soon faded, too. Certain other songs, however, followed a different trajectory. They captured with particular intensity the affection of both performers and the public at large, and held that affection year after year. They may not have always been hits in the familiar sense, may not have reached the top of the pop charts. But to the period's end, such songs as Irving Berlin's "Cheek to Cheek," Cole Porter's "I've Got You Under My Skin," Vernon Duke's "Autumn in New York," the Gershwin brothers' "Embraceable You," and Bart Howard's "Fly Me to the Moon" continued to be played, sung, and listened to in nightclubs and concert halls, on records and radio. In a marketplace of countless musical alternatives, these songs separated themselves from the thousands of other pop ditties of the age like wheat from chaff. By 1960 or so, when the songwriting techniques that had characterized the four previous decades began to fall out of favor, these songs had firmly established themselves as American classics. Although they would never again be the mainstays of popular music, they would continue to be performed, recorded, and purchased, right up to this day. These are the songs that have come to be known as the Popular Standards.

The term *Standards*, like many others in the lexicon of popular music, probably began life as a term used by working musicians to identify the songs that had outlasted faddish attention and stayed in the American ear. As this unique musical universe took shape in the early twentieth century, professional musicians were expected to know by memory every song within it—to know its melody and chords, its "standard" (published) key or tonality, and if a vocalist, to know its lyrics by heart. Before long the yeomen on the business side of the music industry began to use the label, then the broadcasters and the recording execs. It later found its way into the vocabulary of the consumer and Popular Standards is now the helpful and widely accepted label for a rich legacy of words and music.

It is easy to understand why the Popular Standards have so firmly established themselves in the American musical firmament. The Standards are, simply put, excellent pieces of work. Their harmonies are rich, colorful, complex; their lyrics are sophisticated, their rhymes fresh. They display an inventiveness of rhythm and often of form. In these respects alone, the Popular Standards show themselves to be clearly superior—*not* just to other pop songs of their day, but to the vast majority of popular songs of any day before or since. As with any work of art, there is with Popular Standards an elusive quality to their excellence, one that can be heard and felt, but not easily identified. And it is this quality that has kept both performers and their audiences coming back to the songs again and again.

Still, as fine as these compositions are, it is worth asking whether they would have endured without the active collaboration of the jazz performers of their day. Jazz was also coming into its own in 1920. Its musicians, arrangers, bandleaders, and singers tapped the music of Broadway and Hollywood as their principal feeding ground. Big bands and small groups, New Yorkers and Chicagoans, piano-based combos and horn ensembles, scatters, swingers, and beboppers all came to the catalogue. Moored to these works, jazz reached the height of its popularity.

But if the Standards supplied content for jazz, jazz more than returned the favor. Jazz performers became the original keepers of the flame, the Standards' ambassadors to the American public. More important, however, is what these performers did with this music along the way. As practitioners of an improvisational art form, they experimented, varying the rhythms, altering the harmonies, changing keys. They brought different dance models to the Standards—Latin, waltz, foxtrot, whatever. They changed tempos and tonalities. The singers joined in, bringing their individual styles to the songs, aiming to *add* to the material, not simply to reiterate it. Often enough, they delivered interpretations that even the composers could not have imagined, indeed, might have thoroughly disliked. Through endless experimentation, jazz singers and musicians first demonstrated what the Standards were capable of—their extraordinary flexibility, itself a testament to their greatness.

Jazz performers also produced some of the most powerful interpretations of certain Standards—interpretations that were central in raising many a composition to Standard status. Louis

Armstrong's interpretation of Frank Loesser's "A Kiss to Build a Dream On," for example, almost single-handedly made it a Popular Standard, as did the Artie Shaw recording of Cole Porter's "Begin the Beguine." The interpretations came to be almost inseparable from the original compositions. In them, the songs found full voice; without them, the songs might well have been forgotten.

Jazz, then, was an uncredited cocreator of the Popular Standards. Jazz recognized and took inspiration from the excellence of the compositions, but in turn jazz teased out and rewarded that excellence. It brought as much to the construction and elucidation of the Popular Standards as it took from them. In the years since 1960, jazz performers have continued to produce some of the finest interpretations of these songs. Theirs was, and is, a mutual admiration society.

A few further points about Popular Standards:

1. The Popular Standards, like the pop songs of their era, generally were written for performers by professional songwriters who toiled in a business that had clear agendas and boundaries. They wrote for specific projects in theater, movies, and radio. It was their life and their livelihood. With a few exceptions—Duke Ellington, Hoagy Carmichael, and Fats Waller come to mind—they were not performers. Their job was to write music and lyrics for other people. The inherently collaborative relationship between songwriter and performer invited the kind of innovation that allowed these songs to find their best expression, unburdened by the imprint of any one previous artist. If this sounds like stating the obvious, consider that after 1960 or so, this accepted division of labor in popular music ended, and performers who composed (composers who performed)—The Beatles, Bob Dylan, Joni Mitchell—took center stage and have held it ever since.

2. The Popular Standards are almost always *songs*, that is, pieces of music with words. Indeed, most of the future

Standards that had no lyrics at birth—such as "Star Dust," "Satin Doll," and "What's New?"—did not become Standards until lyrics were added. It sounds contradictory, then, that the Standards became the basic repertoire of instrumental jazz. But the reason may lie in the fact that to musicians a Standard is a total work, and though the individual player isn't singing the words, they are part of his/her relationship to the piece. The great tenor sax master Lester Young said he knew all the lyrics of every piece he ever performed.

Although there are hundreds of established Popular Standards, most of them were composed by no more than a couple dozen songwriters. Some of these songwriters—such as Berlin, Porter, Gershwin, and Ellington—have familiar names, while others' names have faded even if their music has not: Kay Swift, Vincent Youmans, Andy Razaf, Arthur Schwartz. In the years 1920 to 1960, countless songwriters plied their trade, but clearly the talent for creating works on the order of Popular Standards was in precious short supply. A similar observation can be made about the performers of the Popular Standards in those formative decades. The Standards certainly owe a debt to the whole universe of singers and musicians who brought these songs into their repertoires; but only a relative handful of those performers can be credited with having raised the Standards to the status of American classics. Their names are in many cases better-known than those of the songwriters: Louis Armstrong, Ella Fitzgerald, Billie Holiday, Bing Crosby, Sarah Vaughan, Mel Tormé, Frank Sinatra, Benny Goodman. The best of their works constitutes an impressive recorded treasury in its own right.

The remarkable proliferation of such fine songs written in the years 1920 to 1960 and the fortune of such extraordinarily gifted performers to give them voice has earned this period the title "The Golden Age of Popular Music." But this label should not convey the impression that to perform or to listen to Popular Standards is merely an exercise in nostalgia. While anyone is free to take them that way, the songs themselves are much more than a bridge to the past. They are in fact a living legacy. The Popular Standards challenge each new generation of singers and musicians to master them, reinterpret them, *own* them. To each new generation of listeners, whatever interpretation they discover, the Popular Standards provide a rewarding musical experience that speaks to the eternal needs of the heart and soul—the way good art always has.

TWO

The Story of Popular Standards

"Without a song the day would never end..."
—Rose, Eliscu, Youmans, 1929

Edith Wharton published her Pulitzer Prize–winning novel *The Age of Innocence* in 1920, just in time to watch the age disappear (if it ever existed). The following decade witnessed profound changes in morals, manners, and fashions, and most Americans had more money in their pockets than ever. They spent an increasing amount of it on entertainment. Popular music, now a full-fledged industry, gathered a healthy share of those dollars and entered a Golden Age, marked by a vast number of mediocre songs, but also by a refined portion that reached new levels of excellence and were destined to become our Popular Standards.

The music rose on the same upward curve that boomed its principal places of origin—a bullish musical theater, vaudeville (still kicking at that time), and by decade's end, a flourishing Hollywood product, the movie musical. These bustling musical engines of the Golden Age obviously had colorful forebears, and following a brief look at them, we'll check out the Broadway and Hollywood musicals that birthed most of the Standards, the legions of musicians and singers who interpreted them in performance, and the magical means by which both song and performance were brought to the American public—recordings and radio.

Popular Music

In the century just passed, within a freewheeling capitalist economy, a vital mix of races and cultures intersected with miraculous new technologies that almost overnight became the primary distribution systems for popular arts and entertainment, including especially the segment that would become known as "popular music." The familiar term is only about one hundred years old. Earlier songs such as those by Stephen Foster and a few others were often considered "popular" (i.e. they were loved and performed by The People), but the two-word label did not gain currency until production of songs became a full-time American *business*. When Charles K. Harris's waltz-ballad "After the Ball" (1892) rang up astonishing sheet music sales of five million copies, the word *hit* was introduced into the language, and a musical gold rush began—a rush to the fortunes that could be made from selling songs, marketed as a *commodity* in the same manner as soaps, cigars, and sausages.

Within the musical establishment of the day, the term *popular music* was derisive. Most of the people who wrote and performed these songs were scorned as upstarts—young people, mostly—immigrant Jews, "Negroes," Irishmen, plus a few hicks from the Midwest with little or no training or exposure to fine music. Music had always been *serious*, its support and enjoyment a badge of the elite. The common people had plenty of church music and folk music and such; surely they could only be corrupted by this rank, popular stuff. Worse still, it was making money. Big Money.

The popular music business in its early decades went by the evocative name of Tin Pan Alley. The men and women of the Alley were the first to think of popular music as a product. They turned it out week after week, year after year, and they knew how to merchandise it. Their product was the stuff of dreams, a tune in search of an audience. From the beginning, popular music was bound up with the stage—in particular, with vaudeville and the somewhat more involved musical comedies. The purveyors of popular music regarded the stage as their best launching pad for new songs; "After the Ball" had originated in a property called *A Trip to Chinatown*. The producers and headliners of the stage spectacles, in turn, looked to Tin Pan Alley to provide them with fresh, crowd-pleasing material. Both benefited greatly from the arrangement.

In the years ahead, the relationship between stage and song would continue to flourish, generating a torrent of popular music even as new technologies would change its shape and means of distribution. And amid this torrent would emerge the Popular Standards.

Vaudeville and Musical Comedy

From the 1890s on, vaudeville was a show business staple and a launching pad for popular songs by the thousands. A simple amalgam of songs, dances, and jokes, vaudeville had its origins in variety, a primitive, unpolished version of vaudeville, and in one of variety's predecessors, the minstrel show.

Musical comedy was distinguished from vaudeville by the presence of a plot, or at least the semblance of a plot, that linked the various elements together. It too introduced many a pop tune. Parentage of American musical comedy is shared by Italian and German opera, the Parisian revue, British Music Hall (especially seen in the enormous influence of Gilbert & Sullivan), and the light and sentimental "little opera" originating in Austria, the operetta. In the late nineteenth century, Americanized productions, while still rooted in those European forms (chiefly the operetta), began adding native elements—the same routines and techniques from minstrelsy and variety upon which vaudeville was drawing. In the early decades of the century, musical comedy was extraordinarily popular, with figures such as George M. Cohan—whose utterly original shows spoke to the audience with American slang and character—leading the way.

The new American musicals did not call for the big voices of traditional operetta. Like vaudeville, they called for actors, comedians, and dancers who could sing with style, but didn't need a two-and-a-half octave range to do it. (Think Fred Astaire, Bob Hope, Fanny Brice.) What they did need were just the kinds of pop tunes that the songsters on Tin Pan Alley were tapping out.

The theatrical tradition represented by the evolving musical comedy would mature in the 1920s into American musical theater, one of the country's most beloved forms of popular entertainment. Out of this would emerge yet another of America's cultural treasures, the movie musical. These two spectacles, in turn, would prove to be the prime source of the Popular Standards.

Tin Pan Alley

There really is no such place in New York as Tin Pan Alley, and there never was. The term was supposedly coined by a songwriter/reporter named Monroe Rosenfeld in 1903 or so, who compared the din of piano-playing song pluggers pounding battered uprights on publisher's row on New York's 28th street to tin pans. The name stuck, even after many of those offices had either gone broke or gotten rich and moved uptown, or later still, had sold their catalogs to the Hollywood studios and the record companies. *Tin Pan Alley* for many years meant, simply, the *business* of popular music, like *Wall Street* is shorthand for the money business and *Silicon Valley* for semiconductors and cyberspace.

The Princess Theater

From 1915 to 1918, future Standards giant Jerome Kern and his collaborators produced in New York's tiny Princess Theater a series of small musicals that mimicked neither heavyweight operettas nor glitzy revues. They were not as "American" as Cohan's flippant productions, but if Cohan had brought slang, streetcars, and American flags to Broadway, Kern upped the ante by simply writing better music. Kern, who had studied in Europe, had clearly digested both the lyricism of operetta—its soaring melodies and rich language—and the snappy rhythms of Tin Pan Alley. For the Princess he imported the brilliant Britishers PG Wodehouse (yes, the same one who wrote the *Jeeves* yarns) to write lyrics, and Guy Bolton to write the books. These sophisticated shows would be a major influence on musicals to come in the '20s.

Vaudeville and the bustling musical comedies of the early twentieth century created rich opportunities for a generation of American songwriter/publishers such as Harry and Albert von Tilzer, Charles K. Harris, and Paul Dresser. Along with dozens of others they were the founders of Tin Pan Alley. Their armies of song pluggers roamed the streets of New York and Chicago, blasting out the words and music of the latest tunes to any producer or performer who would listen. Even operettas playing in legitimate theaters could be hustled to introduce a new song, an "interpolation" totally unrelated to the show.

Once launched, the songs were purveyed to the public largely on sheet music, the song fully detailed on two staves for piano and a vocal staff above it, with melody and lyrics. The upright piano had come into its own as the century turned, and most middle-class homes had a piano and several people in the family to play it. Successful songs sold hundreds of thousands of copies.

The popular songs of the early twentieth century were pedestrian affairs, with simple harmonies common to hymns and folk songs. With few exceptions, the Tin Pan Alley songwriters were self-taught and musically quite unsophisticated. Their legacy of Standards is thin to nil.

Still, if the product of Tin Pan Alley didn't represent cultural finery, it did furnish a training ground for young songwriters who would soon endow American music with a real cultural treasure: the songbook of Popular Standards. It's almost as if those hardscrabble Tin Pan Alley publishers had planned an old-world apprentice system. Among the kids working on the Alley, demonstrating the new tunes for vaudevillians or writing charts for their orchestras, were a fifteen-year-old George Gershwin at Remick, a fellow named Harry Ruby pushing product for the Gus Edwards and von Tilzer houses, and a young composer of recognized talent, Jerome Kern, marking time as a stock clerk over at T. B. Harms. They and dozens like them would soon be the journeymen in the trade, and they would bring to it talent and training, and at times true genius, far beyond the plans and visions of the generation that apprenticed them.

In the years after 1920, recordings would challenge sheet music as the common currency of the music business, and Tin Pan Alley itself would go into decline. But the Tin Pan Alley firms had by then established the financial base upon which the coming Golden Age of popular music would be built.

The New Songwriters

A pervasive show business myth insists that all entertainers and performers from the early years of the century must have sprung from poverty-stricken childhoods on New York's Lower East Side, gotten little or no education in the process, and succeeded on raw talent and grit alone. It's a nice myth, and is the true story of one of the great songwriters of the Popular Standards: Irving Berlin. He's the most famous of them all, so that may explain the prevalence of the myth. But it certainly

TPA, RIP

Bob Dylan, somewhere in the mid-60s, said "Tin Pan Alley is dead. I killed it." More likely it wasn't murder by Dylan or anyone else, simply death of old age. Technology and economics had put an end to the old ways of Tin Pan Alley by 1930. The phonograph was the first culprit, reducing sheet music sales by immense percentages every year. Sure, there were royalties from record sales, but they didn't match those juicy profits from sheet music. Right on the heels of the record boom came the radio craze, which for a while not only hit Tin Pan Alley another lethal blow, but actually paralyzed the phonograph crowd for a few years, denting the already meager royalties from recordings. Technology then struck again when the movies began to talk and sing. The major studios had major money, but saw no reason to spend it on royalties payable to those elderly New York publishing houses. So they just *bought* them.

doesn't fit the others. Cole Porter, Dorothy Fields, Richard Rodgers, Jerome Kern, Harold Arlen, Duke Ellington—they were products of comfortable, middle-class families, with good educations and, for some, considerable privilege.

Several of them apprenticed on Tin Pan Alley, but even as youngsters they brought to their song-plugging chores a much higher degree of musical skill than the older mentors who were teaching them the business. Lorenz Hart, Oscar Hammerstein II, and Richard Rodgers all had the benefit of higher education at Columbia University; Hoagy Carmichael was a graduate in law at Indiana before turning to the songwriting game; Dorothy Fields was the daughter of Lew Fields, one of the most successful and wealthy showmen in New York; Cole Porter was a Yale man. Are these the struggling youngsters of show biz myth?

The future Standards writers, instead, were an urbane, civilized bunch—sophisticated New Yorkers, most of them, well-educated, but seasoned early on in the ways of the theater and show business. How else could they have mastered all the tools they brought to the game? For the lyricists, a knowledge of classic poetry as well as light verse, and a thorough study of all that had gone before, from Shakespeare to Gilbert & Sullivan. For the composers, deep study of harmony and classical theory, plus for many, solid piano training.

But the composers of the Popular Standards were equally products of their own musical era. They were all born within a few years of 1900, just as the new sound called "ragtime" was creeping up on America. The "Maple Leaf Rag," Scott Joplin's masterpiece, had been published in 1899; two years later the American Federation of Musicians (AFM) had passed a unanimous resolution condemning ragtime and urged the members never to play it. That was the perfect way to get young musicians hooked on it, and indeed they were. The repeated, constant syncopations of the music reached them directly as they listened and played, and indirectly, almost by osmosis, from the world around them. Many of the budding songwriters knew also the jazz world and the blues. And if they didn't know those musical styles before 1921, they certainly did afterward; in that year, Eubie Blake and Noble Sissle's all-black musical *Shuffle Along* exposed many an ear to the rhythms of ragtime, jazz, and the blues. These multiple influences would in time be brought to bear on the established song matrix of Tin Pan Alley, one factor in the raising of popular music to a zenith of excellence.

What brought these uniquely capable young talents to the tough, competitive world of show business? Who can say? Richard Rodgers might well have gone into medicine, Vincent Youmans into his father's business, Cole Porter remained a playboy in Paris. Dorothy Fields taught school for a while. A lot of talented people apparently found themselves gathered together around a time and place that must have been very exciting, and potentially profitable, and they probably couldn't imagine themselves doing anything but writing songs.

World War I ended on November 11, 1918. George Gershwin had just turned twenty, and his brother Ira would be twenty-two the next month; Duke Ellington was nineteen, already playing gigs in Washington, D.C., and planning his move to New York; Harry Warren would soon be twenty-five, anxious to end his tour of duty with the U.S. Navy and get back to New York City, and his career in theater and music. Cole Porter was over in Paris and wondering, at twenty-six, if the clever songs he was singing for his partying friends would ever make it to Broadway. Irving Berlin (he was thirty) and Jerome Kern, thirty-three, were already the idols of the younger guys, Berlin an international star with dozens of hits since 1910, his own publishing company, and plans to build a theater on Broadway. The hardworking Kern had finally broken through with a hit song called "They Didn't Believe Me," and had then become the talk of the town with his minimusicals at New York's Princess Theater. Together, they were about to change popular music.

Broadway and Hollywood

It's almost impossible to separate the history of the Golden Age of Popular Music from those of the stage and screen. These were the twin arenas where all the action was—and the money. No songwriter could expect to enjoy a career completely outside these arenas, nor was there any reason to want to. Broadway and Hollywood were themselves in their own Golden Ages, and they offered work to any songsmith who could cut the mustard.

By and large, the composers and lyricists who labored for stage and screen productions were not seeking to write for the ages. They were doing a job and getting paid to do it. They were working from one project to the next, doing their best work on a tight schedule, without time to consider the future of their individual songs beyond high hopes for the vehicle containing them. They must often have been surprised that their songs often came to be embraced by the public with greater affection than the vehicles that launched them. It was a nice twist that the films became, over the years, long-running advertisements for the songs.

This is not to say that a songwriter didn't always harbor a secret hope that such and such a song would be a major hit. Many were during this period, and the ensuing royalty checks were a welcome addition to contract fees. Depending on the deal made with the studio or the theatrical producer, the songwriter(s) controlled exploitation of a song after the vehicle that launched it was shelved. This was often the trajectory of a song that eventually would become known as a Standard, picked up from a revue, a musical, a movie, and transferred to the cabaret or the concert hall, and to radio programs and recording studios. At these junctures, the songwriters knew they were involved in a business as well as an art.

Once launched, the future Standards that came out of Broadway and Hollywood quickly developed identities altogether independent of their origins. Artists performing them, and fans hearing them, often neither knew nor cared that, say, the Mercer/Arlen torch song "One for My Baby" came from 1940s *The Sky's the Limit*, or that the ballad "Someday My Prince Will Come" was written for *Snow White and the Seven Dwarfs*. They were simply fine songs in their own right.

Revues

At their height in the decade following World War I, the type of stage show known as the *revue* was among the most popular and profitable of entertainments, and a fine outlet for the new generation of songwriters. The revues were splashy combinations of songs, dances, and sketches, often topical and usually held together rather tenuously. They were wonderful vehicles for the songwriter because the tunes stood on their own, usually designed to suit a particular performer, but never obliged to spin off a plotline.

George White's Scandals, the *Ziegfeld Follies*, the *Earl Carroll Vanities*—these were the leaders—big shows with lots of chorus girls, comics, and new songs. One of George Gershwin's first hits was the Popular Standard "Somebody Loves Me," in the 1924 George White production. In 1926 the newly formed songwriting trio of DeSylva, Brown, and Henderson placed four hits with the *Scandals*: "Birth of the Blues," "Black Bottom," "Lucky Day," and "It All Depends on You." Harold Arlen's classic torch song "I Gotta Right to Sing the Blues" was introduced in the tenth edition of the Earl Carroll series.

The indestructible *Ziegfeld Follies* introduced the Vernon Duke–Ira Gershwin Standard "I Can't Get Started" in the 1936 edition, and Irving Berlin, after contributing to some of Florenz Ziegfeld's mammoth productions, teamed with producer Sam Harris, and launched four sharply successful revues in their Music Box Theater. These shows set a new tone of intimacy and taste, and Berlin loaded the stage with great songs, including the future Standards "Say It with Music," "Lady of the Evening," and the ballad classics "What'll I Do?" (1923) and "All Alone" (1924). Other revues peppered Broadway in the '20s and '30s, including the *Grand Street Follies*, several editions of *The Little Show* and *Garrick Gaieties*, the first of which launched Rodgers and Hart as a team.

Another type of revue created jobs for young songwriters in the booming nightclubs of New York. In Harlem the *Cotton Club Revues* (later the *Cotton Club Parade*) led the way, hiring the Duke Ellington orchestra and entertainers of the caliber of Cab Calloway and Ethel Waters to present new material by up-and-coming teams like Harold Arlen and Ted Koehler, who delivered great songs and future Standards in "Stormy Weather," "Between the Devil and the Deep Blue Sea," and "Ill Wind."

Musical Theater

Neat lines of development are impossible to discern in the history of American musical theater. It has always mirrored America's healthy chaos of race and ethnicity, and while its roots lay elsewhere on the globe, like jazz it couldn't have grown and matured in any soil but America's. After 1920 the melting pot of musical theater was a bubbling blend of traditional operetta, light musical comedies à la George M. Cohan and Jerome Kern, vaudeville and raucous burlesque, lavish revues— all of it now informed by strong currents of ragtime, the blues, and jazz from African-American composers and performers. Throughout the next four decades, musical theater would, even more than the revue, serve as the principal point of origin for Popular Standards. Rodgers and Hammerstein, Cole Porter, Irving Berlin, Dorothy Fields, Jule Styne, and the Gershwin brothers, among others, would all thrive in this arena. And while the shows themselves would take some time to grow to a high level of sophistication, the music largely found its voice from the start.

In the years before WWII, the plots and characters of most of the shows themselves seem, in retrospect, pretty creaky. But the music? Rodgers and Hart's *Babes in Arms* (1937) provided four evergreens: "The Lady Is a Tramp," "My Funny Valentine," "Johnny One Note," and the wonderful ballad "Where or When." George and Ira Gershwin put four beauties into the score of *Girl Crazy* in 1930: "Bidin' My Time," "But Not for Me," "Embraceable You," and "I Got Rhythm," the last of which not only has become a prime Standard, but is one of the basic chord improvisational patterns in jazz. Jerome Kern, with lyricist Otto Harbach, contributed three love songs to *Roberta* (1933) that are alive and well as Standards: "Smoke Gets in Your Eyes," an almost instant classic, plus "The Touch of Your Hand" and "Yesterdays." In New York, Irving Berlin, after a few years of self-described creative doldrums, composed one of the great scores of the period for *As Thousands Cheer* (1933), with "Easter Parade" and "Heat Wave," and the stunning "Supper Time," which he composed for Ethel Waters, and which is now a Standard.

Not all of these early works featured forgettable plots and topical tomfoolery. Kern and Hammerstein's *Show Boat* (1927) portrayed real people in lifelike situations within a logical but complex story, balanced by music, dance, and comedy. One of the finest in Broadway history, it also happens to have a score that brims with Standards such as "Bill," "Can't Help Lovin' That Man," "Why Do I Love You?," "Make Believe," and of course the classic "Ol' Man River." The Gershwins' *Of Thee I Sing* (1931), a hard-boiled satire lampooning American presidential campaigns, was the first musical to win a Pulitzer Prize. The superb score premiered such future Popular Standards as "Who Cares?" and "Love Is Sweeping the Country."

These impressive shows foreshadowed future American musicals, in which story and music would become more and more fully integrated. In the meantime, the Standards continued to issue forth from the stage. Rodgers and Hart's daring *Pal Joey* (1943) delivered "Bewitched, Bothered and Bewildered" and "I Could Write a Book." Rodgers and Hammerstein's *Oklahoma!* (1943), the first collaboration between these two, produced "People Will Say We're in Love," "Out of My Dreams," and "Oh, What a Beautiful Mornin'. " *Kiss Me, Kate* (1951), generally considered Cole Porter's finest score, bulges with songs that have become Standards: "Always True to You in My Fashion," "So In Love," "Wunderbar," and the superb showbiz opening number that's been borrowed endlessly, "Another Op'nin', Another Show."

Movie Musicals

Major breakthroughs in entertainment technologies always seem to leave the current establishment unprepared. When the "talkies" invaded motion pictures, the industry was already a giant, with millions invested in equipment, personnel, and in the chains of theaters themselves. Their product was *silent* film, and the industry leaders were not anxious to change the status quo. But the upstart Warner Brothers studio had broken the ice with Al Jolson singing a few songs on the primitive soundtracks of *The Jazz Singer* (1927) and *The Singing Fool* (1928). And in short order the movie musical would join musical theater as an essential forum for songwriters and a principal source for Popular Standards.

The first "big" musicals—all talking, with music and dance throughout—came along from MGM in 1929: *Broadway Melody* and *Hollywood Revue of 1929*, the latter introducing the Popular Standard "Singin' in the Rain." (It was of course recycled as the title song of the 1952 film starring Gene Kelly, generally considered the finest of the Hollywood musicals.) Other early productions included Eddie Cantor in *Whoopee* (1930), a Broadway import that premiered the vital Standard "Love Me or Leave Me" by Walter Donaldson. In 1933—after a few bleak years spent by the studios mastering the technical problems of sound-on-film—came *42nd Street*. It was an instant hit, with new stars Dick Powell and Ruby Keeler, daring staging by Busby Berkeley, and great songs by Harry Warren and Al Dubin that set the pace for years to come. The team of Fred Astaire and Ginger Rogers also made their first appearance that year in *Flying Down to Rio*, its score by Broadway's Vincent Youmans sporting the future Standards "Orchids in the Moonlight," "The Carioca," and the title song itself.

New York songwriters came West by the dozens, many to stay for the balance of their careers: Warren and Dubin, Walter Donaldson, Johnny Mercer, Richard Whiting. Some worked on both coasts: the Gershwin brothers, Jerome Kern, Dorothy Fields, and Irving Berlin, who, when he did come to Hollywood, created master scores for Astaire and Rogers, including the Standards "Cheek to Cheek" and "Let's Face the Music and Dance." New names appear in the film credits of the '30s and '40s: Jimmy Van Heusen, Harry Revel, Johnny Burke, Ralph Rainger, Leo Robin, and Mack Gordon. Warren remained the quintessential Hollywood composer, his many movie hits maturing into Standards over the years: "The Boulevard of Broken Dreams," "I Only Have Eyes for You," "Lulu's Back in Town," "September in the Rain," "Where Are You?," "At Last."

Musicals were big moneymakers for the Hollywood studios, their gala years matching those of the Popular Standards. And their legacy is impressive: the "Road" musicals of Bob Hope and Bing Crosby, with dozens of Burke–Van Heusen Standards embedded in their scores ("But Beautiful," "Constantly," "Moonlight Becomes You"); the classic Gershwin films *Shall We Dance, A Damsel in Distress,* and *The Goldwyn Follies,* which introduced "A Foggy Day (in London Town)," "Love Walked In," and "Love Is Here to Stay;" the films of Judy Garland climaxed in 1939 with the all-time classic *The Wizard of Oz,* its score a classic in itself, highlighted by the Harburg/Arlen Standard "Over the Rainbow."

The songs in the Hollywood book of Popular Standards reflect a quality common to most songs of Broadway musical theater of the period: they were not plot driven. Many of the classic films were "backstage" musicals set in show business scenarios, which provided perfect cues for song and dance. The songwriter could invent freely, keeping in mind the voice and style of the performer.

A few changes did take place in the structure of popular songs as they made their way onto the screen. Choruses generally matched the thirty-two-measure format handed down from Tin Pan Alley, but verses were truncated even further than their counterparts in Broadway songs. Composers were also occasionally called upon to meet the extended demands of dance, as in the lengthier Irving Berlin songs for Fred Astaire.

Musicians and Singers

The Popular Standards would have enjoyed little attention following their debuts in forgotten shows and films without the services of the gifted performing artists whose careers spanned the same years. They are as much a part of the history as the original creators. Singers, bands, jazz musicians, vocal groups—all helped spread the gospel, not only in the established arenas of clubs and concert halls, but the newer avenues of radio, records, and for some, television.

But how did they get the music? After all, the day-to-day performers were working different venues: cabaret, nightclub, concert, dance hall, radio, and recording studio. Obviously it was the *business* half of the "music business" that came into play and made the connections. The publishers of the Popular Standards, often owning as much as a 50 percent equity in the songs, hoped that the public would eventually purchase thousands of copies in the form of records and, at least through the 1940s, in sheet music. But at the outset, they saw to it that professional performers got copies as soon as the shows opened. The game was one of hustling and promoting—cajoling, if the performer was a star, up to and including giving her/him a cut of the royalties. Delivery of the words and music to the artist came in the form of "professional copies" for piano and voice, published on newsprint and available for the asking. Orchestrations known as "stocks" for various sized bands and orchestras were prepared by the publisher's stable of arrangers and distributed free or at bottom dollar to singers and orchestras. The object, of course, was to turn the song into a hit as quickly as possible. (There was certainly no thought that it might, fifty-odd years later, still be considered a Standard.)

With sheet music and orchestration at hand, performers now had a "road map" for the new song, and could apply their own stylistic decor, change the key, move the tempo up or down, lay down a Latin beat or a jazz pulse. If the performer was a big name, every effort would be made by the publisher to get the star into a recording studio with the song and feature it on the radio. These techniques applied whether the performer was a vocalist, part of a vocal group, a band leader, a solo pianist—all, it was hoped, would play a part in plugging the song.

The contribution of performers to the establishment of Popular Standards as Popular Standards lay not only in regular use of the material, but in their placing a characteristic imprint upon it. Most of the memorable performing imprints on the Standards originated in, or drew their inspiration from, the world of jazz. From scatting Mel Torme to straightforward Doris Day, from the Count Basie beat to the sweet touch of the Glenn Miller orchestra, jazz was the bedrock. Its forces ranged through vocal and instrumental soloists, small instrumental combos and vocal groups, and to the big swing bands that dominated the '30s and '40s.

The Big Bands

Origination of the big jazz band is often credited to conductor-arranger James Reese Europe, among others. In a career cut short by a tragic death, Europe (1881–1919) became the first African-American to make phonograph records (for Victor, in 1913). During the war, as an officer in the U.S. Army, he was stationed in France as conductor of the 369th Infantry Band. They played the requisite military pieces, but before long were salting them with inflections of a new style of music called jazz then germinating back home. After the war, with Jim Europe home and helping lead the way, jazz made a quantum leap from heretofore small New Orleans–style ensembles to fully orchestrated dance bands. Thus, the Big Bands were originally called jazz bands. *Swing* supplanted *jazz* as the defining adjective in the 1930s, with the bands getting larger and more musically sophisticated, but at the expense, some would say, of their true jazz nature.

The era of the Big Band spanned roughly the years between the two world wars, say, 1920 to 1945. Bands had been around for ages, of course, and plenty were *big*. But to the world of American popular music and the Standards therein, Big Bands meant Tommy Dorsey, Count Basie, Benny Goodman, Glenn Miller, Artie Shaw, Duke Ellington, and a few others. The bands crafted *the* sound of popular music for two decades, blending the improvisational journeys of a solo instrument, like Goodman's clarinet or Coleman Hawkins's saxophone, with the precision of a well-honed orchestra.

Some of the best jazz musicians of the day could be found in bands, like saxophonist Lester Young with Count Basie and drummer Gene Krupa with Goodman. Most bands also included singers, although they tended to be used sparingly. Joe Williams sang for years with the Count Basie band, as did June Christy with Stan Kenton, Billie Holiday and Helen Ward and Peggy Lee with Benny Goodman, Ella Fitzgerald with Chick Webb, and Frank Sinatra with Tommy Dorsey. At mid-century, having served their stints in the Big Band boot camp, these singers, and to a lesser degree the top musicians, would emerge as headliners in their own right.

On tour, the bands played for the dancing couples in the spacious ballrooms of the time. Off the road, from bases in New York and Chicago, they worked the myriad recording and radio dates that would captivate the listeners at home. Their repertoires encompassed whatever was out there at the time: songs from film and theater, pop hits from Tin Pan Alley, and new arrangements of older tunes. Landmark Standards emerged from their splendid treatments of tunes such as Hoagy Carmichael's "Star Dust," which had been around for quite a while, but was never a smash until Artie Shaw's 1941 recording. Other Standards born of the Big Bands include Bunny Berigan's "I Can't Get Started" (1936), "Sentimental Journey" from Les Brown (1945), and "You Made Me Love You," a 1941 Harry James hit.

By the mid-1940s changing times caught up with the Big Bands. Military duty had interrupted the careers of many seasoned sidemen, and when they returned to the competitive music business they often found their old jobs had disappeared. By 1947 the Big Bands of Les Brown, Benny Goodman, Harry James, and Tommy Dorsey had all shut down. Those that had managed to stay in business through the war years had been forced to raise their fees so high that many ballroom owners couldn't afford them any longer, and the nationwide network of dance halls, where young couples had done the Lindy and the fading Fox Trot, were going broke. Crippling strikes by the musicians' union (AFM) 1942–43 and 1948 ruinously affected the health of the Big Bands.

Although a few of the Big Bands—including those of Count Basie, Duke Ellington, and the innovative Stan Kenton—survived all this, turning to the concert halls instead of the dance halls, an era was clearly over.

The Vocalists

In the Big Band days, the singer had been part of the scenery, rising on cue to "take the vocal chorus." In the decades after World War II, the singer, not the band leader, became the star: Frank Sinatra, Billie Holiday, Ella Fitzgerald, and other towering talents, finally were given a chance to deliver on the promise they had shown as band singers. And practically all of them acknowledge their debt to the great Louis Armstrong for the way they delivered the words to a song. There were certainly other jazz musicians who also played and sang, who brought improvisational skills to words as well as music. But Armstrong was one of the first, probably the best, and surely the most visible and accessible to others of his and later generations. His work seemed to say to them, liberate words and melody, honor the song but make it your own. A whole new type of singing would emerge: "jazz singing."

The vocalists continued to perform live, usually in concert halls, usually with an ad hoc orchestra pulled together for the tour. But their real home was the recording studio. There, most of them maintained the Big Band sound behind them, provided by superb studio aggregations under arranger-conductors such as Billy May, Nelson Riddle, Quincy Jones, and Axel Stordahl. Many of these studio masters had also survived that Big Band boot camp in younger days, and rose to new heights of musical excellence, arranging now to showcase a singing star rather than to keep the beat at the dance hall. This was a major change in the texture of jazz/vocal recording.

This shift in balance from band to vocalist didn't shrink the Standard list. Not at all. The singers, newly empowered, revisited old Standards and anointed new ones. Sarah Vaughan helped "Tenderly" into Standard status in the late '40s, around the same time Billy Eckstine championed "My Foolish Heart." The 1931 composition "Prisoner of Love," on which lyricist Leo Robin shared credit with the singer Russ Columbo, was zoomed to a 1,000,000-record sale and permanent Standardism by Perry Como in 1946, and Peggy Lee ran up the same sales in 1952 on Rodgers and Hart's "Lover." The 1950s were a bountiful decade for the American singers—Georgia Gibbs, Jo Stafford, Tony Bennett, Margaret Whiting, Doris Day, Kay Starr, who brought Irving Berlin's "Waiting at the End of the Road" out of obscurity and onto a Standard vector. The Arlen/Mercer song "That Old Black Magic" was practically owned by singer Billy Daniels after Margaret Whiting scored a major hit with it for Capitol Records in the mid-'40s.

Soloists shared the spotlight with superb vocal groups who built on the legacy of earlier trios and quartets such as the Andrews Sisters, the Mills Brothers, and the Modernaires. New heights of vocal daring and sophistication were reached by groups such as the Hi-Lo's, who recorded a classic rendition of Hoagy Carmichael's "Skylark," and the Four Freshmen, who appeared often with the Stan Kenton orchestra and recorded fine versions of "Day by Day" and "Mood Indigo."

Working in an era when LPs supplanted the much-shorter 78 rpm singles many of the top singers also recorded full albums of Standards—including songbooks of the music of Berlin, Porter, Gershwin, and the rest. These LPs were essential in the canonization of these songs, and of their creators.

The Jazz Musicians

No one could have predicted that the Popular Standards would become the principal feeding ground for jazz musicians throughout the Golden Age. The Standards are, after all, a body of *vocal* material, not instrumental. Nor were their composers grounded in jazz, but rather in musical theater. And yet, from the 1920s on, the Standards became the lingua franca of the jazz world. The participation of jazz musicians in the Big Bands, and later in the ad hoc groups backing vocalists, is but a small part of their story. They also practiced their craft in smaller ensembles, bringing together different instruments in every imaginable permutation and combination, and as soloists. As these musicians experimented with new jazz styles—from swing to bebop to cool and beyond—they took the Standards along for the ride.

The instruments they brought to the party were the usual ones: the piano, some drums, a bass viol, trumpets and trombones, clarinets, the occasional flute, and the saxophone—an instrument that orchestras had shunned for almost a century before the jazz folks picked it up around 1920. It blended beautifully with the other instruments, coming in different sizes with voices bearing homely human names: tenor, alto, baritone, soprano. A sax or sax section was soon found in almost every band, and jazz soloists on the instrument took their place among the great interpreters of the Popular Standards.

Louis Armstrong, such a profound influence on the singers of the Golden Age, is also usually credited with originating the practice of tapping the Standards (and lesser pop tunes) for instrumental use as well. Others eagerly followed: trumpeters Miles Davis; reed men from Ben Webster to Johnny Hodges; jazz guitarists Herb Ellis and Remo Palmier. Ditto the pianists: Art Tatum, the crowned king of jazz piano, with a technique that would humble Horowitz, explored the Standards in recording after recording, as did George Shearing, Erroll Garner, Oscar Peterson, Hank Jones, and the rest. They embraced the Standards, fastening their improvisational imprint on this growing library.

The typical outline of a jazz arrangement was established early on. With the chord progression of the song firmly in mind, the written melody was played a time or two, generally by the ensemble; then the players made up new ones as they went along, based on the composer's harmonic design. That's what jazz is all about—making things up. And something about the Standards appealed to jazz musicians, whatever their instrument, coaxing them into wonderfully inventive improvisations, in many cases great leaps away from the song's original intentions, but still a comfortable home to which they could return after the wildest of harmonic adventures. Coleman Hawkins's tenor sax treatment of "Body and Soul," an interpretation that granted the song immortality, is but one case in point.

The jazz musicians gave the Standards a parallel life, a life equal to or perhaps even longer-lasting than that tended by the Big Bands and the vocalists. Although their work was not always mainstream pop music, it is safe to say that without the attention of the jazz world, the Standards might never have made it into American memory banks.

Phonograph and Radio

Since the beginning of the twentieth century technology has driven the arts, especially the popular arts. Popular music would still be moldering in the piano benches of the nineteenth century were it not for the advent of the phonograph and radio broadcasting. Both were critical to the distribution of all those great songs now called Popular Standards. Most of the creators of the Standards began and ended their careers in theater (and its techno cousin, movie musicals). But all of them interlocked with records and radio to market and promote their works.

Ironically, the recording industry and the broadcast business found themselves competitors for a few years, after the latter swept the country in the late 1920s. Radio was free, and records cost seventy-five cents apiece. Why buy a record when you can hear Rudy Vallee singing "I'm Just a Vagabond Lover" on the radio at no cost? All through the early 1930s it was records vs. radio, dog eat dog, winner take all. The rules of the game even severely restricted the broadcast of phonograph records on the air. It took a radio announcer named Martin Block to break the deadlock on his "Make Believe Ballroom" from New York's WNEW in 1935. He winked an eye at the rules, played some new records on the air, ad-libbed some commercials and chatter between them, and waited to see what would happen. He made sales history. A few years later the local "disc jockey" was a fixture in most cities. Top Forty radio arrived (or Top Ten or Top One Hundred), as the recording industry belatedly realized that its old enemy, radio, was its best super-salesman and that listeners, especially young listeners with plenty of pocket money, would go out and buy the latest hit single *if they heard it on the radio!* (It didn't hurt that the price of records was slashed to thirty-five cents at about the same time.) From then on, the erstwhile rivals would be allies in the great game of popular music.

As these tandem technological marvels exploded in popularity over the coming decades, they replaced sheet music as the primary means by which the general public came to know a song. They exposed millions of listeners not simply to particular songs, but to a vast array of individual performers interpreting these songs; this was a revelation and a treat in itself. But in the process, these mechanisms of distribution also played the decisive role in winning a permanent place for the Standards in America's heart.

Records

Recorded sound and a device with which to play it back, had been invented by the indefatigable Thomas Edison in 1877. Emile Berliner had improved upon the breakthrough with a machine that recorded on disks rather than Edison's fragile cylinders, and by the turn of the century, a whole music business had grown up around the new technologies. Columbia Records, founded around 1890, and Berliner's Victor "Talking Machine" Company (one day to be RCA-Victor), established in 1901, were soon hustling scratchy recordings featuring the latest Tin Pan Alley hits, and singing stars like Bert Williams and Nora Bayes and Al Jolson. The idea caught on quickly; phonographs and record collections began to appear in homes across the country.

Over the coming decades, phonograph records would become the number one point of contact between popular music and the listening public. They received a tremendous boost in 1925, when the Orthophonic (electric) recording process replaced the acoustic process as the industry standard, immensely improving the quality of recorded sound. By 1927, sales of single records had reached over 100 million copies and of phonographs, almost one million. Once past an ugly skirmish with radio during the early days of the Depression, when sales dropped to as low as six million copies in 1932, the record business picked up where it had left off.

Columbia, finally getting wise to America's love of swing, signed up some of its stars, including Duke Ellington and Benny Goodman. American Decca signed other stars, such as Bing Crosby and the Mills Brothers. And the stars brought to their labels their growing affection for the Popular Standards. A fresh generation of jazz and jazz-inflected performers was on the rise, and throughout the Golden Age, the record business rose with them.

As long as 78s were the common coin, however the blessing was somewhat mixed. The rigid three- to four-minute time squeeze of a 78 rpm record didn't have much tolerance for lengthy numbers. Any composition that ran longer had to be cut to fit, sometimes mercilessly. The first thing to go from the original was often the song's verses, those expository phrases that alternated with the catchier chorus. The singer and the band would each take a chorus, then time was up. To fans familiar only with the recorded versions (that is, to most fans), the chorus alone became the entire song, and the often-lovely verses were forgotten. Here again technology and commerce, one driving the other, exerted perhaps more influence on the popular music of the twentieth century than did the songwriters and performers.

The Orthophonic Revolution

While the development of Orthophonic recording made for much-improved sound quality on phonograph records, its implications for popular music went far beyond that. The narrow range of the acoustic process had limited access to recording by many voices and instruments (including the piano). The Orthophonic revolution opened the door to a new breed of vocalists who no longer had to belt their songs to the distant back wall of the music hall, but could croon ballads into the warm intimacy of the carbon microphone. Bing Crosby was one of the first to understand that a microphone was his *instrument*. Ruth Etting, Gene Austin, and others followed.

With the appearance in 1950 of microgroove, long-playing recordings (LPs) complete *albums* of Popular Standards began to appear from Peggy Lee, Sarah Vaughan, Mel Torme, Doris Day, Frank Sinatra, Ella Fitzgerald, and all the others. The time limits imposed by the old 78s became an unhappy memory. Performers could stretch out if they wanted to, and jazz musicians could start indulging in ten-minute takes, singers in longer and more inventive outings, even restoring the neglected verses. The very creation of these albums—quite a few of which were songbooks devoted to distinct composers, including Berlin, Gershwin, Porter, Ellington, and Kern—went a long way toward definitively establishing their songs as classics.

Broadcasting

Guglielmo Marconi perfected wireless transmission of sound in 1901, and in 1916 a bright young entrepreneur (and future commercial broadcasting titan) named David Sarnoff foresaw every home in America equipped with a "simple radio box."

By the 1920s, Sarnoff's prediction was beginning to come true. And after almost knocking off the recording industry, radio broadcasting joined records in spreading popular music far and wide, and helped to found and perpetuate the Standard canon in America.

The impact of radio broadcasting on the care and feeding of Popular Standards during their shared Golden Years cannot be overestimated. In spite of (or perhaps enabled by) their commercialization, the networks and the local stations programmed lots of good music over the years, broadcast *live*. Both NBC and CBS offered up regular shows, such as the *Camel Caravan* or the *Bell Telephone Hour*, which carried full orchestras, featured stables of soloists and special guests, and could program several dozen songs on every outing. Broadway show tunes, jazz, Big Band swing, current pops from film musicals were all part of the daily diet. Songs by the songwriting masters were staple fare, not yet known as Standards perhaps, but heading in that direction (and paying healthy royalties in the meantime).

A quick glance at just a few of the major programs illustrates the breadth and consistency of radio's partnership with American popular music. *Your Hit Parade*, which debuted on NBC in 1935 and continued on radio (and then TV) until 1958, was the most popular and influential network program that purveyed popular music. Its staff vocalists over time included Doris Day, Dinah Shore, and Frank Sinatra; its orchestra leaders Axel Stordahl, Lennie Hayton, and the versatile Johnny Green, composer of the Popular Standards "Body and Soul" and "I Cover the Waterfront." *Arthur Godfrey Time* first appeared on CBS in the mid-1940s and propelled Godfrey into national stardom, his casual style and ad-lib approach shattering the formal aura of network radio. Godfrey had a special ear for jazz and show tunes, and surrounded himself with superb New York musicians like Dick Hyman, Lou McGarity, Andy Fitzgerald, and Hank Jones. He and his singing guests—a wide range of Broadway and film artists—championed the Popular Standards, as did the superb jazz vocalists often featured, such as Lurlean Hunter, Ethel Ennis, and Joe Williams. Pat Boone, Julius LaRosa, Rosemary Clooney, and Vic Damone got their start on Godfrey's programs, which ran on CBS for over thirty years. Among the other important and enduring programs of the era: *Kraft Music Hall*, hosted for a time by Bing Crosby; *Major Bowes Original Amateur Hour*, the debut venue for such stars-to-be as Steve Lawrence and Frank Sinatra; *The Bob Hope Show*; *The Kate Smith Show*; and so many more. Besides their live shows, the national networks also frequently served up remote broadcasts of the big dance bands.

The number of radio stations, even in major cities, was for years pretty limited, and few were independent. Most were affiliated with one of the chains, and in the evening hours especially carried the major productions fed by the networks from the broadcast centers of New York, Chicago, Hollywood, and for a time, San Francisco (NBC). The local stations themselves were often too small to employ live musicians. Instead, they tended to rely on "transcription" services, which delivered fine quality 16" 33-⅓ rpm disks, cataloged and supplemented each month, often accompanied by scripted programs with plenty of Standards included. These transcription companies paid the royalties and looked after the licensing. Once the rules regarding on-air record play were relaxed, local DJs added their voices, and their own library of single records to the mix.

The End of the Golden Age

It was around 1960, or just after, that the jazz inflected performance styles that had characterized the previous four decades were dethroned as *the* sound of popular music, ending the Golden Age of Popular Standards. Throughout the 1950s, jazz singing had been jockeying for position in the new world of R&B and doo-wop, and was clearly losing ground. The new composers/performers were not drawn to the Standards. The Beatles, the Rolling Stones, Bob Dylan, and most of the others preferred to write their own songs, in part to allow them to express the sort of highly personal or sharply political sentiments which were rarely given voice in the Standard library. And even if the newcomers had sought out the Standards, their heavily amplified, guitar-based approach hardly lent itself to the complex formulations of Gershwin, Arlen, Porter, et al.

At the same time that Rock/Folk/R&B and company were pushing the sounds of the Golden Age off stage, the traditional breeding ground of the Popular Standard, the Broadway musical, was developing in ways that dramatically reduced single song output. Great works for the theater such as *Carousel, West Side Story*, and *My Fair Lady*—priding their unity of book, lyrics and music—contributed to the slowdown. As music and story grew ever more closely bound, individual songs became increasingly difficult to pry from the score to stand on their own. Hollywood musicals were following Broadway's lead, and were falling out of fashion with mass audiences anyway, soon to disappear almost entirely. By the mid-'60s the number of potential Standards gleaned from theater and film musicals had fallen to almost zero.

Once the *demand* for songs written in the style of the Golden Age evaporated, there was little to entice a new generation of songwriters to address the *supply* side. A devoted minority struggled to compose within the disciplines of the Golden Age, in spite of a shrinking market. Most however, simply answered the call of the contemporary music industry, writing for the market of their time just as the older crowd had for theirs.

The Popular Standards, while no longer topping the charts, were hardly forgotten. Plenty of veteran performers like Sinatra, Armstrong, Torme, and Fitzgerald, were not about to jettison their well-honed standard repertoires, even as they occasionally added new pop material. Their immediate successors—Tony Bennett, Rosemary Clooney, Geroge Shearing, and quite a few others—continued to carry the torch. Singers like Johnny Mathis and Nancy Wilson, meanwhile, built careers in the 1960s and 70s based in part on the old songs. These and

Latter-Day Standards

Although the output of new compositions written according to Golden Age conventions slowed to a relative trickle after 1960, some of these works have proven to be worthy successors to the Popular Standards. Quite a few have justifiably taken their place alongside the longer-established tunes in the repertoires of many singers and musicians. These latter-day Standards include such film themes as "Windmills of Your Mind" (1968), "The Way We Were" (1973), and "New York, New York" (1977)—and from the theater, surely Stephen Sondheim's "Send in the Clowns" (1973).

dozens of other dedicated performers can probably be credited with canonizing the Standards once and for all.

Popular Standards at the Millennium

The era of the Popular Standards is now fixed in time. Their resurrection as a mainstream style is not only unlikely, but would probably be unwise. Most popular music belongs to a particular time and place, and is, like skirt length, beards, and slang, a matter of fashion. That the Popular Standards have survived their time and place is proof of their excellence and a lasting credit to their creators. The "Great American Songbook" is a body of work that followed the rules and sensibilities of its time, and remains viable on its own terms without the crutch of nostalgia. Most of the Broadway and Hollywood musicals whose scores gave birth to popular Standards have been long since shelved. The Popular Standards that survived them have not. They have earned a life of their own, an established niche in American music, and one of its most remarkable components.

Whatever the cultural and technological upheavals to come, the popular Standards are safe and sound. Young performers explore them. Jazz musicians rediscover those pungent, complex harmonies and melodies—Wynton Marsalis (trumpet), Ken Peplowski (reeds), Frank Vignola (guitar), Bill Charlap (piano), going "way out" as did their elders, but returning home to the rich confines of the Popular Standards. And in a line of succession that leads from Armstrong and Crosby, through Fitzgerald and Sinatra, new voices are also appearing with gratifying regularity, infusing the genre with fresh vitality and style as a new century begins: Mary Cleere Haran, Michael Feinstein, Harry Connick, Jr., Jane Monheit, Ann Hampton Callaway. Whatever's next, the American Songbook of Popular Standards is off the page, on the stage, and into the world's sound systems to stay.

THREE

Popular Standards Deconstructed

"There Goes That Song Again..."
—Sammy Cahn and Jule Styne, 1944

A song—any song from any age—is made up of two elements: words *and* music. Each element is rooted both in tradition and accepted practice. When one or both elements of a song transcend convention and reach new levels of excellence and inspiration, we recognize special and unusual gifts in its creator(s). When *hundreds* of songs by dozens of artists attain such heights within a brief span of years, we anoint those years as a Golden Age, a mysterious renaissance of sorts, and wonder at the forces that brought it about. We're curious to dissect the songs themselves, seeking to uncover elements in them—in their detail or their essence or their architecture itself—that were new or radical.

In the case of the Popular Standard, the dissection is initially disappointing, revealing nothing in the basic *structure* of the song that differs from that of the run-of-the-mill pop tune. Both adhere to formats descended from the past—from folk songs and marches, dance tunes and hymns—evolving by the late nineteenth century into a near-mandatory matrix for the American popular song. But a closer look reveals major innovations *within* that structure, clearly setting the Standards apart from the avalanche of popular songs that surrounded them.

Innovations in the *words* include consistent use of internal rhyme, a comfortable reliance on slang and the American vernacular, and topicality. In their *music*, the Standards exploit fully the aggressive beat and syncopations of jazz and its predecessor, ragtime, the characteristic harmonies of the blues, and the full musical palette of chromaticism. Beyond these specifics are the subtle ingredients of inspiration and craftsmanship possessed by the individual songwriters themselves.

Structure

Capital letters are employed by the professionals in the music business to identify the "phrases," or sections, of songs. There's nothing mysterious about these ABCs (and occasional Ds). They're simply a handy form of shorthand. AABA, for instance, indicates that the first two phrases (A and A) are musically identical (or very close to identical), the third phrase (B) is quite different, but somehow related. (It's known in the trade as the *bridge* or the *release*.) The final phrase (A) is a repeat of the opening. The letters refer only to the musical content of the phrase, not the words, but knowing the words is often a big help in parsing the song and identifying its ABCs. Take for instance the nifty novelty hit from 1925 that has become a singalong standard, "Yes, Sir! That's My Baby."

A   Yes, Sir, that's my baby,
      No, sir, don't mean maybe,
      Yes, sir, that's my baby now.

A   Yes, ma'am, we've decided,
      No, ma'am we won't hide it,
      Yes, ma'am, you're invited now.

B By the way, by the way,
When we reach the preacher I'll say:

A Yes, sir, that's my baby,
No, sir, don't mean maybe,
Yes, sir, that's my baby now.

The first phrase (A) embodies the primary melodic theme, the length of the phrase, and in this case even the title. The second phrase (A again) serves up the same melody exactly, different lyrics. The third phrase (B) has a different melody, but one that connects and returns easily to the final A; the lyrics of B themes can embellish or contradict the As, but in this song, simply reinforce them. The final phrase (A yet again) makes the song a perfect AABA, repeating both words *and* music.

In this example the brevity of the phrases is helpful to illustrate a basic AABA. In most of the classic AABA Standards, the phrases are lengthier, and more graciously outfitted in words and music. They include the love song closely identified with the Bogart-Bergman film classic *Casablanca* "As Time Goes By," Irving Berlin's "Blue Skies," the Arlen/Harburg song "It's Only a Paper Moon," and "Someone to Watch Over Me," by George and Ira Gershwin. AABA was not invented on Tin Pan Alley. It's ancient and somehow feels logical and natural, and is still very much around. The Beatles song "Yesterday," for instance, is a perfect fit.

Consider now another form common to many Popular Standards: ABAC. It turns up in the Tin Pan Alley hit that has long since cued the seventh-inning stretch at the ball game.

Stretch and sing:

A Take me out to the ball game,
Take me out to the crowd

B Buy me some peanuts and Cracker Jack,
I don't care if I never get back, let me

A   Root, root, root for the home team,
      If they don't win it's a shame,

C   So it's one, two, three strikes you're out
      At the old ball game.

Note that the middle A theme ("... root, root, root ...") starts out on the same melody as the first A, but climbs up the scale at the end, so it's a bit different. Superscript numbers are used in describing song phrases that act this way, saying yes, it *is* ABAC, but with a slight difference in the second A, to wit: ABA^{1}C. Lots of Popular Standards follow the ABAC map: the early Rodgers and Hart success "Manhattan," the Gershwins' "Embraceable You," and the holiday hummer that everyone can check for ABAC compliance, Irving Berlin's "White Christmas."

There are many Standards that avoid repetition of phrases altogether: the beloved "Always" by Berlin spins out four separate musical phrases, ABCD, as do Jerome Kern's challenging "All the Things You Are" and, surprisingly, the 1910 proto-Standard "Some of These Days." All these variants, however, from ritual AABA to meandering ABCD, are almost always accommodated in just thirty-two measures of music. Four phrases eight measures long: $8 \times 4 = 32$. Neat.

Some prime Popular Standards are considerably more complex. Think of Cole Porter's "Night and Day." It is an alphabet soup: ABA^{1}BCB^1. Or the Irving Berlin classic "Cheek to Cheek." For openers "Cheek to Cheek" is double the length of most songs of its time, some of its phrases sixteen measures long, others just eight, and it scans out AABBCA. But such lengthier works are exceptional.

The writers of Popular Standards generally adhered to the customary thirty-two measures, meaning the length of the *chorus*. Those thirty-two measures (or "bars") are the ones ringing in our heads—for instance, those ABACs from "White Christmas." But "White Christmas" also has a *verse*, and so do "Manhattan," "Always," "All the Things You Are," "Some of These Days," and for that matter, "Take Me Out to the Ball Game." Most Popular Standards, especially those which were generated for musical theater, have a verse tucked in their original scores. A *verse*?

The Popular Standards were composed during a time when the basic structure of popular song—the offspring of folk and traditional music—was changing almost daily. Early hits from Tin Pan Alley had generally told long stories, well developed in a series of verses, each employing the same melody, every verse followed by a melodically distinct and perhaps catchier chorus, a brief melodic refrain that enunciated the moral of the story, or the joke, or the catchphrase that would grab the public's fancy. The chorus could be as brief as eight measures, with words constant throughout. No performance of the song was complete without the whole agenda: as many as eight or ten verses, which set the scene, introduced the characters in the song, and told the story, each verse followed by a quick chorus. In the decades leading up to the Golden Age, the storytelling verse found itself shrinking, increasingly neglected in favor of the chorus. Choruses soon doubled the length of their predecessors, and began to tell a story themselves, albeit a more succinct one. By prime times on Tin Pan Alley, two verses usually sufficed, still, however, carefully telling us who/what/where/when will be celebrated in the chorus.

The writers of the Standards continued the trend, further bulking up the chorus at the expense of the verse. Like most Standards the Irving Berlin song, "All By Myself," features a verse. But it is shorter and notably less specific than the typical Tin Pan Alley verse. Although still presaging the sentiment of the familiar chorus, it is of less importance to the song as a whole:

Verse   I'm so unhappy, what'll I do?
        I long for somebody who will sympathize with me,
        I'm growing tired of living alone,

I lie awake all night and cry, nobody loves me,
that's why.

Chorus   All by myself in the morning ... etc.

Many a Popular Standard has just this sort of brief, scene-setting opening verse and then it's all chorus after that. And there are even some Standards in which the verse has been abandoned altogether.

If the verses of the Popular Standards are unfamiliar even to those who know the choruses fluently, there's a good explanation for this: Many of the best-known recordings of the songs leave the verses off. Initially this was a byproduct of technology; the 78 rpm records that for decades were the common currency of the recording industry held only three minutes of music. Verse and chorus could not both fit. Something had to give, and it was inevitable that the chorus would win out over the verse. With the passage of years, the chorus alone became the entire song as it was heard on records and radio. But the verses are still an elemental part of many of these songs—Happily, a new generation of Standard singers, in cabaret and recording studio, have begun to dust off the verses and put them back on the page with the chorus.

Words

Professionals long ago started calling words "lyrics." The top of the first page on almost every piece of sheet music, on the left just below the title, reads "*Words* by . . .", but *lyrics* is probably better. Words can be so many other things—prose or poetry, prattle or proclamation. *Lyrics* mean only those words that go with music.

Lyrics, for instance, are *not* poems. We do not attend readings of the poems of Irving Berlin or Johnny Mercer or Oscar Hammerstein II, though their lyrics are as deep in our collective memory as the words of our major poets, if not deeper. Poetry is meant to stand on its own. The words of a poem, even the spaces between them, must alone deliver a message and create the rhythm appropriate to that message. Lyrics don't bear a similarly full burden, but are in partnership with music—its melody, harmony, and rhythm underscoring lyrical content and message.

Everyone asks the songwriter: "Which comes first? Music or words?" Ira Gershwin said he always wanted the tune first, and that he and his brother worked no other way. And indeed, there are many other examples of Popular Standards for which the music not only came first, but was already popular before the words were added: "Misty," "Star Dust," and "What's New?" Oscar Hammerstein, after working with others on a music-first basis, turned to constructing lyrics first during his long partnership with composer Richard Rodgers. So it seems the answer to that common question is probably that it's a fifty-fifty operation. With longtime collaborators like Burke and Van Heusen or Rodgers and Hart, the two functions probably came along side by side, each partner adding, subtracting, giving and gaining ground, compromising until a final product emerges. Certainly those few who created both words *and* music throughout their careers, e.g., Irving Berlin and Cole Porter, were driven alternately by a melody that needed words, or a phrase that begged for a melody.

Those who write both lyrics and poetry claim that lyrics are the more difficult. Music may free the lyricist from certain responsibilities, but it imposes other tasks at least as difficult as those demanded of the poet. The lyrics must cohabit with the music. The lyricist must understand the path of the melody and remain in league with its harmonic and melodic twists and turns, mirroring its breaks, its continuities and repetitions, its very logic. The careful lyricist, for instance, will try to supply the singer with an open vowel sound during whole notes, especially high ones at phrase endings. Breathing space must be provided, and successive consonants must be those that roll easily off the tongue. These functional demands often oblige the lyricist to abandon a perfect rhyme or clever metaphor. Even with theater songs, given somewhat more elbow room in range and style, the lyricist is restricted in the length and metric structure of a line. Willing adherence to all these limits or rules is surely one of the defining skills of the great lyricists, or as one of them put it, quoting Goethe, ". . . in limitations he first shows himself the master." A good lyricist is a person with an open mind, and is a master of give-and-take.

Lyrics in the days of the Popular Standard remained bound largely to the rules and rhyme schemes of classic poetry. They scan and they rhyme (modern poetry seldom does either of those things, but never mind). The masters who wrote the Standards knew those rules, bent and amended them often, but honored and obeyed them, too. Off rhymes, for instance, were to be avoided. In a run-of-the-mill pop tune, it's okay to rhyme, say, *time* with *shine* because the vowel sounds match, but it's a rare move in the lyrics of the Standards. Perhaps this attention to poetic excellence is what brings performers back to them again and again.

Good rhyming, without resorting to the hackneyed *moon, June, tune,* is the mark of the superior lyricist. Obvious rhymes on accented beats were typical of early Tin Pan Alley songs. For example, the familiar 1892 song "Bicycle Built for Two":

> Daisy, Daisy, give me your answer *do,*
> I'm half crazy over the love of *you,*
> It won't be a stylish *marriage.*
> I can't afford a *carriage*
> But you'd look *sweet*
> Upon the *seat*
> Of a bicycle built for *two.*

The rhymes fall on the strong beats at the end of the lines. The writers of the Popular Standards, however, explored more complex rhyme schemes, or simply dropped a formal rhyme scheme altogether. More original still, these innovative wordsmiths peppered their lyrics with internal rhymes, rhymes within lines, rhymes between their main rhymes. Larry Hart's "Manhattan" (his first hit with partner Richard Rodgers) is a rich sampler of the technique:

> We'll have Man-*hattan*, the Bronx and *Staten* Island,
>   *too*,
> It's lovely going *through* the *zoo* . . .

Or from Irving Berlin's "Everybody Step":

> Ev'rybody step to the syncopated *rhyth-m*
> Let's be goin' *with* 'em when they begin . . .
>
> Ev'rybody step if you want to see a *glutton*
> When it comes to *struttin'* over the ground . . .

Berlin was also a master of the simple, direct sentence that sounds like conversation, but has tiny rhymes tucked in:

> What'll I *do* when *you* are far away and I am *blue?* What'll
>   I *do?*

Popular song lyrics were first injected with slang on a free-swinging, regular basis by the master showman George M. Cohan around the turn of the last century. Youngsters on Tin Pan Alley like Irving Berlin got the message, and before long the heretofore stilted language of popular song lyrics had morphed into a syntactical stew of words and forms incorporating the English language as spoken by the People—the American people: street language, slang, vernacular, idiom, colloquialisms. The "baby" of "Yes, Sir! That's My Baby" is no infant, nor is the "daddy" in Cole Porter's "My Heart Belongs to Daddy" anyone's father. Broke? Say it like Dorothy Fields did: ". . . diamond bracelets Woolworth doesn't sell, baby . . ." Infatuated?

Check out Larry Hart's lyric: "...I'm so hot and bothered that I don't know my elbow from my ear..."

At the same time, the language became richer: more vivid, more literate. And as they juxtaposed elegant language with slang and topical references, it became, simply, more *fun*. To listen closely to the lyrics of the Standards is to encounter words one would never have expected to find in a popular song: asbestos, pollyanna, gossamer, paragon (Cole Porter); chalice, crystalline, implacable (Johnny Mercer); sequestering, chintz, unphotographable (Larry Hart). Topical touches? Ira Gershwin was a master, his "I Can't Get Started with You" refers to Greta Garbo, J. P. Morgan, Lifebuoy soap, Jim Farley and *The New Yorker* without missing a beat or a timely rhyme. Porter parlays Popeye and L. B. Mayer in "It's DeLovely," and E. Y. "Yip" Harburg somehow gets the zipper, Nylon, and bubble gum into "The Springtime Cometh." The total effect is to conjure up a tuned-in, cosmopolitan universe—to flatter and invite the listeners to the party with the assumption that, of course, they too catch all the clever allusions and sophisticated chatter.

The Popular Standards would not have secured the nation's enduring affection, however, if in all their cosmopolitan cleverness they did not also have something to say about the trials and joys of our own lives. The lyrics of most Popular Standards indeed mask in their well-groomed smartness, messages about the eternal longings of the human heart—messages that seem always to feel intimate and personal. The Standards, after all, remain wedded to the one subject that has occupied the attention of popular music since its invention—romantic love.

Irving Berlin, it is said, when asked the secret for writing a successful song, replied "Just think of a new way to say 'I love you.'" The Popular Standards comply, their titles alone promising to satisfy his formula—including the necessary variations for love lost, unrequited, regained, and imagined. His own include the profound "How Deep Is the Ocean?" and the lighthearted "I'm Putting All My Eggs in One Basket." Larry Hart said it many ways: "My Heart Stood Still," "I Could Write a

Book," "My Funny Valentine." Cole Porter's include a story of love's beginnings in "I've Got You Under My Skin," and its ending as "Just One of Those Things." The Standards see love from every angle, and in the process have created some of the most provocative and indelible images of romance and heartbreak ever given voice.

Music

Just as the primary lyricists reached for variety and sophistication in language, the new crowd of popular composers adopted harmonies that many of the old Tin Pan Alley men would have considered mistakes. Not that there was anything really "new" in harmony that hadn't turned up somewhere over the centuries. But in the hands of the Popular Standards composers, Tin Pan Alley's steady diet of tried-and-true tonic/dominant/subdominant chords, (the I-V-IV) which had been for years the meat and potatoes of popular music, were tossed into a spicy stew of extended and altered chords.

A musical term for much of this is *chromaticism*. It's the perfect word because its Greek root is *chroma*, which means *color*, and that's what the chromatic scale provides in music: color. Think of it this way: the seven white keys in the C-scale on the piano (eight when you get back to C above middle-C) are a diatonic scale—that is, a scale with eight tones. (Forget the murky Greek background of *diatonic*. In modern music it means the eight notes in that scale.) But what about the others—those five black keys encountered on the way up the scale to the octave? There have been times when they were called "foreign," and periods in Western music when they were considered subversive and dangerous, those chromatic half-steps, those *colorful* steps. But the nineteenth-century Romantics plied them lavishly (Chopin, Wagner, Lizst), and then came those daredevil French impressionists Debussy and Ravel with their wild harmonic flights and whole-tone mind-benders, and all bets were off. The leading songwriters of the Golden Age, many of whom had been well-schooled in classical composition (or were suitably impressed by colleagues who had), embraced the previously off-limits freedom of chromaticism. They refused to be tied to the old Tin Pan Alley ground rules. (Dissonance was *okay*: internal modulations *worked*.)

The relative sophistication of the musical vocabulary of American popular song can be clearly seen by comparing a typical chord progression from a Tin Pan Alley phrase circa 1915 with one from the Golden Age. It's the difference between grade school and graduate school. The first might look something like this:

$$C \rightarrow C^7 \rightarrow F \rightarrow Fm \rightarrow C \rightarrow G^7 \rightarrow C$$

The second, richly chromatic, something like this:

$$Fm^{6+9} \rightarrow A\flat^{9\flat5} \rightarrow Dm^{9+11} \rightarrow D\flat^{7+9} \rightarrow Cm^7/F \rightarrow B^{7+\#5} \rightarrow B\flat^6$$

One needn't know music nor hear those chords to perceive that those little letters and numbers mean *colors*, dark or light, that stimulate suspense and provide relief, always hinting at mystery.

Like European chromaticism, the African-American music known as the blues—which had made its way in the century's early decades from the Mississippi Delta into mainstream popular music—was another ingredient in the musical melting pot that characterizes the Standards. Viewed only from a structural standpoint, the blues demand strict adherence to a prescribed twelve-measure pattern in both words and music. The chord progression was, and remains today, a rather precise one involving the basic I-IV-V chords. The form originated on the folk level, and a few other blues were published after 1910, but W. C. Handy's "St. Louis Blues" (1914), *the* blues standard, was the first to be widely heard and imitated, and it set the pattern for years to come.

The unique harmonies of the blues derive from the consistent use of minor sevenths on all the chords, and flatted thirds in-termittently upon the I-IV-V chords. This is achieved improv-isationally when the blues are sung—a bending of the notes between major and minor thirds.

The composers of the Popular Standards published essentially no blues *as such*—that is, individual songs in the twelve-measure I-IV-V matrix of the tradition. But in many Standards, the flatted thirds and portions of the basic twelve-bar progres-sion are incorporated. "Blue notes" can be found in hundreds of Standards, even though very few of the songs themselves are full-fledged blues. George Gershwin's songs, from his earliest days on, are drenched in these inflections, as in "Somebody Loves Me," with its bluesy minor third clothing the downbeat in fourth measure ("...I wonder WHO..."). Duke Ellington, in the Standard "I Ain't Got Nothin' but the Blues" shrinks the customary twelve measures to eight in the main phrase, but adheres nonetheless to the chord progression.

A final, critical ingredient in many a Popular Standard was the syncopated rhythm of ragtime and jazz, both, like the blues, of African-American origin. Syncopation is an elusive concept, but it can be described simply as a relentless urge to avoid remaining always *on* the beat with melody and words—"square," as they used to say. The imperative was always to work *around* the beat: before it, after it, inside of it. Constant syncopation, born of ragtime, was already embedded in popular music by 1917 when along came jazz, in which musical meter was fractured even more recklessly than in the suddenly old-hat ragtime. By the time most of the composers of Popular Standards turned twenty-one, syncopation was simply a part of the musical environment.

It is not easy, however, to set the complexities of syncopation onto published sheet music. The shifting accents of syncopation are tricky to score; a forest of ties and dotted eighths can blacken the page and intimidate the timid sight-reader. (Difficult piano tricks like George Gershwin played, for instance, in his own version of "I Got Rhythm" don't show up in the common published edition.) Songwriters must often *imply* syncopation with accents in the lyric or other clues, and depend on jazz musicians and show folk to get the message across in performance. Syncopation is an ever-present undercurrent in American popular music of the Golden Age—and especially in the hands of Gershwin, Duke Ellington, Harold Arlen, Hoagy Carmichael and a few others, it was the rhythmic foundation upon which their songs were built.

It is one of the sweetest turn of events in the history of the arts that the youthful composers of America's Popular Standards were bilaterally smitten by elegant chromaticism on one side of their brains and earthy blues on the other, with the syncopating freedom of ragtime and jazz melding the two in a constant flow of rhythmic invention and excitement. No wonder they changed the world.

Performance

The life of a Popular Standard begins, obviously, with its creators—the composer and the lyricist. Its life after birth is entrusted to performers, who either sustain or disdain it. If they like it (and it likes them), they're welcome to make it their own. In the process they may change it or rearrange it, add or subtract from its content, experiment with it, and imprint it with their own style. Having been written for the marketplace, the Standards were designed to be ready at a moment's notice to take on the needs and ideas of any artist, whatever they may be. But the Standards have proven more amenable to widely diverse interpretations than anyone could have imagined.

They have found a comfortable home among solo players on piano, sax, guitar, vibes, flute, clarinet, steel drum, and fiddle. They've thrived equally under the care of small ensembles and big bands, mixing and matching instruments in all conceivable combinations. They've served countless singers, alone and in groups of various shapes and sizes, with voices of every description: belters, crooners, scatters, shouters, and talkers. They have been rendered in every jazz idiom: swing, bebop, cool, fusion, lite; translated into Latin rhumbas, mambos, cha-chas, merengues; and covered in doo-wop, soul, reggae, R&B, rock, country, and hip-hop. They have even been given the classical treatment. Their verses have been struck out and reinserted, their chorus stretched and shrunk. They have been sped up, slowed down, converted from foxtrots to waltzes and back again, and improvised almost beyond recognition. The adaptability of the Popular Standard is one of its defining characteristics, one of the main reasons it remains artistically alive today.

If ever there was a relationship defined by the word *symbiosis*, it is that of the songwriter and the performer, joined in the glorification of the American Popular Standard. Thousands of musicians and singers, in and out of jazz, have carried the good news of the great songs. Both performers and songs—and, of course, the listening public—have benefitted mightily from the relationship.

FOUR

The Songwriters

"I Let a Song Go Out of My Heart"
—Duke Ellington, 1938

One of the mysteries of American musical history is that a relatively small number of songwriters were responsible for virtually all of the vast treasury of music known as the Popular Standards. But the fact remains; and below is an all-too-incomplete survey of the lives and achievements of those songwriters—composers and lyricists alike. Most are the obvious names, recognized by general consensus among writers and critics, professionals in the music business, collectors and fans. These are the major figures, the ones who spent their lives in the business. A few figures stand out by virtue of the size and importance of their particular contributions: Harold Arlen, Irving Berlin, Hoagy Carmichael, George Gershwin, Ira Gershwin, Oscar Hammerstein, Larry Hart, Jerome Kern, Cole Porter, Richard Rodgers. Their biographies are presented in somewhat greater detail than others. But in every case the references to individual songs, and to the musicals and films in which they were born, represent only a random sample of that artist's credits and accomplishments.

Although their work did produce a handful of early Standards, the major figures in American operetta in the first decades of the twentieth century—Sigmund Romberg, Rudolph Friml, Victor Herbert—are omitted. Likewise, the great names in American musical theater and film working primarily since 1960 are not included: Alan Jay Lerner, Frederick Loewe, Sheldon Harnick, Johnny Mandel, Leonard Bernstein, Comden and Green, John Kander, Fred Ebb, Michel Legrand, Meredith Willson, Henry Mancini, and Stephen Sondheim, to mention only a few. The works of these and other artists are without question among the finest in the history of American music, and an occasional late-issue Standard surfaces from them (e.g., Sondheim's "Send in the Clowns"). But like their operetta grandparents, they in effect belong to a genre all their own.

Harold Arlen (1905–1986): Harold Arlen was born Hyman Arluck in Buffalo, New York. His father was a cantor who had his son singing in the synagogue choir at age seven, and studying piano, perhaps to become a teacher. The boy had other ideas. He did want to sing, but loved pop songs and Broadway, and he was also one of those kid piano players in the 1920s who got hooked on the new sound called jazz. He always said that his career as a songwriter "just happened"—that all he had ever wanted to do was just sing and play. At age fifteen he launched The Snappy Trio, then changed the name to The Southbound Shufflers when the paid jobs started coming in. As they grew into dance-band stature, they became the chic Buffalodians, with Arlen playing piano, singing, and writing the charts. Before long he found himself in New York City, working in the pit band for George White's Scandals of 1928, and paying his dues in vaudeville, theater, and radio. Among his mentors were the masterful Fletcher Henderson, who would later score most of Benny Goodman's best arrangements, and the renowned songwriter Harry Warren. Warren hooked him up with an aspiring lyricist by the name of Ted Koehler, leading to a lasting partnership that would produce hit after hit, including the future Standards "Stormy Weather," and "I've Got the World On a String."

The next step in this remarkable career that "just happened," was Arlen's teaming with lyricists Ira Gershwin and E. Y. Harburg for the Broadway revue *Life Begins at 8:40*, (1934). It was with Harburg, in Hollywood a few years later that Harold Arlen would compose the music for what is surely an American classic, "Over the Rainbow," for Judy Garland in *The Wizard of Oz*. There were two dozen other film scores by this no-longer-accidental songwriter, and they launched a lot of Standards, especially the collaborations with Johnny Mercer. It was with Mercer, too, that in 1946 Arlen composed the score of the all black musical Broadway musical *St. Louis Woman*, containing the great Standard "Come Rain or Come Shine." His collaborators on the book for this show were the distinguished African-American writers Countee Cullen and Arne Bontemps. *House of Flowers* (1954), starring Pearl Bailey and Diahann Carroll in her Broadway debut, brought Arlen into collaboration with novelist Truman Capote. He then renewed his partnership with E. Y. Harburg for the 1957 Broadway hit *Jamaica*, starring Lena Horne.

Harold Arlen was unique among American popular composers. His early passion for jazz and his many associations with black artists and writers blended somehow with the cantoral influences of his youth, producing songs and harmonies that were his alone, and could probably result only from such a made-in-America heritage. And he was a pianist—a good one. That has to explain why so much of his work, like that of those other gifted pianists Gershwin and Ellington, has always inspired eager improvisation in the world of jazz.

Irving Berlin (1888–1989): "What do I care for the world's affairs," runs one Irving Berlin lyric, "as long as I can sing its popular songs." And Berlin could sing—did so all his life, albeit in a husky, nervous tenor. But the songs that danced in his head are the important ones—songs that would reflect and shape American culture for a century. He began turning them into a livelihood as a youngster, singing for pennies on the streets of New York until he was old enough and good enough to perform at Pelham's Café on the Bowery, or make the rounds as a song plugger for Harry Von Tilzer's Music Company. By then he was sixteen.

He had arrived in his adopted country at age four. With his parents and siblings, he joined the thousands of immigrants jammed into New York's Lower East Side, when it was considered the worst slum in the Western world. The exact place of his birth is uncertain, but it was within what is now known as Byelorussia. What is certain is that his family had to flee from there or die in the pogroms being carried out by the Cossacks of the Czar. Israel Beilin (some sources say Beline) was born on May 11, 1888. Afterward, 101 months of May would pass before he died on September 22, 1989. In that remarkable span of years he brought to market, by one count, 451 hit songs, of which 282 made the Top Ten, and 35 Number One. The total number of copyrights hovers somewhere around a thousand, and heaven knows how many more were tossed out, rewritten, renamed, dumped in the trunk, or simply forgotten. His first song, "Marie from Sunny Italy," earned him a grand total of thirty-seven cents. Just four years later, "Alexander's Ragtime Band" became an international hit, sold a million copies of sheet music, and changed the course of the music business for a century to come. Irving Berlin, in the footsteps of his friend and mentor George M. Cohan, stamped an indelible "American" in front of the new stuff critics were calling "popular" music.

Berlin defies categorization. He had no musical training as a child, nor much education of any kind except the stern lessons learned on the streets of New York. His native language was Yiddish, but no lyricist has ever captured so perfectly the words and rhythms of his second language, the English of American cities and streets. A composer as well as a lyricist, he often took the lead in widening the musical parameters of popular music as it developed over the years toward more creative and sophisticated uses of harmony and structure. He was always ahead of the curve, never simply a clever chameleon who could change with the times. Most of his peers didn't or couldn't shelve old habits and adapt to the unforgiving musical upheavals of the new century, from ragtime to jazz to swing, from vaudeville to theater to film, from records to radio to television. Berlin did, in words *and* music.

Irving Berlin as artist—composer, lyricist, man of the theater—took no backseat to Berlin the businessman. While still in his twenties, he formed his own publishing company, allowing him to control both the publishing and composing royalties to his growing body of work. He also published the work of others, and built a prestigious company bearing his name that thrives yet today. He controlled his own work with a strong but often generous hand, assigning the royalties from some of his most lucrative compositions to the Army Emergency Relief Fund, the Boy Scouts and Girl Scouts, and other organizations. His eye for business even took him into New York real estate—the real estate of the theater business, of course. He and producer Sam Harris formed a partnership and built the busy and beautiful Music Box Theater on 45th Street.

Irving Berlin's first Broadway show was *Watch Your Step*, starring the famous dance team of Irene and Vernon Castle. He wrote twenty songs for that show, including "Play a Simple Melody," the first of his show-stopping contrapuntal duets, and a smash hit years later for Bing Crosby and son Gary. His last show was *Mr. President* (1962), unless you count the booming revival of *Annie Get Your Gun* (1966). He added a new song to the score at that time, and brought Ethel Merman back to play Annie Oakley.

American Popular Standards have emerged from multiple sources: musical theater, film musicals, the big dance bands, and Tin Pan Alley (meaning loosely those songs that come directly from a music publisher, without production auspices of any kind). Most songwriters manage success in one or two of these venues, but Berlin mastered them all. Examples abound—musical theater: "There's No Business Like Show Business" from *Annie Get Your Gun* (1946); film musicals: "Cheek to Cheek" from *Top Hat* (1935); Tin Pan Alley: "Alexander's Ragtime Band" (1911), "Always" (1925), and "Love and the Weather" (1947); dance bands: "Marie," a little waltz Berlin had composed in 1928 for a movie and forgot about until 1937, when the Tommy Dorsey orchestra recorded a novelty jump-tune version, a big hit that put them on the charts.

Several of Irving Berlin's songs have become American anthems, or perhaps more accurately folk songs of twentieth century America. "God Bless America" is as well-known as "The Star Spangled Banner" (and a whole lot easier to sing); "Easter Parade" and "White Christmas" have marked those holidays for years. (Berlin, by the way, considered "White Christmas" his best song.)

This strong-willed and talented man knew more than his share of pain and loss. He was wrenched from his homeland at the age of four; his father died when he was eight; his first wife Dorothy Goetz, died of typhoid shortly after their honeymoon, and though his second marriage a decade later to Ellin Mackay was a happy and lasting one, blessed by the birth of three daughters, the couple suffered through the death of an infant son.

Professional songwriters are supposed to be just that, and Irving Berlin could for sure write a good song in fifteen minutes and often did. But a closer look at certain of his enduring songs indicates that many of them came from his heart. He said as much about "When I Lost You," the aching song of remembrance inspired by the death of his young wife. And although he wouldn't confirm it, there is a sense that his haunting ballads of the 1920s—"What'll I Do?" "Remember," "All Alone," and "Always," must also have been expressions of a personal nature. If they weren't, he was all the more ingenious as a craftsman by making them seem so. Standards today by any measure, his love songs, whatever their inspiration, have became the stuff of dreams for millions.

That opening line, "... as long as I can sing its popular songs ..." is from his tune "Let Me Sing and I'm Happy." During most of a century, Irving Berlin wrote down the songs in his heart so *we* could sing them. They have, indeed, made us very, very happy.

Lew Brown (1893–1958): A lyricist in the successful songwriting troika of DeSylva, Brown, and Henderson, Lew Brown started young, racking up his first hit at age nineteen with the veteran Tin Pan Alley composer Albert von Tilzer, "I'm the Lonesomest Gal in Town." He was born in Odessa, Russia, emigrating to New York with his parents at age five. He kept up a busy career on Tin Pan Alley, then found his way to the Broadway stage after becoming part of the DeSyla/Brown/Henderson team, scoring revues such as the *George White Scandals* and musicals including the highly successful *Good News* (1927). Brown also collaborated with the composer Harry Warren and had a hand in several film scores, including *Stand Up and Cheer* and *Just Imagine*. Among the Standards bearing Lew Brown's name are "That Old Feeling," "I'd Climb the Highest Mountain," and "Together."

Johnny Burke (1908–1964): The Bob Hope/Bing Crosby "Road" movies showcased many of Johnny Burke's best lyrics, with music by his longtime partner Jimmy Van Heusen. He was born in Antioch, California, and spent most of his time writing for Hollywood, but did undertake a couple of theater musicals, *Nelly Bly* and *Carnival in Flanders*, neither of which brought him much success. Other film scores included *Lady in the Dark* and *If I Had My Way*. Perhaps his best-known Standard is the Erroll Garner tune "Misty," to which he added lyrics of a perfect fit after Garner had already claimed a hit record as a piano solo. Burke also collaborated with Harold Spina and Arthur

Johnston, and wrote words for a multitude of Standards, including "Pennies from Heaven" and "What's New?"

Irving Caeser (1895–1996): The man who wrote the words for "Tea for Two," like his fellow New Yorker Irving Berlin, kept an eye on the popular music business for over a century. His collaborators included a couple of youngsters named George Gershwin and Vincent Youmans, and a couple of veteran operetta composers named Sigmund Romberg and Rudolph Friml. *No, No, Nanette* (1925), with Youmans, was Caesar's claim to Broadway fame, which introduced not only his tea-drinking Standard but another evergreen called "I Want to Be Happy." With the twenty-one-year-old Gershwin he handed Al Jolson one of his biggest hits at the Winter Garden, "Swanee," (1919), and wrote the words for many other Standards, including a swinging "Crazy Rhythm" and a tender "If I Forget You."

Sammy Cahn (1913–1993): The lyricist who was responsible for the Standard "Call Me Irresponsible" was born on New York's Lower East Side, and like most of his fellow songsmiths got an early start, partnering with Saul Chaplin to write for vaudeville. They garnered their first hit with the Jimmy Lunceford orchestra in 1935, and a million-seller for the Andrews Sisters in 1937, "Bei Mir Bist du Schoen." A long collaboration with composer Jule Styne followed in the 1940s, spawning a succession of Popular Standards such as "I'll Walk Alone" and "It's Been a Long, Long Time."

Then, in the 1950s, in partnership with composer Jimmy Van Heusen, Sammy Cahn wrote some fine lyrics for his friend Frank Sinatra, picking up a couple of Oscars for "High Hopes" and "All the Way." A busy man through a consistently successful career, Cahn wrote for Broadway (*High Button Shoes, Skyscraper, Walking Happy*) and for Hollywood, notably Sinatra's *Robin and the 7 Hoods* and *The Joker Is Wild.*

Hoagy Carmichael (1899–1981): Most Popular Standards are successful not only as songs, but also as vehicles that inspire jazz settings and improvisation. It's a mystery, then, why only a few composers of Standards came from the world of jazz, or were themselves performers. Sure, many of them "played some piano," but only a handful did so publicly as part of their professional lives. Duke Ellington did so, prominently of course, as did Fats Waller; George Gershwin was a superb pianist with close ties to jazz, but his life as a songwriter was lived mainly in theater and film. So Hoagy Carmichael brought unusual versatility to the game. He was a skilled pianist nurtured in the jazz tradition of cornetist Bix Beiderbecke and other Midwestern players; he was a singer with an average voice but an unforgettable style that served him well all his life; he often wrote his own lyrics ("Rockin' Chair" and "Hong Kong Blues").

Hoagy (Howard Hoagland) Carmichael was born in Bloomington, Indiana, the home of Indiana University, where he earned a law degree in 1926. By the time he got the degree, however, he'd become so smitten by music that, except for a brief crack at law clerking in Florida, he opted for a career in the music business and never looked back. It seemed inevitable. He was influenced as a child by a strong-minded, ragtime piano-playing mother, and in his teens, studying with an African-American professional pianist from Indianapolis, he was captivated by jazz. It all came together through his friendship with Beiderbecke. His future would be music.

Hoagy Carmichael moved to New York in 1929 and there worked with a number of pioneer jazz figures including Louis Armstrong, Mildred Bailey, the Dorsey brothers, and Red Norvo. By 1930 the good songs were coming, and Carmichael was becoming a national celebrity. He also became a movie star along the way, having moved West in 1937 under contract to Paramount Pictures. He kept writing songs of course, often now with lyricists Frank Loesser and Johnny Mercer, but soon found himself on the other side of the camera, appearing in fourteen films, the best-known probably "To Have and Have Not," (with Bogart and Bacall). Carmichael always stepped up eagerly to the next new thing in media and the music business, taking on radio and television in their earliest days, and shining as a performer, a complete music man wherever he went. In his eighty-odd years, the man who composed "Star Dust" seems to have lived a dozen lives.

B. G. "Buddy" DeSylva (1895–1950): In his busy life as a composer, lyricist, and producer, New York–born DeSylva seemed to be everywhere at once. If he wasn't writing Broadway shows with his partners Lew Brown and Ray Henderson, he was in Hollywood producing movies. The list of his collaborators reads like the roster of the Songwriters' Hall of Fame: Gus Kahn, George Gershwin, Jerome Kern, Richard Whiting, Vincent Youmans, and a dozen others. He was the producer and co-librettist for the Broadway musicals *DuBarry Was a Lady and Panama Hattie*, was in and out of the publishing business, and served as a director of ASCAP for many years. From all these endeavors his name appears on many a Popular Standard: "Birth of the Blues," for instance, and "Look for the Silver Lining."

Howard Dietz (1896–1983): Like Rodgers and Hart and Comden and Green, the team Dietz and Schwartz seemed for years an inseparable and successful partnership. Both also worked with others in the trade, but their dual credits dominate the title pages of their many Popular Standards: "Dancing in the Dark," "Alone Together," "I See Your Face Before Me," "I Guess I'll Have to Change My Plan," are just a few of them. Besides Arthur Schwartz, the New York–born lyricist Howard Dietz wrote musicals with the composers Jerome Kern (*Dear Sir*, 1924), George Gershwin (*Oh, Kay!* 1926), and Vernon Duke (*Sadie Thompson*, 1944). Dietz was extremely prolific as a songwriter, but pursued a parallel career as a successful executive in the motion picture business (Goldwyn, MGM, Loew's).

Walter Donaldson (1893–1947): One of the most consistently productive of the major composers of Popular Standards, Donaldson was already turning out hit songs as early as 1915. His smash hit of 1919: "How Ya Gonna Keep 'Em Down on the Farm? (After They've Seen Paree)" celebrated the end of the Great War (WWI), a raggy song in which Donaldson and his lyricists Sam M. Lewis and Joe Young foresaw what historians and novelists soon confirmed—that America's Age of Innocence was over. Sure enough, the new decade was soon dubbed the Roaring '20s, with underscoring in large part by Donaldson's parade of popular songs, some with words by his longtime partner, Gus Kahn ("Yes Sir! That's My Baby," "That Certain Party"), others for which he wrote both words and music: ("Little White Lies," and "At Sundown," perennial jazz standards.)

Donaldson was the ultimate pro, a canny craftsman writing for the fickle pop-tune market, his work seldom involving full scores for theater or film, just letter-perfect thirty-two-bar inventions that unfailingly caught the public's fancy. Perhaps if this busy man had found the time or opportunity to compose more frequently for theater and film, his immense talent would be better appreciated today. His best-known works, after all, are from such projects: "Carolina in the Morning," from *The Passing Show* of 1922; "My Blue Heaven," included in *Ziegfeld Follies* of 1927, and "Love Me or Leave Me," from *Whoopee*, (1928).

Walter Donaldson, like his contemporary Harry Warren, was a talented, ambitious youngster from Brooklyn, who was good enough at the piano to get jobs at an early age with New York publishing houses. He entertained American troops during the war, then returned to New York after the Armistice, became a veteran Tin Pan Alley denizen, migrated to Hollywood when the movies started to sing, composed a string of hits—many to become Popular Standards—coming thick and fast all the while. His last major success was the 1940 collaboration with Johnny Mercer, "Mister Meadowlark."

Al Dubin (1891–1945): Dubin/Warren was for years a credit that graced many a great song from Hollywood's golden years of the film musical. Alexander Dubin was born in Switzerland, but grew up in Philadelphia, moved as a young man to New York to pursue his dream of writing songs, went off to war and returned to Tin Pan Alley with a few hit songs in the 1920s. He soon settled in Hollywood, pairing with Joe Burke to create a number of Popular Standards including "Tip-Toe Through the Tulips" (1929), followed by his highly productive years with Harry Warren. Together they scored prime musicals such as *42nd Street, Dames* and several of the Gold Diggers features. The Dubin/Warren team's Standards stand out: "Lullabye of Broadway," "I Only Have Eyes for You," and of course, "42nd Street."

Vernon Duke (1903–1969): Vladimir Dukelsky was born in Parafianovo, Russia, and was raised in Kiev, where he studied theory and composition. His plans to pursue a career in the world of symphonic and dance music were interrupted when, with his family, he fled Russia in 1919, spent some time in Paris, London, and in New York, where he was befriended by George Gershwin. He soon found himself composing for the Broadway theater, first in partnership with E. Y. "Yip" Harburg (*Walk a Little Faster*, 1932), then with Ira Gershwin for *Ziegfeld Follies* of 1936, the show that introduced the venerable Standard "I Can't Get Started." As Dukelsky, he continued composing for the ballet and the concert stage, had another Broadway triumph with *Cabin in the Sky*, (1940, with lyrics by John LaTouche), and considerable success in film, including the heartbreaking task of completing George Gershwin's score for *Goldwyn Follies* following Gershwin's sudden death in 1937. His many Popular Standards include "Taking a Chance on Love" and "Autumn in New York."

Edward Kennedy "Duke" Ellington (1899–1974): The nickname "Duke" was fastened on Ellington when he was still a child, but it was clearly an insight into his future. He was to take his place among the true royalty of American composers. Ellington fit no category in the rough-and-tumble business of American music. He wrote songs, yes, quite a number of them Standards, for which he composed the music, with lyrics by Johnny Mercer, Bob Russell, and a few others. But he was not a creature of Tin Pan Alley, cranking them out for the market. He seldom wrote for the theater or film, despite occasional outings in both. His superb orchestra, for a time a contemporary of the other Big Bands, was never the same kind of vehicle, however it might appear to be in size and instrumentation. Ellington was perhaps the greatest American *composer* (not songwriter) of his era, and he did his work on an instrument unlike that of any of the others. That instrument was his orchestra.

Duke Ellington was born and raised in a middle-class black family in Washington, D.C. He was studying piano as a kid, and his yen for music led him to study some of the player-piano rolls so ubiquitous in those days—especially rolls made by young masters like James P. Johnson. He had grown to manhood, after all, in exactly the years of ragtime's reign, say 1900 to 1920. Scott Joplin's "Maple Leaf Rag" was published the year he was born, and in the happy rush of ragtime fever, the great Eastern stride players like Johnson quickly emerged. Like many notable pianists of his generation, the young Duke actually learned fingering and style by following the keys of the player piano, over and over. Along with his formal private training, and some arduous practicing, he had become in his teens a competent stride pianist, with a growing command of harmony and arranging.

Before he was twenty he was booking himself and small ensembles at parties and dances in the Washington area, and testing the waters in New York. After some ups and downs, he formed a small band he called the Washingtonians and landed a steady engagement at a midtown New York club. In 1927 this orchestra began an open-ended engagement at Harlem's Cotton Club, then the zenith of big-time New York. The Ellington story from that moment on is a story of growth and success, remarkably free of the cycles and strains that would plague other musical organizations in the decades to come.

Even before the Cotton Club break, Duke Ellington had begun to assemble the cadre of superb musicians who would be as potent a factor in his composing art as they would be contributors to the sound of the orchestra itself. Their names are legend in their own right, and over the ensuing years would include Johnny Hodges, Harry Carney, Bubber Miley, Cootie Williams, Oscar Pettiford, Rex Stewart, and Louis Bellson. The relative consistency of personnel enabled Ellington to produce work of astonishing precision and consistency.

In 1939, the brilliant arranger/pianist Billy Strayhorn joined the organization, as did Ben Webster on tenor sax. The next three years produced what many Ellington experts consider the period of his greatest work, his own composing endeavors augmented by those of Strayhorn, who is credited with composing the Ellington trademark theme "Take the A Train." This familiar piece provides an example of how Ellington's approach differed from other figures of his time. "Take the A Train," like the Standards "Sophisticated Lady," "Mood Indigo," "Satin Doll," and most of the other "songs" credited to Duke Ellington, began as instrumentals, some for various soloists, others arising from ensemble improvisations guided by Ellington or Strayhorn. Words were then added, sometimes much later, and while certain pieces did become hits and Standards, many of the after-the-fact lyrics are of marginal quality. For instance there are words to "Take the A Train," but nobody sings them. The Standard "Satin Doll" with Johnny Mercer's fine lyric is an exception, as is Mitchell Parish's for "Sophisticated Lady." Several tunes with lyrics by Bob Russell stand up well, e.g., "Don't Get Around Much Anymore."

Duke Ellington spent very little time on these popular things, although all were certainly a cut above average for their day in terms of harmonies and structure. His composing efforts lay increasingly with major instrumental works, enlarging upon hundreds of shorter orchestral pieces. Concerts of these larger works became a regular activity for the orchestra, highlighted by the 1943 Carnegie Hall concert in which Ellington premiered his fifty-minute suite *Black, Brown and Beige*. At the Metropolitan Opera House in 1951, he introduced a work called *Harlem*, and in 1955 at Carnegie Hall, abetted by a symphony orchestra, an extended piece called *Night Creature*.

There is no career in twentieth-century American music like his. Duke Ellington prospered. He was able to keep his large, well-paid orchestra together for decades, and rode out the post-war collapse of most other large music organizations. Royalties from his published Standards, both the vocals and instrumentals, provided steady income through the slow times. He was on tour constantly—the U.S., Europe, all over the world—and when he wasn't touring he was in the recording studios. Musical innovations now taken for granted were his: the extended works in defiance of the three-minute limitations imposed by the 78 rpm single record; jazz concertos, literally built around the skills and styles of individuals in his orchestra, such as Barney Bigard's "Clarinet Lament" or "Echoes of Harlem" with trumpet master Cootie Williams.

In the 1960s and still going strong, Ellington turned his hand to sacred works. They constituted "his worship" he once said, and were presented in live concerts and on records. He was also taking time for small group sessions with favorite jazz musicians such as Max Roach, Louis Armstrong, Coleman Hawkins, and Count Basie. But Billy Strayhorn died in 1967, and Ellington's favorite alto man Johnny Hodges three years later. The Duke carried on through the early '70s with some talented new sidemen, but in 1974 he was stricken with cancer. He died just a few weeks after his seventy-fifth birthday.

Duke Ellington was a man of immense talent and generous spirit, born to a time and place that he seemed instinctively to comprehend, as if he were foreordained to create a legacy of beauty and integrity. He seemed immune to the ever-present demons of the entertainment business, and with a steady hand inspired his associates to the heights of their own creativity. Such a balance of stamina, talent, and wisdom doesn't often come along. Duke Ellington will not be replaced.

Dorothy Fields (1905–1974): An early marriage and jobs as a lab assistant and schoolteacher might seem odd preparation for the career of a woman who would become one the American musical theater's most prolific lyricists and librettists. But Dorothy Fields, born into a celebrated show-business family in New York, had found as a youngster she was pretty good at writing light verse just for the fun of it. She met a struggling young songwriter by the name of J. Fred Coots (who would struggle no longer after 1934, when the royalties started coming in on his perennial hit "Santa Claus is Comin' to Town"). They agreed that their songs were pretty bad, but good enough to get a meeting with the established composer Jimmy McHugh, who helped Fields land a job writing material for the Cotton Club revues in Harlem. She and McHugh, meanwhile, collaborated on a new song for a show called *Delmar's Revels*, with stars-to-be Bert Lahr and Patsy Kelly. The song, "I Can't Give You Anything but Love," was dropped after one night, but got another chance in one of the Lew Leslie *Blackbirds* revues just then becoming chic in New York. One critic called it "a sick, puerile" song, then watched it sell 3 million copies.

That was 1928. From there on, the career of this talented, hardworking woman was a whirlwind of success, working with many of the major composers in both film and theater. She shared an Oscar with Jerome Kern for "The Way You Look Tonight" (1936). Her collaborators also included Sigmund Romberg, Harold Arlen, Burton Lane, and Arthur Schwartz, with whom she wrote the score for the Broadway hit *A Tree Grows in Brooklyn* (1951). All the while, with McHugh and others, she was racking up hits that would become Standards as the years went by: "I'm in the Mood for Love," "Don't Blame Me," "On the Sunny Side of the Street."

Dorothy Fields had a gift for writing lyrics that were informal and elegant in the same breath. She could match the sweep of a Kern melody ("Lovely to Look At") or the smart aleck tone of a McHugh toe-tapper ("Diga Diga Doo"). And when she wasn't writing lyrics, she was working, often with her brother Herbert Fields on the books for musicals, including Cole Porter's *Something for the Boys* (1943), *By the Beautiful Sea* (1954) with composer Arthur Schwartz, and *Up in Central Park* (1945) with the ageing king of operetta, Sigmund Romberg. (The score included the beautiful Standard "Close As Pages in a Book.") Perhaps her most enduring book will be the one she and Herbert Fields wrote for the Irving Berlin classic *Annie Get Your Gun* (1946). Dorothy Fields was still working at top speed into the 1970s. Her partner was now Cy Coleman, the shows were *Sweet Charity* (1966) and just one year before she died in 1974, *Seesaw* starring Tommy Tune. She died of a heart attack in New York City on March 28, 1974.

George Gershwin (1898–1937): The first musical comedy to win the Pulitzer Prize was *Of Thee I Sing*. The prize went to the librettists, George S. Kaufman and Morrie Ryskind, and the lyricist Ira Gershwin, but incredibly, did not mention the composer, George Gershwin. His score was the talk of New York. The show was a broad political satire and it ran during the clamorous election year of 1932. It was seen as another highly original work that pushed the musical theater another step toward cohesion of music with plot and character. A few Standards were born—"Who Cares?" and "Love is Sweeping the Country"—but most of the songs were glued to the story line, superb in that function.

In two more years George Gershwin would complete his masterpiece, the opera *Porgy and Bess*. It was based on the novel *Porgy* by DuBose Heyward, and Heyward served as librettist, sharing credit for the lyrics with Ira Gershwin. It was not a success in 1935, and ran a mere 124 performances. It had opened in Boston to considerable acclaim, but in New York the critics were uncertain. Some wasted words quibbling whether the work was a musical or an opera. Others were troubled by the subject itself—an extraordinary portrayal of the lives of black Americans. Kinder voices would soon hail it as a folk opera, and the highest refinement of the book musical, boasting what was unquestionably one of the finest scores in Broadway history. Five years after George Gershwin's death, *Porgy and Bess* was restaged in New York, with Todd Duncan and Anne Brown from the original cast. It was then unanimously recognized as a true masterwork.

George Gershwin, with his brother and others, certainly composed his share of Standards, but he is lastingly famous for works of much broader ambition and appeal. He was the most persistent in establishing an injection of jazz idiom into musical theater. And Gershwin sought from the beginning of his career to move from Tin Pan Alley to musical comedy and then to "serious" composing—that is, larger works for piano and orchestra. His best-known major work remains the *Rhapsody in Blue*, premiered in 1924 by the Paul Whiteman orchestra at Aeolian Hall in New York, with the composer at the piano. Then came *Concerto in F* (1925) and *An American in Paris* (1928). All are rich in the idioms of the blues and jazz, more so than any of his theater works.

But he was not idle on Broadway. Gershwin, already a slick pianist at age fifteen, had started as a Tin Pan Alley song plugger. After a job at Remick Music and a few others, he was taken on by the vigilant Max Dreyfus of Harms Music, who put Gershwin on a $35-per-week retainer and told him to get busy and write some songs. It wasn't long before he had his first huge hit, "Swanee," introduced in 1919 by Al Jolson in the show *Sinbad*. Into the early 1920s Gershwin contributed to several editions of *George White's Scandals*, the 1924 edition giving birth to the Standard "Somebody Loves Me." From then on, with brother Ira as his lyricist, Gershwin rolled out a string of hit shows, including *Lady Be Good* (1924), *Strike Up the Band* (1927), and *Girl Crazy* (1930), which was revived as *Crazy for You* in 1992 and racked up over 1600 performances. These shows premiered many a Standard-to-be: "Fascinating Rhythm," "The Man I Love," "I've Got a Crush On You," "Soon," "Embraceable You," and "But Not for Me."

The Gershwin brothers' ventures in Hollywood produced

three major films in quick succession: *Shall We Dance* (1937), with Fred Astaire and Ginger Rogers and a superb score that included "They Can't Take That Away from Me," *A Damsel in Distress* (also 1937), and *Goldwyn Follies* (1938), released after Gershwin's death. The score was completed with the help of Vernon Duke, and provided a splendid legacy in the two beautiful Standards "Love Walked In" and "(Our) Love is Here to Stay."

George Gershwin's sudden death on July 11, 1937, shocked America. Toward the end, his friends had noticed his frequent bouts of depression, which some dismissed as due merely to his dissatisfaction with Hollywood and his desire to return to major new projects in New York. He had also complained of severe headaches, and according to his friend, the pianist Oscar Levant, Gershwin had recently suffered a blackout while performing the *Concerto in F* with a Los Angeles orchestra. Levant and others urged him to take a long rest, but there was really nothing to be done. He died as he had lived, moving on to the next big event, this one his last—a quick death from a brain tumor.

Three thousand, five hundred people stood in the rain at his funeral at New York's Temple Emanu-El. The novelist John O'Hara bespoke everyone's disbelief and sorrow. "I don't have to believe it if I don't want to."

Ira Gershwin (1896–1983): His aunt had already given Ira Gershwin some beginner's lessons, and the family decided a piano of his own should be purchased to fire the boy's enthusiasm. It had to be hoisted through a second story window to get it into the Gershwin flat on Second Avenue in New York, and as soon as it was in place, Ira's little brother George sat right down, and to everyone's astonishment began to play. Turned out he'd been spending hours observing the neighbor's player piano and imitating the notes and chords it played. From then on the new piano got plenty of use, but Ira Gershwin realized it was his brother who had the real stuff, and he changed course, to grow up and become one of America's finest lyricists.

The credit phrase "by George and Ira Gershwin" is so often heard it's easy to forget that Ira Gershwin collaborated with many others, both before and after his long partnership with brother George. They did collaborate briefly on one song early in both careers—"The Real American Folk Song Is a Rag" (1918), but soon after that George suddenly got very famous, and the modest Ira decided to slip behind a pseudonym for a few years. Naming himself after another brother and his sister, he became Arthur Francis, and with the up-and-coming Vincent Youmans wrote a hit show in 1921 called *Two Little Girls in Blue*, which introduced the perky Standard "Oh Me! Oh My!" In 1924 a couple of shows, *Primrose* and *Lady, Be Good!* were so successful (and Ira had gotten so good at his craft), that he ditched the imaginary Mr. Francis for good, and the "by George and Ira" credit took over from then on.

In the years after George Gershwin's death (1937), Ira Gershwin gradually entered into new collaborations. With Harold Arlen, he wrote lyrics for the film *A Star Is Born*, which introduced a Judy Garland signature song, "The Man That Got Away" (1954). Other film collaborators included Harry Warren (*The Barkleys of Broadway*, 1949), Burton Lane (*Give a Girl a Break*, 1953), and, in the picture that included one of his finest hits "Long Ago and Far Away," (*Cover Girl*, 1944) Jerome Kern. Other distinguished collaborations for theater and film included works with Kurt Weill, Aaron Copland, and Arthur Schwartz. In addition to the dozens of Popular Standards created in partnership with his brother, Ira Gershwin wrote "I Can't Get Started" with Vernon Duke, and with Harry Warren "Cheerful Little Earful" and "My One and Only Highland Fling."

In the many years he survived after George's death, Ira Gershwin became the "keeper of the Gershwin flame," attending to the details of his brother's estate, dealing with their manuscripts and other articles of personal and professional importance, many of which are now part of the permanent Gershwin exhibition in the Library of Congress. He was assisted in much of this during the last seven years of his life by the singer/pianist Michael Feinstein, who became his secretary, archivist, and friend, and who has championed the work of the Gershwin brothers in performance and recordings as part of his own ongoing celebration of the American Standards and the men and women who created them.

After a long life full of honors and respect, Ira Gershwin died in Beverly Hills, California, on August 17, 1983.

Mack Gordon (1904–1959): Like Harry Warren, Al Dubin, and dozens of other New York songwriters, Mack Gordon made the move to Hollywood and became a major name in the world of the film musical. Gordon was born in Warsaw, Poland, but arrived in New York as a child, grew up to perform for a time in vaudeville, wrote for a few Broadway musicals (*Meet My Sister*, *Ziegfeld Follies* of 1931), and then headed West. A composer and a lyricist, he produced literally hundreds of songs for dozens of movies, including *Wake Up and Live*, *Orchestra Wives*, and *Mother Wore Tights*. His principal collaborators were Harry Revel and Harry Warren, and many cherished Standards were the result: "Stay As Sweet As You Are," "There Will Never Be Another You," and "You'll Never Know" are only a few of them.

Johnny Green (1908–1989): A few of the leading composers of Popular Standards were also superb pianists, and Johnny Green was one of them. Early in his career he was an accompanist to Ethel Merman and to Gertrude Lawrence, for whom he composed the masterpiece, "Body and Soul." In an incredibly busy career, Green was also a bandleader, arranger, and conductor. A major figure in Hollywood, he was for many years musical director at MGM, and won several Academy Awards for scoring and conducting such classics as *Easter Parade* (1951) and *An American in Paris* (1953). He also composed major works such as the symphonic suite Raintree County and found time to collaborate with Edward Heyman and others to create a cluster of

Popular Standards, including "I'm Yours," "Out of Nowhere," and "I Cover the Waterfront."

Oscar Hammerstein II (1895–1960): Oscar Hammerstein died in 1960, but in 1996 three of his shows were playing on Broadway. Two of them had won Tony Awards for Best Musical Revival: *Show Boat* and *The King and I. State Fair* was a Tony nominee.

If ever a man were destined for a life in the theater, it was Oscar Hammerstein II. Hammerstein I, his grandfather, was a celebrated opera impresario and theater owner. Oscar's father was the director of Hammerstein's Victoria, the most popular vaudeville house of its time, and his uncle Arthur was a Broadway producer. Oscar II was born into this illustrious family in New York City on July 12, 1895. As a young man he was taken under the wing of the veteran author and lyricist Otto Harbach, which in turn led to a collaboration with the composer Vincent Youmans and a Broadway hit, *Wildflower* (1923). But his most significant partner before Richard Rodgers was Jerome Kern, beginning with *Sunny* in 1925, which led to their 1927 masterwork *Show Boat*, unanimously considered the first truly modern musical. It's score included a plethora of Popular Standards, such as "Can't Help Lovin' Dat Man," and "Make Believe." With other collaborators the busy Hammerstein published "One Kiss" (with Sigmund Romberg), "Indian Love Call" (with Rudolph Friml), and with the team of Kalmar and Ruby, the Standard that became a Louis Armstrong standby, "A Kiss to Build a Dream On."

Hammerstein's long experience as a lyricist, when melded with the seasoned talents of the composer Richard Rodgers, would coalesce some years later in their first collaboration. It completed the evolution, begun with *Show Boat*, toward the musical play in which the music, still fully scored, supports a real plot and well-defined characters. The show was *Oklahoma!* It opened on March 31, 1943, at the St. James Theater in New York, and ran for an unprecedented 2,248 performances. For the next seventeen years there was no stopping this new team.

They conceived and wrote a series of musicals that were not only hits, but were properties that further attested to the growing strength and maturity of musical theater: *Carousel, South Pacific, The King and I, The Sound of Music.*

Many who worked with him declared Oscar Hammerstein to be a true poet, who brought a greater degree of sensitivity and high art to the writing of lyrics than any of his predecessors. He was a friend and mentor to many; his most famous "student," Stephen Sondheim, has continued to broaden the scope and power of the American musical in his own way.

Otto Harbach (1873–1963): At various times in his long and productive life, Otto Harbach was an English professor, a newspaperman, and an advertising copywriter. He was born in Salt Lake City and worked in the West as a young man, but came to New York in time to collaborate as lyricist and librettist with several of the masters of American operetta, including Rudolph Friml and Sigmund Romberg. These relationships led to subsequent pairings with Jerome Kern, George Gershwin, and Vincent Youmans, and a rich endowment of Popular Standards was the result: "The Touch of Your Hand," "Smoke Gets in Your Eyes," "Yesterdays," and his first hit, "Cuddle Up a Little Closer," written in 1908 for the musical *The Three Twins.* Harbach was a charter member of ASCAP and its president from 1950 to 1953.

E. Y. "Yip" Harburg (1898–1981): The popular song that marked the Great Depression was written by Edgar Yipsel Harburg, with music by his first collaborator, Jay Gorney. It was 1932's "Brother, Can You Spare a Dime?" That same year, on a much happier note, Harburg teamed with Vernon Duke on the upbeat Standard "April in Paris." Harburg was born and raised in New York City and was a pal of Ira Gershwin in high school and at CCNY. With Gershwin he would later coauthor the Broadway and film production *Life Begins at 8:40.* Music for that show was composed by Harold Arlen, who was Harburg's primary partner on a number of Hollywood and Broadway shows, climaxing with the classic film *The Wizard of Oz* (1939) and its unforgettable Standard "Over the Rainbow." Other composers with whom he worked during his long life were Johnny Green, Burton Lane, and Jerome Kern. "It's Only a Paper Moon" is his, with Arlen.

Lorenz (Larry) Hart (1895–1943): The partnership had clicked from the beginning. The Varsity Shows at Columbia University brought Larry Hart and Richard Rodgers together, and the partnership endured for twenty-five years, spawning hit shows that transformed American musical comedy. The Columbia shows in those days were a hotbed of creativity. (Rodgers's partner-to-be Oscar Hammerstein II had also cut his teeth there.) Rodgers, bound for Columbia but still in high school, was already writing songs and looking for a lyricist when he met the older Larry Hart, who had been at Columbia but was now working for the Shubert theatrical organization. In 1919 they had a glimpse of Broadway with their tune "Any Old Place with You," interpolated in a so-so show called *A Lonely Romeo*. The following year several of their songs were included in *The Poor Little Ritz Girl*, a moderate success. After a few years of hard knocks the team of Rodgers and Hart finally got off the ground for good with the success of the Broadway revue, *Garrick Gaieties*, in 1925. Their consistent teamwork together produced dozens of Popular Standards: "Blue Room," "My Heart Stood Still," "Falling in Love with Love," "My Funny Valentine," "A Ship Without a Sail," "You Are Too Beautiful," "There's a Small Hotel," and lots more.

Larry Hart insisted on literacy and urbanity in the words of his songs, and with Rodgers and their frequent collaborator on book, Herbert Fields, coaxed musical theater toward greater cohesion of music, lyric, and plot. A look at some of his lyrics may be the best way to study the man. After he and Rodgers, for instance, had spent a few years working in Hollywood, he could dismiss the pretensions of West Coast sophistication with "...hate California, it's cold and it's damp..." (in the 1937 Standard "The Lady Is a Tramp"). He found flippant language to mask the pain and loneliness that follows a romantic breakup: "...wish you were there again, to get into my hair again..." ("It Never Entered My Mind" 1940). Hart was the master, not only of the intricate internal rhyme, but of the offhand use of common rhymes in uncommon ways: "We'll have a blue room, a new room, *for two* room..." ("Blue Room" from *The Girl Friend,* 1926).

When Rodgers asked him to work on the musical that would open under the name *Oklahoma!,* Hart said no, it wasn't for him—all those cowboys and corn. Rodgers partnered instead with Oscar Hammerstein and made theater history when the show opened in March of 1943. Rodgers and Hart, meanwhile, were also working that year on a revised production of their 1927 hit, *A Connecticut Yankee.* They had written six new songs for the show, which opened in mid-November, and was a critical success. Hart had been ill, but attended the opening. A few days later he was found in a hotel room, alone, and was rushed to a hospital, where he died of pneumonia on November 22, 1943.

Ray Henderson (1896–1970): The third man in the songwriting trio often dubbed "DBH" by writers and collectors was Lew Henderson—born Raymond Brost in Buffalo, New York. De-Sylva, Brown, and Henderson were a major force in musical theater, and with Henderson the music man, turned out a lot of Standards, including "Sunny Side Up" and "Button Up Your Overcoat." Without DeSylva's participation, he and Lew Brown wrote the perennial torch song "The Thrill is Gone" (1931), which inspired a hit version in 1970 by B. B. King. Henderson also worked with Irving Caesar and Ted Koehler, and in 1926, with words by Mort Dixon, created an essential Standard, "Bye Bye Blackbird."

Gus Kahn (1886–1941): "Love Me or Leave Me," "It Had to Be You," "I'll Never Be the Same"—a few Gus Kahn Popular Standards that bring him well into the span of the Golden Years of the genre, even though his career began in earlier Tin Pan Alley days with collaborators Grace LeBoy (his wife) and Egbert Van Alstyne. Persistent and prolific, he worked with almost everyone in the trade during the '20s and '30s, among them Walter Donaldson, Richard Whiting, B. G. DeSylva, Vincent Youmans, George Gershwin, and Harry Warren. A native of Germany, Kahn arrived in the U.S. at age five, grew up in Chicago, got into vaudeville as a sketch writer, and brought those skills to the Broadway stage in shows like *Whoopee* (1928) and *The Passing Show* of 1922, and to the Hollywood musical in *Kid Millions, Flying Down to Rio,* and *Ziegfeld Girl.*

Bert Kalmar (1884–1947): You can thank Bert Kalmar (and Harry Ruby, with an assist by Oscar Hammerstein) for one of Louis Armstrong's biggest hits, "A Kiss to Build a Dream On." Armstrong introduced it in a movie called *The Strip* (1951), recorded it for Decca, and made it into a hit. It's been a Popular Standard ever since. Kalmar and Ruby were one of those long-term teams, and though they worked with a few others from time to time, were solid partners on Broadway, then in Hollywood for years, where they contributed to films such as *The Cuckoos, Horsefeathers,* and *Check and Double Check.* Kalmar, a New York native, started as a kid magician, worked as a comedian and sketch writer in vaudeville, and brought it all to a successful career not only as a lyricist, but as the author of a variety of screenplays. His own screen biography was named after a Kalmar/Ruby song, *Three Little Words* (1950), starring Fred Astaire.

Jerome Kern (1885–1945): Interviewers often asked James Hubert "Eubie" Blake (1883–1983), the celebrated African-American composer/performer, to name the person who most influenced him in his own early efforts to compose for the theater. His answer was always Jerome Kern. "We all listened to him, those harmonies! *Nobody* was doing those things!"

"Those things" were the songs in the Princess Theater shows. The Princess was a tiny house (299 seats) and Kern, with his lyricists, took full advantage of this intimacy. Audiences accustomed to grandiose operettas or splashy extravaganzas such as the *Ziegfeld Follies* were led for the first time through song after charming song by means of clever plot devices and believable characters. There were four Princess shows, the most successful of which was *Very Good Eddie* (1915). They weren't yet providing Standards-to-be like Kern's Broadway scores would do soon enough, but they set in motion a major break with old rules and practices that would encourage other young talents such as Rodgers and Hart, the Gershwins, and Kern himself to champion this new approach to musical theater. Songs had heretofore been spotted willy-nilly between jokes and sketches. Now, with increasing urgency, they had to *fit*.

Jerome Kern was born in New York City of a middle-class German-Jewish family; his father was a merchant and his mother an amateur pianist and devoted music lover. Kern was given piano lessons as a child, and played in every school production he could wangle. After high school he studied for a while at the New York College of Music, then went off to Europe, studied a little, listened a lot, and wound up in England, where he met two other young men who also yearned for a life in the theater—P. G. Wodehouse and Guy Bolton. Both would soon be Kern's collaborators in the Princess and Broadway shows that lay ahead.

Back in New York, Jerome Kern became a protégé of the respected publisher Max Dreyfus, who put Kern to work writing songs for interpolation into various European and American operettas, an invaluable apprenticeship for the young composer. Ten years passed before a Kern song became a hit, but it finally happened with "They Didn't Believe Me," included in the score of *The Girl from Utah* (1914). Then came the Princess shows, and the thirty-year-old Jerome Kern was declared an "overnight success." Into the 1920s, Kern worked with some of the best lyricists in the business, including Anne Caldwell, Otto Harbach, and a gifted young author and lyricist under Harbach's aegis, Oscar Hammerstein II. There were over two dozen shows, with major successes in *Sally* (1920) and *Sunny* (1925), but except for his song "Look for the Silver Lining," there was no hint yet of the fount of Standards that Kern's genius would soon produce. Then came 1927 and *Show Boat*.

It was based on the Edna Ferber novel, with book and lyrics by Oscar Hammerstein II. If the exciting Princess shows had brought a new breath of life to American musical theater ten years earlier, *Show Boat* now nursed it triumphantly into maturity. Henceforth, the "musical comedy" must move beyond mere sketch and song and dance, and strive to incorporate the basic elements of the drama. This challenge seemed then to inspire music of greater depth and complexity. Major credit for the literary excellence and character development of *Show Boat* must belong to Hammerstein as author and lyricist, and to Edna Ferber's novel, itself a landmark in American culture. But without Kern's brilliant score, these achievements might well have gone unnoticed. Furthermore, Kern seems even to have inspired himself to new heights as Standards now bloomed from every new show that followed: *Sweet Adeline,* (1929), *The Cat and the Fiddle* (1931), *Music in the Air* (1932), *Roberta* (1933), which costarred a young dancer/comedian by the name of Bob Hope, and launched the classic "Smoke Gets in Your Eyes." Among other Popular Standards born in these shows are "Don't Ever Leave Me," "The Song is You," "I Won't Dance," "Lovely to Look At," and "Yesterdays."

Like most New York composers, Jerome Kern spent time in Hollywood during the '30s. He worked with Fred Astaire and Ginger Rogers in *Swing Time* (1936), winning the Academy Award with "The Way You Look Tonight" (lyrics by Dorothy Field). He won another Oscar in 1941 for "The Last Time I Saw Paris." He returned to Broadway in 1939 with *Very Warm for May*, which failed at the box office, but premiered the superb Standard "All the Things You Are." Returning to Hollywood, Kern composed songs and scores for a number of films including *The Joy of Living* (1938) and *Can't Help Singing* (1942). He found new collaborators in Johnny Mercer ("I'm Old-Fashioned," 1942) and Ira Gershwin ("Long Ago and Far Away," 1944).

In 1945 Jerome Kern had begun work on a musical based on the story of the Wild West sharpshooter Annie Oakley. It would mark his return to Broadway after a six-year absence. In a remarkable convergence of Broadway talent, the producers were to be Richard Rodgers and Oscar Hammerstein, with Hammerstein, his creative partner on *Show Boat*, doing the lyrics for the new show, and Herbert and Dorothy Fields the book. The project ended in abrupt tragedy. Kern, in New York to first put the finishing touches on a scheduled revival of *Show Boat*, suffered a cerebral hemorrhage and died on November 11, 1945. A reluctant Irving Berlin was finally convinced to undertake *Annie Get Your Gun*, which of course became a smash and a classic.

The world of American musical theater was a small and exclusive world. Involved in this one property were Kern, Berlin, Fields, Rodgers, and Hammerstein. Ironically, as the musical theater was by 1940 moving from one triumph to another, soon to reach a peak of creativity, two of its irreplaceble captains were already gone—George Gershwin in 1937 and Jerome Kern in 1945.

Burton Lane (1912–1997): A New Yorker by birth, composer Burton Lane nevertheless spent most of his productive years in Hollywood, heading there shortly after he and his lyricist Harold Adamson got some attention with their songs for Earl Carroll's *Vanities and Artists and Models* in 1930. Lane worked on more than thirty pictures for MGM and Paramount, including *Royal Wedding* and *St. Louis Blues*. He couldn't stay away from his hometown, though, and returned on two occasions to collaborate on a couple of Broadway's most beloved musicals: *Fi-*

nian's Rainbow (1947), with lyrics by E. Y. Harburg, and *On a Clear Day You Can See Forever* (1965), with book and lyrics by Alan Jay Lerner. Lane's Standards, mostly from film scores, include "How About You?," "Too Late Now," and "That Old Devil Moon."

Frank Loesser (1910–1969): Another native New Yorker who spent a few years in Hollywood paying his dues, Frank Loesser found success there after a year or so of scuffling, with songs like "The Moon of Manakoora" for Dorothy Lamour in *The Hurricane*, and "Two Sleepy People," a joint venture with Hoagy Carmichael for the Bob Hope film *Thanks for the Memory* (1938). After wartime service he returned to both film and theater. He won an Oscar in 1949 for "Baby It's Cold Outside" from *Neptune's Daughter*. Now determined to write both words and music, Loesser came to New York in 1948 with *Where's Charley?*, a Broadway hit for Ray Bolger, and then two years later, launched his "Musical Fable of Broadway," the smash success *Guys and Dolls*. This was followed by *A Most Happy Fella* in 1956, music, lyrics and book by Loesser, and *How to Succeed in Business Without Really Trying*, another long-running smash. Loesser's Popular Standards, other than hits from these shows, include "Small Fry" and "Heart and Soul" with Carmichael, "I Don't Want to Walk Without You," (Jule Styne) and "The Lady's in Love with You" (Burton Lane).

Jimmy McHugh (1894–1969): A Boston kid with good piano skills, Jimmy McHugh broke into the business as a rehearsal pianist and a song plugger, and wrote a forgettable Tin Pan Alley hit in 1916 called "Carolina, I'm Coming Back to You." It wasn't until the late 1920s that his remarkable bundle of hits/Standards began to take hold, largely the result of a collaboration with the lyricist Dorothy Fields. It was a long-lasting association, and produced major Standards, including "Don't Blame Me," "I'm in the Mood for Love," and "On the Sunny Side of the Street." He worked with Fields in theater and film projects for many years, and also collaborated with other lyricists on film scores, producing Standards such as "Where Are You?" and "You're a Sweetheart" with Harold Adamson.

Johnny Mercer (1909–1976): A self-described greenhorn, up from Georgia to New York to become an actor, Johnny Mercer decided on a different job. Picking it out for himself, he declared himself a songwriter when he was not yet twenty years old. Nothing had happened in the acting business except for a couple of walk-ons that required him to sing, and right away he decided he could write better songs, words and music—though his best work in the future would be as a writer of lyrics. Not that he wasn't musical, too, he just hadn't had that much training as a kid. He had a good ear and a distinctive, casual singing voice that would sell a lot of records when the time came. His decision to write songs would prove a sound one. He wrote over 1500 of them in partnership with most of the top composers. He became the ultimate craftsman, gifted with a sense of language and the American vernacular. He could make you laugh with "Jubilation T. Cornpone" and break your heart with "Days of Wine and Roses." He could write a nonsense lyric like "Jeepers Creepers" with Harry Warren, set words to Lionel Hampton's difficult, nearly atonal "Midnight Sun" (rhyming "chalice" with "palace" and "aurora borealis"). With Harold Arlen he wrote "One for My Baby," "Skylark" with Hoagy Carmichael, "Too Marvelous for Words" with Richard Whiting. Jerome Kern, his favorite of all the great composers for the theater, was his partner for the Fred Astaire/Rita Hayworth film *You Were Never Lovelier* (1942), resulting in two major hits—"Dearly Beloved" and "I'm Old-Fashioned." He won four Academy Awards, two in a row (1961 and 1962) with "Moon River" and "Days of Wine and Roses," both of them Standards. He took on the difficult job of adding words to "Satin Doll," a Duke Ellington/Billy Strayhorn work so intrinsically composed of extended jazz riffs that the imposition of a lyric would seem not only impossible but superfluous. Mercer did it with the hipster slang of the '50s, a cool, sassy lyric that singers dug immediately, turning words and music into a Standard.

When Johnny (John H.) Mercer was a kid in Savannah, Georgia, his training in popular music was unique—much of it really of his own making. He had no formal musical training, but as he grew up he found he had an almost photographic memory of popular songs. He studied them, analyzed how the words and the melodies fit together, and tried to understand why some songs worked and others didn't. By the time he went up to New York at age nineteen, he knew all the words and melodies of hundreds of popular songs, could sing them, and had made them his own. His first songwriting job in New York was for the third edition of *The Garrick Gaieties* in 1930, where he worked alongside a couple of other ambitious youngsters named Vernon Duke and E. Y. "Yip" Harburg. He first lyric was a routine thirty-two bars called "Out of Breath (and Scared to Death of You)," but his songs must have been good enough, because before long he was hired as a staff writer for the Paul Whiteman Orchestra. Whiteman's once-a-week radio show demanded Mercer write a song per week, and he did his job handily, cranking out songs for stars on the show like Al Jolson and Jack Teagarden.

Hollywood called, and Mercer began a long residency on the West Coast. One of his first films was *Rhythm on the Range* with Bing Crosby, for which he wrote both words and music, providing a hit song for Crosby with the cowboy spoof "I'm an Old Cowhand (from the Rio Grande)." At the same time he was a busy singer himself, with hit records not only of his own songs ("Ac-Cent-Tchu-Ate the Positive" with music by Harold Arlen, 1944), but with songs by other Hollywood songwriters, such as his number one record of the 1946 Burke/Van Heusen number "Personality." That same year his collaboration with Harry Warren, "On the Atchison, Topeka, and the Santa Fe," won the Oscar for Best Song. And the hit single was released on the new Capitol label, of which he was a cofounder. Mercer the businessman was not only a partner in this extremely successful new company, he brought talented newcomers such as Margaret Whiting and Dean Martin to the label.

Johnny Mercer loved New York, and in the midst of his prosperous Hollywood years, he returned and went straight for Broadway. Just to prove he could do it, perhaps, he wrote words and music for the 1951 Phil Silvers musical *Top Banana*, and in 1956, with Gene dePaul doing the music, had a Broadway hit with *Li'l Abner*.

Mercer's songs have exhibited remarkable staying power. Broadway revues and cabaret shows featuring his work have come and gone regularly since his death, and producers continually go back to his songs in search of material for young performers. Movie producers, dubbing old songs on soundtracks of new films, dig deep into the Mercer catalog—the soundtrack of the Marlon Brando film *The Freshman* (1990) for instance, or Harvey Fierstein's *Torch Song Trilogy* (1988). A full menu of Mercer is provided on 1997's *Midnight in the Garden of Good and Evil*, produced and directed by the faithful fan of jazz and Standards Clint Eastwood. The story takes place in Mercer's hometown of Savannah, so Eastwood scored the film in toto with Mercer songs—two older recordings (Sinatra and Bennett) and the balance, new soundtrack versions by k.d. lang, Joe Williams, Diana Krall, and even the star of the film, Kevin Spacey.

In 1939 Johnny Mercer wrote words and music for a song called "You Grow Sweeter as the Years Go By." So does your music, Mister Mercer.

Ray Noble (1903–1978): A classically trained pianist, a bandleader, a composer acting as his own lyricist, and a British citizen who, toward the end of his career, played the roles of pompous Brits in American cinema. That's a capsule bio of Raymond Stanley Noble, whose superb orchestra, playing New York's Rainbow Room in the mid-1930s, included as sidemen Glenn Miller on trombone, Charlie Spivak on trumpet, and Claude Thornhill at the piano. Noble composed the jazz Standard "Cherokee," (which does also have words, but no one seems to have sung them), and a list of sweet love songs, Standards all: "The Very Thought of You," "Love is the Sweetest Thing," "I Hadn't Anyone Till You," and the last tune of the evening played by every dance band since 1931. "Goodnight Sweetheart."

Mitchell Parish (1900–1993): It is probably the most-performed, most-recorded Popular Standard of the twentieth century. Dance hall and radio emcees for years have been introducing it as "Hoagy Carmichael's Immortal 'Star Dust'!" It is also Mitchell Parish's immortal "Star Dust." He wrote the words, bringing a true labor of love to a difficult melody written as an uptempo piano piece by Carmichael. Parish was born in Shreveport, Louisiana, but grew up in New York City, where he studied at Columbia and NYU, sharpening his considerable literary skills. He was a staff writer in music publishing houses, wherein his unsung (and sometimes uncredited) work as a lyricist graced many a future Standard, especially those first conceived as instrumentals. Parish set words to Duke Ellington's "Mood Indigo" and "Sophisticated Lady," Peter DeRose's "Deep Purple," and Leroy Anderson's "Sleigh Ride."

Cole Porter (1892–1964): J. O. Cole had become a millionaire in the coal and timber business, and when his daughter Kate Porter gave birth to a boy on June 9, 1892, in Peru, Indiana, it was decided the family surname should be the boy's given name. Kate, a woman of culture and education, had the boy studying violin and piano from age six, but Grandfather wanted him to become a lawyer and packed him off to prep school and then on to college. Cole Porter didn't want to be a lawyer. He wanted to write songs, and he wanted to write both words and music, too, like his idol, Irving Berlin.

He managed to get a show on Broadway called *See America First*, but it closed after two weeks. He was twenty-four years old, had graduated from Yale, tested the waters at Harvard Law, and decided a life in music would be more fun. But Broadway at this stage wasn't much fun either, so with a war going on in Europe he went overseas. Biographical fact and fiction collide during the war years, Porter claiming he'd joined the French Legion in the African desert, and with a portable piano, sang for the troops—well enough for the French government to award him the Croix de Guerre for boosting morale. After the U.S. entered the war he turned up in Paris, assigned to instruct the doughboys in the art of French gunnery practices. It's more likely he wasn't in either army but was involved, however patriotically, with a privately sponsored food relief agency. This would explain how he found time to rent a luxurious flat in Paris, join the social whirl, and meet his wife-to-be, the wealthy divorcée Linda Lee Thomas.

Back in the U.S.A. after the war, he wrote another Broadway flop called *Hitchy-Koo* of 1919. One song survived the show, "An Old Fashioned Garden," an old-fashioned Tin Pan Alley kind of song so completely unlike the sophisticated songs for which he was known that it's possible he wrote it as a spoof. Returning to Paris, he married the wealthy Mrs. Thomas, and the parties got bigger and better. Guests included Noël Coward and Elsa Maxwell, who told him the clever songs that he was singing to amuse his guests were far too chic for American tastes. But just wait, she said, your time will come. Meanwhile, he was working steadily to sharpen his skills, and was studying with the demanding French composer Vincent d'Indy.

Broadway success had eluded him for over ten years, but in 1928 the producer E. Ray Goetz, who was married to Irene Bordoni, the "French Doll" of Broadway, sensed that Porter's sophisticated songs would be just right for his wife's elegantly risqué touch. He was right. The show was *Paris*, and Cole Porter finally broke through with his special brand of song. A big hit was the perennial "Let's Do It (Let's Fall in Love)." The parenthetical qualifier served, by the way, to misdirect radio and recording watchdogs, but even the folks in Dubuque got it.

1929 became a busy year for Porter, with the opening of his

Wake Up and Dream in March, and his first major hit *Fifty Million Frenchmen* in November. The former introduced one of his all-time best songs, the powerful "What is This Thing Called Love?" With *Fifty Million Frenchmen*, critics were suddenly proclaiming Cole Porter's lyrics the equal of the urbane Larry Hart's, and with good cause. The show included the Porter Standard "You Do Something to Me," and the sassy favorite "You've Got That Thing." Porter's hand was strengthened increasingly now by his association with top producers and directors, and by the challenge of composing for great stars of musical theater—Fred Astaire, Ethel Merman, Bert Lahr, Mary Martin, Sophie Tucker. The hit shows came thick and fast and the hit songs—many to become Standards—came along apace. In late 1932, *Gay Divorce* premiered, (the movie title was changed to *The Gay Divorcée*) introducing the great Porter classic "Night and Day."

The extravagant successes of the 1930s did nothing to prepare Cole Porter for the tragedy that would strike him down on October 24, 1937. Riding horseback at the estate of a friend on Long Island, his mount slipped on a muddy hill and fell on him, crushing both his legs. His injuries were so severe that a double amputation was urged, but Porter refused, and would fight through the rest of his life the trials of repeated surgery and constant pain, forced increasingly to depend on painkilling drugs. That he continued to create his great works for musical theater remains one of the most inspiring stories of raw courage in the face of misfortune in the annals of show business, or any business for that matter.

For another twenty years, through the 1940s and '50s, Cole Porter's musicals were consistently more successful than those of any other composer except Richard Rodgers. Touching just the high points, this is the roster: *Anything Goes* (1934, with Ethel Merman), *Jubilee* (1935), *Red, Hot and Blue!* (1936, Merman again, with Bob Hope and Jimmy Durante), *DuBarry Was a Lady* (1939); *Panama Hattie* (Merman, 1940), *Let's Face It*

(1941, starring Danny Kaye), *Mexican Hayride* (1944, with June Havoc), *Seven Lively Arts* (1944, Bea Lillie), *Kiss Me Kate* (1948, with Alfred Drake originally—and a very successful revival in 1999), *Out of This World* (1950), *Can-Can* (1953, with Gwen Verdon stealing the show in her first major starring role), and *Silk Stockings* (1955, starring Don Ameche). A wealth of Popular Standards came from these and other Porter scores: "I Get a Kick Out of You," "Just One of Those Things," "My Heart Belongs to Daddy," "I Love You," "Ev'ry Time We Say Goodbye," and "It's All Right with Me" are just a handful of them.

Cole Porter's wife died in 1954, and his Broadway successes concluded with *Silk Stockings*, but he somehow found the reserves to score the film *High Society*, which introduced his last hit, the unadorned "True Love." He finally underwent the bitter climax of his twenty-year battle with pain and disability—the loss of his right leg, and he withdrew from public view, fell into severe depression and failing health, and died in Santa Monica, California, on October 15, 1964.

Ralph Rainger (1901–1942): The only New York credits in native son Ralph Rainger's c.v. would read "member of a two-piano team for the *Ziegfeld Follies*." Rainger was a busy and accomplished man—a law graduate (Brown University) who studied music with Clarence Adler and Arnold Schoenberg and became a superb pianist, the favorite accompanist of such Broadway luminaries as Libby Holman and Clifton Webb. But his skills as a composer didn't surface until he went to Hollywood and teamed up with lyricist Leo Robin. Their Academy Award winner "Thanks for the Memory," from *The Big Broadcast* of 1938 became Bob Hope's signature for the rest of his life. Their many film scores birthed wonderful Popular Standards, many introduced by Bing Crosby: "June in January," "With Every Breath I Take," "If I Should Lose You." The partnership ended tragically when Ralph Rainger died in a plane crash in October of 1942.

Andy Razaf (1895–1973): Born in the United States (Washington, D.C.,) but nonetheless a member of the royal family of Madagascar, Andy Razaf's full name was *Andreamentania Paul Razafkeriefo*. He became a leading contributor to the black musical revues breaking ground on Broadway around 1930, including *Hot Chocolates* and Lew Leslie's *Blackbirds*. His principal collaborator was Thomas "Fats" Waller, and he wrote the lyrics for the Standards "Ain't Misbehavin' " and "Honeysuckle Rose," plus other characteristic Waller tunes including "The Joint Is Jumping," "Keepin' Out of Mischief Now," and "Black and Blue," the minor-key lament that later gave title to a Broadway musical (1989), as did "Ain't Misbehavin' " to the 1978 hit revue of Waller's life and work.

Leo Robin (1900–1984): Both before and after the death of long-time collaborator Ralph Rainger, lyricist Leo Robin worked widely with other composers. Like Rainger, Robin had originally studied law (University of Pittsburgh). He had also studied at Carnegie Tech's drama school and worked as a reporter. By the mid-'20s he was writing for Broadway, collaborating with Vincent Youmans on *Hit the Deck* (1927), and working on various other productions. Then came the Hollywood years with Ralph Rainger—a wealth of major movies and song hits, many to become Standards—cut off by Rainger's sudden death in 1942. Leo Robin stayed in the game, collaborating with Jerome Kern on the 1946 film *Centennial Summer*, and with Jule Styne on the Broadway hit *Gentlemen Prefer Blondes* (1949). Besides the many Standards produced by the Robin/Rainger partnership, Robin's works include "In Love in Vain" (with Kern, 1946), "Prisoner of Love" (with singer Russ Columbo, 1931), and dozens of others.

Richard Rodgers (1902–1979): Maybe he foresaw that someday they'd name a New York theater on 46th Street after him and put his face on a postage stamp, so he didn't take that job selling children's underwear when he was twenty-two. He'd been considering it. He'd been writing songs since he was sixteen, even then in partnership with Lorenz (Larry) Hart, but except for friendly pats on the back for amateur shows at Columbia College, nobody was very excited about his work. But then, like all struggling young talent in show business fiction, he got his "big break." *Garrick Gaieties*, a revue, opened in New York. The show had been produced as a fund-raiser for the Theatre Guild, but had gone over so well the Guild reopened it for a commercial run in May of 1925. Richard Rodgers thereupon abandoned forever the idea of selling anything but music for the rest of his life. *Garrick Gaieties* had seven songs by Rodgers and Hart, including the Standard "Manhattan," knit together with cheeky topical sketches, still within the time-honored revue framework, but smart and contemporary. It presaged half a century of success in which Rodgers and his partners would implement new creative demands in the American musical theater.

Richard Rodgers's happy home life as a child surely ordained his lifelong diligence and devotion to his work. He was born and raised in a prosperous New York City household, his father, a physician, and his mother, a schooled pianist. He showed little interest in the piano as a child, except to sit and improvise. His real love was for the theater and the operettas so popular at the time by Victor Herbert and Sigmund Romberg. Then in 1916 he saw a performance of Jerome Kern's *Very Good Eddie*, and it changed his life. He knew that he and some of the critics were right—that the Kern musicals at the Princess Theatre heralded a new era of musical creativity. Rodgers devoured them, going repeatedly to see *Oh, Boy!, Oh Lady! Lady!, Leave It to Jane*. Kern, he said, was his hero.

There were a few hard years, not of poverty or desperation but just plain failure, before Richard Rodgers could become "an overnight success." His early disenchantments with show business motivated him to go back to school, and he spent two years at the Institute of Musical Art, refining his spotty lessons as a child. Continued disappointments brought him to that critical point: should he keep trying theater or sell underwear? Then, lo, *Garrick Gaieties* opened, unfolding with it a life of fame, wealth, and hard, hard work. Rodgers, when asked why he kept on writing music, once famously replied, "It's my job."

That job with Larry Hart as his partner lasted twenty-five years and spawned twenty-seven musicals, including *On Your Toes* (1936), *Babes in Arms* (1937), *The Boys from Syracuse* (1938), *Pal Joey* (1942), and their big hit of 1927, *A Connecticut Yankee*. These shows produced Popular Standards that are almost uncountable, and which have been staples of both jazz and vocal artists for years: "It's Easy to Remember," "I Didn't Know What Time It Was," "The Lady Is a Tramp," "Yours Sincerely," "Where or When," "This Can't Be Love," "Lover," "Little Girl Blue"—an endless list. With Hart, Richard Rodgers's final production was in 1943, a revival of *A Connecticut Yankee*, followed by Hart's untimely death in November of that year, the same year that Richard Rodgers's second partnership was launched. His new colleague was Oscar Hammerstein II, their first show together another landmark in American musical theater.

Oklahoma! ran for five years and grossed $7,000,000, a box office record; its national company toured for ten years grossing $20,000,000, played in theaters all over the world, and set a new record as the longest-running show in the 287 years of London's famed Drury Lane. Rodgers and Hammerstein, as Rodgers and Hart had done before them, continued to strengthen and enlarge the content and purpose of the staged musical. With Larry Hart, Rodgers had brought urbanity and sophistication to the form, along with a growing effort to develop plot-driven songs and full character development. With Hammerstein the movement reached full maturity. Their subsequent hits, classics all, include *Carousel* (1945), *South Pacific* (1949), *The King and I* (1951), *Flower Drum Song* (1958), and *The Sound of Music* (1959), perhaps the most successful and frequently performed of all American musicals. Another bounteous set of Popular Standards has emerged from the Hammerstein collaboration, including "People Will Say We're in Love," "If I Loved You," "You'll Never Walk Alone," "Some Enchanted Evening," "Something Wonderful," "This Nearly Was Mine," and many, many more.

Oscar Hammerstein II, Richard Rodgers's second comrade-in-arms, died in August of 1960, but Rodgers, his work ethic and muse still intact, soldiered on. In 1962 he produced *No Strings*, his partner—Richard Rodgers, writing both music and lyrics. In 1965 the show was *Do I Hear a Waltz?* his lyricist the young and already proven Broadway figure Stephen Sondheim, whose mentor as a youngster had been that same wise man of the theater, Oscar Hammerstein. Rodgers kept his hand in with movie scores and rewrites, survived a heart attack in 1969 and a laryngectomy in 1974, but still showed up for his job. With Sheldon Harnick he wrote *Rex* (1976) and in 1979 *I Remember Mama*, with lyrics mostly by Martin Charnin.

The value of Richard Rodgers's contribution to the music of America is inestimable. With his two partners he clearly led the way in the development of American musical theater into a mature and meaningful form, and in the process composed dozens of Standards that continue to grow and flourish on their own.

It was a job well done.

Harry Ruby (1895–1974): Ruby was a denizen of Tin Pan Alley, a young man with a good touch on the piano, born and raised in New York, with some time spent honing his skills as an accompanist on the vaudeville circuits. In 1920 he and the lyricist Bert Kalmar formed a partnership that would last until Kalmar's death in 1947. Most of the Popular Standards with Ruby as composer were products of that partnership, although he occasionally donned a lyricist's hat to create others such as "Give Me the Simple Life" with pianist Rube Bloom (1945) and "Maybe It's Because" with Johnnie Scott (1949). Red Skelton and Fred Astaire played Kalmar and Ruby in the film *Three Little Words* (1950).

Arthur Schwartz (1900–1984): Another lawyer turned songwriter, the Brooklyn native Arthur Schwartz graduated from NYU and Columbia, taught English in New York high schools, and practiced law for a while in the mid-'20s before turning his full attention to composing songs. In 1928 he met Howard Dietz, the lyricist destined to become his longtime collaborator. Broadway musicals and films followed, including *Three's a Crowd*, *The Band Wagon*, and *Flying Colors* on stage, and *Thank Your Lucky Stars* and *You're Never Too Young* on film. Like Dietz, he also became involved in film production, his credits including the Cole Porter film biography *Night and Day*. Most of Schwartz's Popular Standards were cowritten with Dietz, but he also collaborated with Edward Heyman, Johnny Mercer, Frank Loesser, and with Dorothy Fields (e.g., "Make the Man Love Me" from the 1951 musical *A Tree Grows in Brooklyn*).

Jule Styne (1905–1994): Born in London, growing up in Chicago after age seven, Jule Styne was aimed at a career as a concert pianist, and performed with the Chicago Symphony at age nine. However, he chose to pursue songwriting instead, and proved, in his long and productive life, to have made a wise choice. He composed for Broadway and for motion pictures. His Broadway scores included *High Button Shoes* and *Gypsy* (with Stephen Sondheim), his film scores *My Sister Eileen*, *The Kid from Brooklyn*, and *The West Point Story*. There were dozens more, and hundreds of songs in collaboration with Hall of Fame occupants Sammy Cahn, Frank Loesser, Comden and Green, Bob Merrill, and Leo Robin: "I Don't Want to Walk without You," "Small World," and "Everything's Coming Up Roses."

Jimmy Van Heusen (1913–1990): Edward Chester Babcock changed his name at age sixteen when he got a job as a radio announcer in his hometown of Syracuse, New York. As Jimmy Van Heusen, his songwriting career began soon thereafter, supplying material for the celebrated Cotton Club in New York City. In a long and profitable career, his collaborators would include

Johnny Mercer, Sammy Cahn, and Eddie DeLange, but his Hollywood partnership with the lyricist Johnny Burke created one of those pairings, like Rodgers and Hart and Kalmar and Ruby, that for years would bring a steady flow of fine songs to the Popular Standard list. Their words and music decorated dozens of films at Paramount, including twenty with Bing Crosby—eight of them the wacky "Road" films costarring Bob Hope. They endowed the Standards repertory with "Imagination," "Polka Dots and Moonbeams," the luminous "Like Someone in Love," and dozens more. After the fertile Hollywood years with Burke, Van Heusen's collaboration with Sammy Cahn earned a couple of Oscars with "All the Way" in the 1957 Sinatra film *The Joker Is Wild*, and "High Hopes" in 1959.

Thomas Wright "Fats" Waller (1904–1943): Only a few of the creators of the American Popular Standard were also successful performers. Many of the composers were fine pianists; a few were bashful singers. "Fats" Waller could do it all. He was one of the finest jazz pianists of the century in the demanding "stride" school of the Harlem players; he was an entertainer of the first rank, a singer and a comedian; he was an organist—one of the first to bring the instrument into the field of jazz. But his accomplishments as a composer have outlived his exuberant performing career, and his great songs, most of them with lyrics by Andy Razaf, are essential Popular Standards: "Honeysuckle Rose," "Black and Blue," "My Fate Is in Your Hands," "Keepin' Out of Mischief Now," and the song that lent its title to the grand Broadway review of Waller's life and work, "Ain't Misbehavin'" (1978).

Harry Warren (1893–1981): Salvatore Guaragno was an ambitious Brooklyn kid who hung around theaters and clubs in New York, changed his name to Harry Warren, and worked as a pianist and drummer in pickup bands, and as a stagehand and sometime actor. He served in the U.S. Navy during World War I, then put in time as a handyman and assistant director at the

Vitagraph Studios. He turned up in Hollywood just as the "talk-ies" came in and found it a perfect home, composing some three hundred songs for over fifty pictures. Although many of his songs are well-known Standards, the name "Harry Warren" seems to conjure up no cachet of glamour or legend as do, for instance, the names of George Gershwin or Cole Porter. His best-known project is probably *42nd Street*, the big Busby Berkeley movie for Warner Brothers (1932). It spawned the title tune—a hit then and a Standard today, due in part to its revival as the title of Broadway's 1980 version of the old film, revived yet again in 2001 at a new theater actually on 42nd Street in New York City. The 1980 version enjoyed a long, long run, with many prime Warren numbers interpolated, but the name Harry Warren did not appear in the credits.

This is a man who was among the most successful and productive of Hollywood composers and won three Academy Awards for Best Song of the Year: *And the winners are!*... "Lullaby of Broadway" (with Al Dubin, 1935), "You'll Never Know" (with Mack Gordon, 1943), and "On the Atchison, To-peka, and Santa Fe" (with Johnny Mercer, 1946)—three first-rate popular songs, hits of their day, and two of the three solid Standards. Other Warren Standards include "The More I See You," "I Only Have Eyes for You," "You're My Everything," "I'll String Along with You," and "September in the Rain" as well as dozens more.

The singer/pianist Michael Feinstein, who served as secretary (and friend) to Harry Warren in his last years, has consistently championed the Warren legacy. His songs have always been known, his name should now join them.

Richard Whiting (1891–1938): The longing of sweethearts separated by the war in France was perhaps best expressed in the 1918 ballad "Till We Meet Again," one of Dick Whiting's first hits, with words by Raymond Egan. A native of Peoria, raised in a musical family but largely self-taught as a pianist and composer, Whiting sang on the vaudeville stage, then took staff jobs in the music publishing business, first in Detroit, then New York. He scored a couple of tepid Broadway musicals in the early '30s, then was sent to Hollywood, working first at Paramount Pictures, then Fox and Warner. Among his many film scores were *Hollywood Hotel*, *Cowboy from Brooklyn*, and *The Big Broadcast of 1936*. His many collaborators included Johnny Mercer, Leo Robin, and Bud DeSylva, and the resulting songs include the Standards "Too Marvelous for Words," "She's Funny That Way," "My Ideal," and "Sleepy Time Gal." Whiting's daughter is the singer Margaret Whiting, whose recordings and performances have kept hundreds of Standards in fine fettle for many years.

Spencer Williams (1889–1965): A New Orleans man, pianist/composer Williams, like so many of the early jazz men, went north to Chicago in 1907, then over to New York, where he began turning out hit songs that would last the century. One of his first collaborators was Fats Waller ("Squeeze Me" 1918). His best-known Standard is probably "Basin Street Blues" (1928), for which he wrote both words and music. His collaboration with Jack Palmer produced the essential jazz melodies "I Found a New Baby" and "Everybody Loves My Baby," and with Benny Carter, the ballad "When Lights are Low" (1936). Williams spent much of his life in Europe, working in France with Josephine Baker, in England with Carter and others, and during much of the 1950s, was in Sweden.

Victor Young (1900–1956): Incredible accomplishments in a relatively short life—that would characterize the career of Chicago-born Victor Young. He spent much of his childhood in Poland, where he became a concert violinist of great promise, returning to the U.S. during World War I to follow that discipline, to which he added those of conducting and arranging. His work with the Ted Fio Rito dance band led him to popular music and to jobs in Chicago and New York with radio shows and show bands. In 1936 he moved to Hollywood, where he was a major player in conducting and composing at Paramount and Columbia Pictures, receiving twenty Oscar nominations along the way. His scores include that of the classic film *Shane*. His many successful songs seem almost an afterthought for this talented man, but plenty of Standards are among them. With lyrics by his principal collaborators Ned Washington, Edward Heyman, and Joe Young, they include "Street of Dreams," "Stella by Starlight," and "My Foolish Heart."

Vincent Youmans (1898–1946): There were those who called him "another George Gershwin" in the early days of his career. Vincent Youmans, born and raised in New York, was a child prodigy at the piano and received a fine musical education plus a few years at Yale studying engineering. Following service in the U.S. Navy, Youmans tackled the Broadway musical, collaborating with Herbert Stothart on *The Wildflower* (1923). In 1925's *No, No, Nanette*, he had a smash hit (ditto its 1971 revival, which he wasn't around to enjoy). The Popular Standards "Tea for Two" and "I Want to Be Happy" came from that score. Other stage successes followed: *Hit the Deck* and *Great Day*, and a film score that set new standards of excellence in the infant world of the Hollywood musical. It starred for the first time the Fred Astaire/Ginger Rogers team and was loaded with fine new songs, including "Carioca," "Orchids in the Moonlight," and the song in the title *Flying Down to Rio* (1933). Youmans's brilliant career was interrupted soon thereafter, when he contracted tuberculosis. He fought it for years before his death in a Colorado sanitarium in 1946.

r, a shot from a .38-caliber pistol on the streets of N
ns on New Year's Eve, 1913. He would look back a fe
later and realize his life was changed at that moment—
it foreshadowed events that would one day lead him ou
the world, away from the poverty that had surrounded hir
a child. He was arrested on the spot and sentenced to a tern
the New Orleans Colored Reformatory, or the Waif's Home
it was called. What changed his life was the battered cornet
resented him when he was asked to join the Waif's Home
rass Band. This "jail," run by Black adults for Black children,
was tough but benign, and it was there that young Louis Armstrong was taken under the wing of an unsung hero of American
music, Mr. Peter Davis. Davis recognized a gift in the boy and
insisted he learn to play.

Released after a couple of years and already a capable player
of the marches and classical overtures championed by Mr. Davis, the Armstrong kid now became an apprentice to the great
New Orleans cornetist Joseph "King" Oliver. So began his
schooling in the hustling conservatory of New Orleans streets.
The subject was jazz, and classes were held in the local honky-
tonks when he wasn't delivering coal or selling newspapers to
help his mother Mayanne and little sister pay the bills at home.
His musical command and personal confidence were maturing
fast, and at seventeen he joined the Kid Ory band, a leading
New Orleans outfit, further polished his skills there, then signed
on with the pianist/bandleader Fate Marable, the man to know
if you wanted to play on the riverboats churning between New
Orleans and St. Louis. Next it's off to Chicago to play with his
onetime mentor King Oliver, whose Creole Jazz Band had become the hottest ticket at the Lincoln Gardens on Chicago's
south side. Staying in the Windy City from 1922 to 1924, Louis
Armstrong filled the difficult role of second cornet to the King,
and played brilliantly on the forty-odd records cut by the band.
He had meanwhile married Oliver's pianist Lil Hardin, who
encouraged him to move on to New York, where he promptly
joined the jazz band of Fletcher Henderson.

The Performers

"I'll Sing You a Thousand Love Songs".
—Al Dubin/Harry Warren, 1936

The singers and musicians who have, over the years,
based their repertoires on the Popular Standards
can be counted in the thousands. A special few have not only
brought credit to the original compositions, but also have added
their own creative passions, helping to establish the songs permanently in the musical canon. Below is a survey of several
dozen performers whose stylistic innovation and sheer volume
of work has led them to be regarded as the established masters
of the genre.

The list is mostly limited to those performers who made their
careers during the Golden Age and are, by and large, no longer
with us. Happily, their music is: Frank Sinatra, Ella Fitzgerald,
Bing Crosby, Sarah Vaughan, Louis Armstrong, Nat King Cole,
Lester Young, Coleman Hawkins. Also included are performers
who began their careers in the formative decades and contined
to carry the torch into the years that followed: Rosemary Cloo-

ney, Tony Bennett, Johnny Mathis, Ray Charles, Miles Davis, John Coltrane. (Several performers who were more important to the creation of the Popular Standard—Duke Ellington, Hoagy Carmichael, Thomas "Fats" Waller—are listed in The Songwriters.)

Although few are likely to find fault with the figures whose names have been included in this survey, there is plenty of room for honorable disagreement as to those left off. There are so many fine performers, a line must be drawn somewhere. Count Basie and Benny Goodman are the only Big Band leaders among the names below, so selected because they were also acknowledged masters on their own instruments. All the renowned Big Bands of the late '30s and early '40s played a certain role in the selling of the Popular Standards, but it was a limited one, so the big names in that branch of the business are respectfully omitted here: the Dorsey brothers, Harry James, Artie Shaw, Glenn Miller, Les Brown, and others. They are fully credited elsewhere when their work intersected that of prominent singers, instrumentalists, and songwriters. Much the same is true of the many singing groups of the period—the Andrews Sisters, the Modernaires, the Boswell Sisters, the Mills Brothers, and the Ink Spots. While they all performed and recorded their share of Popular Standards along the way, they were generally more involved with introducing popular hits that accorded with *their* style and capabilities, and thus did not range widely through the body of Standards, as did the primary vocal and instrumental soloists.

The survey stops short of the whole slate of performers who have appeared with gratifying regularity since the 1960s, championing the Standards in their own way: Michael Feinstein, Cassandra Wilson, Mary Cleere Haran, Diana Krall, Wynton Marsalis, Andrea Marcovici, Ann Hampton Callaway, Harry Connick, Jr., Jane Monheit—these and others are infusing the genre with fresh vitality and style, and are surely worth discovering. Special mention, however, must be made of Linda

Ronstadt. In 1983, this famous pop singe[r] leap of faith and embarked (in collaborati[on] ranger Nelson Riddle) on a series of albums doing, she helped make the Standards hip ag[ain] a whole generation of singers (and listeners) dards on for size.

Louis Armstrong (1901–1971): This man from Ne[w]

without question the twentieth century's dominan[t] American music. He not only perfected and legitim[ized] solo power of his instrument (the cornet, then the tru[mpet]) was the musical godfather to several generations of pl[ayers] all the other instruments in jazz as well. It is imposs[ible to] overestimate his effect on the music of the century—no[t only] in jazz but in popular music, as he invented new ways to [bridge] the two and reach the public with his music. He did it a[cross] radio, movies, television. And in the recording industry? [He] played and sang his way through the blues, the ballads, ear[ly] jazz marches and shouts, show tunes, and most of the pop tunes from Tin Pan Alley over five or six decades, including a lavish list of Popular Standards.

Whole books will be written about Armstrong's influence on *vocal* music and the singers who learned from him how to apply the techniques of instrumental jazz to the human voice. And beyond the music, here was a man who built bridges over the chasms of racism, bringing through his music a closer understanding of the world we live in. His good nature and generous stage persona surely cloaked anger and frustration with the racist pressures that surrounded black musicians of his time. By the same token, they also cloaked an inner soul who fought hard for his art, and for the understanding of his race.

Until a bona fide birth certificate was uncovered not too long ago, it was believed (because it had always been his claim), that he was born on the Fourth of July in the year 1900. Actually, it turns out to have been August 4, 1901. That means he was twelve instead of thirteen when he was arrested for firing into

The Armstrong story from here on becomes a blur of travel, record dates, and more travel, always to bigger and better jobs. Coming back to Chicago in late 1925, he formed his own group, the Hot Five (and on occasion the Hot Seven). Recordings by these combos during 1925–1928 are considered classic Armstrong, each of his sidemen jazz giants in their own right: the pianist Earl "Fatha" Hines, Johnny and Baby Dodds, Kid Ory, and in the augmentation to seven, the talented Don Redman on alto sax, the same Redman who, as an arranger, would profoundly influence the swing bands soon to come in the economically depressed but musically booming 1930s. These recordings made Louis Armstrong into a star, selling in Europe as fast as in the U.S.A.

It was at this point that Louis Armstrong found himself expanding from material based on the blues and the jazz-endowed New Orleans marches into solo trumpet and vocal renditions of the popular songs of the day. It's been a basic premise of jazz ever since that any good song is grist for the jazz mill. State the melody just once, then improvise on it and the chord progression supporting it. Louis Armstrong got there first with the convention that is taken for granted in jazz today—that each player should solo in turn, once the ensemble has made the opening rundown of the tune. The soloist becomes the core; the band sets the stage and keeps the beat. Armstrong was honing his unique vocal persona, too, and began regularly to "scat" the vocal—to sing or vocalize with nonsense syllables apart from the song's written lyric. A good scat singer actually imitates an improvising horn, taking off in ad-libbed flights like a trumpet or trombone.

Armstrong's fame in Europe led to many tours—Britain, Scandinavia, and France. He lived most of 1934 in Paris, came back to New York in 1935, and made a movie in Hollywood in 1936 with Bing Crosby called *Pennies from Heaven*—the first of many films in which he would appear. Along the way during all these years he had been recording constantly, not only with his own band, but with some of the great singers, including sessions in the '20s with Bessie Smith, and later with Billie Holiday and Ella Fitzgerald. From the mid '40s on, he returned to a small ensemble called the All Stars, his sidemen varying, but always of the best—Joe Bushkin and Marty Napolean on piano, bassist Milt Hinton, Trummy Young on trombone, Edmond Hall on clarinet, and many others. Throughout these busy and lucrative years he recorded Standard after Standard for Columbia, Decca, and Verve—playing and singing, sometimes in elaborate orchestral settings under arranger-conductors such as Gordon Jenkins and Russ Garcia. He enjoyed several major hits toward the end of his life, including his "Mack the Knife," and of course "Hello Dolly" in 1964, winning the Grammy as Best Song of the Year.

Louis Armstrong died at home in Corona, Queens, New York, on July 6, 1971. Most of his vast recorded work has been reissued, and the magic of the man lives on every day, in the playing and singing of countless musicians and singers for whom he was a model of professionalism, devotion, and talent. Those who knew him said he was gentle, a "natural" man, but obviously an engine of implacable drive and the will to play and to succeed. Fifteen years after his death his recording of "What a Wonderful World" was played on the soundtrack of the Robin Williams film *Good Morning, Vietnam*, and millions of new admirers got to know Satchmo, as he was nicknamed many years ago.

Louis Armstrong worked his way through a century of bigotry and racism armed with the sheer force and beauty of his music, and the power with which it endowed him. His legacy is of many parts—musical and ethical—a great and dedicated man who rose from poverty to the heights of world fame.

Fred Astaire (1899–1987): The Austerlitzes of Omaha were well-to-do, and their son and daughter, Fred and Adele, had dancing and music lessons from an early age. They were soon dancing all over the world in cabarets and vaudeville as Fred and Adele Astaire, made their first movie (with Mary Pickford) in 1917,

The Performers

"I'll Sing You a Thousand Love Songs"
—Al Dubin/Harry Warren, 1936

The singers and musicians who have, over the years, based their repertoires on the Popular Standards can be counted in the thousands. A special few have not only brought credit to the original compositions, but also have added their own creative passions, helping to establish the songs permanently in the musical canon. Below is a survey of several dozen performers whose stylistic innovation and sheer volume of work has led them to be regarded as the established masters of the genre.

The list is mostly limited to those performers who made their careers during the Golden Age and are, by and large, no longer with us. Happily, their music is: Frank Sinatra, Ella Fitzgerald, Bing Crosby, Sarah Vaughan, Louis Armstrong, Nat King Cole, Lester Young, Coleman Hawkins. Also included are performers who began their careers in the formative decades and contined to carry the torch into the years that followed: Rosemary Clooney, Tony Bennett, Johnny Mathis, Ray Charles, Miles Davis, John Coltrane. (Several performers who were more important to the creation of the Popular Standard—Duke Ellington, Hoagy Carmichael, Thomas "Fats" Waller—are listed in The Songwriters.)

Although few are likely to find fault with the figures whose names have been included in this survey, there is plenty of room for honorable disagreement as to those left off. There are so many fine performers, a line must be drawn somewhere. Count Basie and Benny Goodman are the only Big Band leaders among the names below, so selected because they were also acknowledged masters on their own instruments. All the renowned Big Bands of the late '30s and early '40s played a certain role in the selling of the Popular Standards, but it was a limited one, so the big names in that branch of the business are respectfully omitted here: the Dorsey brothers, Harry James, Artie Shaw, Glenn Miller, Les Brown, and others. They are fully credited elsewhere when their work intersected that of prominent singers, instrumentalists, and songwriters. Much the same is true of the many singing groups of the period—the Andrews Sisters, the Modernaires, the Boswell Sisters, the Mills Brothers, and the Ink Spots. While they all performed and recorded their share of Popular Standards along the way, they were generally more involved with introducing popular hits that accorded with *their* style and capabilities, and thus did not range widely through the body of Standards, as did the primary vocal and instrumental soloists.

The survey stops short of the whole slate of performers who have appeared with gratifying regularity since the 1960s, championing the Standards in their own way: Michael Feinstein, Cassandra Wilson, Mary Cleere Haran, Diana Krall, Wynton Marsalis, Andrea Marcovici, Ann Hampton Callaway, Harry Connick, Jr., Jane Monheit—these and others are infusing the genre with fresh vitality and style, and are surely worth discovering. Special mention, however, must be made of Linda

Ronstadt. In 1983, this famous pop singer took a professional leap of faith and embarked (in collaboration with veteran arranger Nelson Riddle) on a series of albums of Standards. In so doing, she helped make the Standards hip again, and inspired a whole generation of singers (and listeners) to try the Standards on for size.

Louis Armstrong (1901–1971): This man from New Orleans is without question the twentieth century's dominant figure in American music. He not only perfected and legitimatized the solo power of his instrument (the cornet, then the trumpet), he was the musical godfather to several generations of players on all the other instruments in jazz as well. It is impossible to overestimate his effect on the music of the century—not only in jazz but in popular music, as he invented new ways to link the two and reach the public with his music. He did it all— radio, movies, television. And in the recording industry? He played and sang his way through the blues, the ballads, early jazz marches and shouts, show tunes, and most of the pop tunes from Tin Pan Alley over five or six decades, including a lavish list of Popular Standards.

Whole books will be written about Armstrong's influence on *vocal* music and the singers who learned from him how to apply the techniques of instrumental jazz to the human voice. And beyond the music, here was a man who built bridges over the chasms of racism, bringing through his music a closer understanding of the world we live in. His good nature and generous stage persona surely cloaked anger and frustration with the racist pressures that surrounded black musicians of his time. By the same token, they also cloaked an inner soul who fought hard for his art, and for the understanding of his race.

Until a bona fide birth certificate was uncovered not too long ago, it was believed (because it had always been his claim), that he was born on the Fourth of July in the year 1900. Actually, it turns out to have been August 4, 1901. That means he was twelve instead of thirteen when he was arrested for firing into the air, a shot from a .38-caliber pistol on the streets of New Orleans on New Year's Eve, 1913. He would look back a few years later and realize his life was changed at that moment— that it foreshadowed events that would one day lead him out into the world, away from the poverty that had surrounded him as a child. He was arrested on the spot and sentenced to a term in the New Orleans Colored Reformatory, or the Waif's Home as it was called. What changed his life was the battered cornet presented him when he was asked to join the Waif's Home Brass Band. This "jail," run by Black adults for Black children, was tough but benign, and it was there that young Louis Armstrong was taken under the wing of an unsung hero of American music, Mr. Peter Davis. Davis recognized a gift in the boy and insisted he learn to play.

Released after a couple of years and already a capable player of the marches and classical overtures championed by Mr. Davis, the Armstrong kid now became an apprentice to the great New Orleans cornetist Joseph "King" Oliver. So began his schooling in the hustling conservatory of New Orleans streets. The subject was jazz, and classes were held in the local honky-tonks when he wasn't delivering coal or selling newspapers to help his mother Mayanne and little sister pay the bills at home. His musical command and personal confidence were maturing fast, and at seventeen he joined the Kid Ory band, a leading New Orleans outfit, further polished his skills there, then signed on with the pianist/bandleader Fate Marable, the man to know if you wanted to play on the riverboats churning between New Orleans and St. Louis. Next it's off to Chicago to play with his onetime mentor King Oliver, whose Creole Jazz Band had become the hottest ticket at the Lincoln Gardens on Chicago's south side. Staying in the Windy City from 1922 to 1924, Louis Armstrong filled the difficult role of second cornet to the King, and played brilliantly on the forty-odd records cut by the band. He had meanwhile married Oliver's pianist Lil Hardin, who encouraged him to move on to New York, where he promptly joined the jazz band of Fletcher Henderson.

The Armstrong story from here on becomes a blur of travel, record dates, and more travel, always to bigger and better jobs. Coming back to Chicago in late 1925, he formed his own group, the Hot Five (and on occasion the Hot Seven). Recordings by these combos during 1925–1928 are considered classic Armstrong, each of his sidemen jazz giants in their own right: the pianist Earl "Fatha" Hines, Johnny and Baby Dodds, Kid Ory, and in the augmentation to seven, the talented Don Redman on alto sax, the same Redman who, as an arranger, would profoundly influence the swing bands soon to come in the economically depressed but musically booming 1930s. These recordings made Louis Armstrong into a star, selling in Europe as fast as in the U.S.A.

It was at this point that Louis Armstrong found himself expanding from material based on the blues and the jazz-endowed New Orleans marches into solo trumpet and vocal renditions of the popular songs of the day. It's been a basic premise of jazz ever since that any good song is grist for the jazz mill. State the melody just once, then improvise on it and the chord progression supporting it. Louis Armstrong got there first with the convention that is taken for granted in jazz today—that each player should solo in turn, once the ensemble has made the opening rundown of the tune. The soloist becomes the core; the band sets the stage and keeps the beat. Armstrong was honing his unique vocal persona, too, and began regularly to "scat" the vocal—to sing or vocalize with nonsense syllables apart from the song's written lyric. A good scat singer actually imitates an improvising horn, taking off in ad-libbed flights like a trumpet or trombone.

Armstrong's fame in Europe led to many tours—Britain, Scandinavia, and France. He lived most of 1934 in Paris, came back to New York in 1935, and made a movie in Hollywood in 1936 with Bing Crosby called *Pennies from Heaven*—the first of many films in which he would appear. Along the way during all these years he had been recording constantly, not only with his own band, but with some of the great singers, including sessions in the '20s with Bessie Smith, and later with Billie Holiday and Ella Fitzgerald. From the mid '40s on, he returned to a small ensemble called the All Stars, his sidemen varying, but always of the best—Joe Bushkin and Marty Napolean on piano, bassist Milt Hinton, Trummy Young on trombone, Edmond Hall on clarinet, and many others. Throughout these busy and lucrative years he recorded Standard after Standard for Columbia, Decca, and Verve—playing and singing, sometimes in elaborate orchestral settings under arranger-conductors such as Gordon Jenkins and Russ Garcia. He enjoyed several major hits toward the end of his life, including his "Mack the Knife," and of course "Hello Dolly" in 1964, winning the Grammy as Best Song of the Year.

Louis Armstrong died at home in Corona, Queens, New York, on July 6, 1971. Most of his vast recorded work has been reissued, and the magic of the man lives on every day, in the playing and singing of countless musicians and singers for whom he was a model of professionalism, devotion, and talent. Those who knew him said he was gentle, a "natural" man, but obviously an engine of implacable drive and the will to play and to succeed. Fifteen years after his death his recording of "What a Wonderful World" was played on the soundtrack of the Robin Williams film *Good Morning, Vietnam*, and millions of new admirers got to know Satchmo, as he was nicknamed many years ago.

Louis Armstrong worked his way through a century of bigotry and racism armed with the sheer force and beauty of his music, and the power with which it endowed him. His legacy is of many parts—musical and ethical—a great and dedicated man who rose from poverty to the heights of world fame.

Fred Astaire (1899–1987): The Austerlitzes of Omaha were well-to-do, and their son and daughter, Fred and Adele, had dancing and music lessons from an early age. They were soon dancing all over the world in cabarets and vaudeville as Fred and Adele Astaire, made their first movie (with Mary Pickford) in 1917, and premiered on Broadway the same year in *Over the Top*. Thus began the career of Fred Astaire, the *dancer*, and books have been, and will be, written about that Astaire, whom many consider America's greatest. When Adele quit the business in 1931, Fred went to Hollywood just in time to meet up with the new opportunities in film musicals, did a couple with a rising young star named Ginger Rogers, after which the two would make dance history.

But Fred Astaire the *singer*? Irving Berlin claimed he'd rather have Astaire sing his songs than anyone in the business. His version was often the first, not only on film but on record, of the classy movie songs that would become Standards, especially jazz Standards. Johnny Mercer and Cole Porter also loved to write for Astaire's thin, reedy, unpretentious voice—probably because of his fluent attention to the lyrics and the meaning behind them. He recorded dozens of Popular Standards, some with the best jazz musicians in the business, including a 1950 Irving Berlin album with Oscar Peterson on piano.

Mildred Bailey (1907–1951): A first-rate musician and a singer of substantial fame, Mildred Bailey not only influenced many who came after her, but also pioneered the role of women in jazz and popular music. She was the first woman to co-manage a commercial swing band, and the first to be featured on radio with a major dance orchestra, that of Paul Whiteman. Bailey's growing fame was generated almost entirely through radio broadcasts and follow-up recordings. Hers was a sweet, clear voice of rather high pitch, and she sang with perfect intonation. With her jazz-flavored style, many assumed she was of African-American descent, and while she did credit black artists such as Ethel Waters and Bessie Smith as strong influences, she was proud that her own heritage was partially Native American, of the northwestern Coeur d'Alene tribe.

While with the Whitman orchestra she married Red Norvo— the first player to legitimize the xylophone, then the vibra-phone, as a jazz instrument. She and Norvo toured with their own band, and billed as "Mr. and Mrs. Swing," had a long-running radio show on CBS. She later was featured on Benny Goodman's *Camel Caravan* radio show. But despite her accomplishments and success during the 1930s, her career was in decline, as well as her health, and she broke down completely after she retired in the late 1940s. But for the support of old pals Bing Crosby, Jimmy Van Heusen, the singer Lee Wiley, and the composer Alec Wilder, she might have died alone and penniless. After a few hapless "comeback" performances with the Ralph Burns Orchestra, she died in 1951 at the age of forty-four.

Count Basie (1904–1984): It took a kid from Red Bank, New Jersey, to bring Kansas City jazz to New York, and just when they were beginning to call it "swing." Young Bill Basie had studied piano with his mother, listened spellbound to his seniors, the early Harlem piano giants, and even gotten a few informal organ lessons with his idol, Fats Waller. He was touring with a vaudeville act on the Keith circuit when he found himself stranded in Kansas City, still in his early twenties. After scuffling for a year or so, he landed a job with a well-known K.C. band led by the pianist Bennie Moten. (The two of them fronted the band on twin pianos.) He stayed until Moten's death in 1935, then pulled together the remnants of the band into a nine-piece, hard-swinging outfit working the Reno Club in Kansas City. They had a regular radio show on a local station, but the New York producer John Hammond happened to be in the area one night, caught a broadcast, and insisted that Basie expand the band, bring it to New York, and as it turned out, make history.

By 1937, through a round of recordings on Decca and broadcasts that now went coast-to-coast, the Basie Band became internationally famous. Basie's was a "swing" band, in keeping with the new buzzword, but of all the competing Big Bands of that time, his retained the deepest roots in jazz. Dancers loved his band because of the robust beat; jazz fans heard his reliance on the blues as the bedrock under his work. His sidemen were the best in the business: Lester Young, Buck Clayton, Vic Dickenson, and Clark Terry, to mention just a few.

Basie had staying power. Most of the Big Bands broke up soon after the war, or struggled along without much of a future. Count Basie seemed to shift gears easily from the dance pavilions to the nightclubs to the concert stages, recording all the while on major labels and leaving a stunning legacy of his best work. The tight, swinging Basie sound, his piano increasingly minimalist, became more arranged as the years went by. Many jazz critics found it overly packaged, but those "packagers" turn out to be some of the best arrangers in the business, including Neal Hefti, Manny Albam, Johnny Mandel, and Sammy Nestico.

William Basie, the "Count"—tough as they come—was still touring when he was well into his 70s, but his health began to fail in the early 1980s, and he died in Hollywood, Florida in April of 1984. The Basie recording legacy is vast, and much of it is available in first-class CD reissues. Additional good news is that the Basie "Ghost" bands have kept the Basie beat and book truly alive, touring steadily all over the world.

Tony Bennett (1926–): Anthony Benedetto, who started jobbing around New York under the name Joe Bari, had been taking notes on how to sing by listening to his idols—two women by the names of Mildred Bailey and Billie Holiday—and one guy named Frank Sinatra, who later would always say to anyone who asked, "Tony Bennett is the best singer in the business." He may also have meant that Bennett was possibly the most attractive *performer* amongst the singers, extremely potent in live performance. His high baritone voice may lack the creamy smoothness of Como and Damone, or for that matter Sinatra, but his full range and the emotional impact he lent it have served him well for decades.

One night in 1950 he had the distinction of placing second to an unknown singer named Rosemary Clooney on TV's popular *Arthur Godfrey's Talent Scouts*. That was okay with him because second place led a few months later to a tour with Bob Hope and a contract with Columbia Records. Like others of his generation and style, however, his career was derailed for a while with the advent of rock. Columbia Records dropped him, but he continued to record on other labels, including his own. A good thing, too. Some of his best work emerged on those recordings, including albums with Ruby Braff and pianist Bill Evans. Lately, back at Columbia Records, he's been recording just about anything he wants to, including plenty of Standards. His tribute in 1999 to the memory of Duke Ellington, *Bennett Sings Ellington: Hot and Cool*, is considered one of the best albums ever, by anybody.

Tony Bennett recently told an interviewer that he thinks the music of Gershwin, Berlin, Kern and the others is truly "classical." Although considered in its own time as simply part of popular music, it must now be recognized, he said, as art.

Ray Charles (1932–): Rhino Records has marketed a collection of Ray Charles recordings from the period 1959–1977 entitled *Standards*. While it doesn't include all the Standards he has recorded in his prodigious career, it helpfully sifts them from his many hits in other styles. Critics and trade publications struggle to invent dual, even triple labels for this talented man—a jazz singer with soul; the man who brought rhythm and blues to country and western, a gospel-inspired rock star. His husky, rangy voice is perfectly suited to every category, to each of which he applies his mastery of the sliding note— melisma. One of the few singers who has always worked from the piano, his vocal/piano synergy is key to his style.

Ray Charles Robinson was born in Albany, Georgia. He lost his vision at age six (from glaucoma) and was orphaned at fifteen. He was determined from childhood to succeed in music, and has ascribed that determination to the three factors he knew could defeat him: he was Black, born in the South, and blind since childhood. At the St. Augustine (Florida) School for the Deaf and Blind he studied composition and various instruments. Using the Braille system he taught himself piano and saxophone and became adept at arranging and composing. After jobbing around for a while in Florida, Seattle, and New Orleans, he landed a contract with Atlantic Records, and promptly delivered his first million-seller, "What'd I Say."

In the late 1950s he moved over to ABC Records, where he became more eclectic than ever, recording pop tunes and best-selling country and western music, and sprinkling Popular Standards into his dozens of recording sessions. Huge hits through the 1960s ("Busted," "You Are My Sunshine") added to his stack of Grammy Awards, and in 1987 he received the Grammy Lifetime Achievement Award.

Rosemary Clooney (1928–): "Come On-a My House" sold a million records in 1951 and was the number-one hit for six weeks. No, it did not become a Standard. It was a ditty—but it proved to be Rosemary Clooney's recording breakthrough, and with other novelties such as "This Ole House" and "Botch-a-Me," was her bread and butter for a few years. But they were nothing like the kind of material she longed to record—ballads, love songs—*Standards*. Happily, however, she is now doing just that, and has been since the 1970s.

With her little sister Betty, Clooney starred on a radio program in Cincinnati when she was thirteen. At seventeen she joined the Tony Pastor Orchestra, and toured for several years. She credits those grueling dance-band junkets for developing not only her confidence, but her warm and powerful alto voice, her loving attention to the words of a song, and her jazz-inflected sense of timing. Those big recording hits of the 1950s opened doors for her in Hollywood, where her best and most lasting film was *White Christmas* (1954) with Bing Crosby. But her movie career was brief, and at the same time the music business was changing, affording less and less chance for Clooney to record her favorite songs, her way. Intense personal problems, meanwhile, led to a breakdown in 1968, but with Crosby's help she recovered, and returned to music at his insistence with sell-out performances in New York and London. The career of one of America's most beloved figures in music was thus courageously renewed and continues to flourish. Her recordings for Concord (twenty-nine to date) are masterful, her voice still warm and rich with a mature style that's now all her own.

Nat "King" Cole (1917–1965): Among the honorary pallbearers at the funeral of Nat "King" Cole in April of 1965 were Count Basie, Jack Benny, Jimmy Durante, and Robert F. Kennedy. He was forty-five years old when he died, a victim of lung cancer after a lifetime of heavy smoking. In his brief years of celebrity, Nat Cole pointed the way through some of the great barriers between Blacks and Whites in mid-century America, "building bridges" as he put it, between the two races, who "needed badly to get to know each other." Music, he felt, was the way he could help to build such a bridge. It was never easy. Hailed as the first African-American to have his own network television series (1956–57), he saw it fail when not one sponsor would "take a chance" on a show hosted by a Black performer.

Nathaniel Adams Coles (he dropped the *s* early in his career) was born in Montgomery, Alabama, but was just four years old when the family moved north to Chicago. His father was a Baptist minister. His mother, Perlina Coles, was a pianist and a soprano in the choir, and she saw to it that Nat and his three brothers got music lessons. At age twelve he was the church organist, and by high school was running a fourteen-piece dance band, booking dates for cash. He was the pianist, never the vocalist. Still in his teens and on the road with a touring company of the famous Black musical *Shuffle Along*, his fame as a pianist spread. His role model was Earl "Fatha" Hines, and before long he was working gigs in Los Angeles with his trio, already recognized as one of the finest young jazz pianists on the scene.

An odd nightclub incident is said to have started him singing when a patron demanded to hear the words as the trio was playing the Standard "Sweet Lorraine." Cole reluctantly obliged, and the audience loved him, so he began to add a cautious vocal every now and then. Turned out he not only had a beautiful baritone voice, but used it with perfect diction and intonation, a gift perhaps of his church singing as a kid. He signed the trio with Capitol Records in 1943, and in November of that year broke out with a national hit, playing *and* singing his own tune "Straighten Up and Fly Right." After that the hits came thick and fast, with Cole's vocal style getting more and more popular. In 1946 he added a string section for the first time, and launched the lasting holiday Standard by Mel Tormé, "The Christmas Song."

In 1950 his approach was changed for good with the release of a lush ballad with full orchestra, "Mona Lisa." It sold 3 million copies—one of the biggest sellers of all time, and from then on audiences knew him only as a singer, and a beloved one. ("Too Young" and "Unforgettable.") Fortunately, he also recorded some superb jazz dates on piano in the '40s with Lester Young, Illinois Jacquet, and others in Jazz at the Philharmonic. But Nat Cole devoted the last fifteen years of his life to recording ballads, many of them Standards to this day.

In 1991 Nat Cole's daughter, Natalie, recorded an album called *Unforgettable.* The title track was a duet she sang with her father's voice from his 1951 recording with Nelson Riddle's orchestra, mixed across forty years by means of remarkable recording magic. The album went platinum, and swept the Grammy Awards that year. It triggered prompt reissue of many of her father's recordings, and a new generation discovered that Nat "King" Cole was indeed, unforgettable.

Perry Como (1912–2001): Ted Weems didn't have the hottest dance band in the country, but during the 1930s he was on network radio every week with a program called *Beat the Band,* and in 1936 he hired a young singer from Pennsylvania to join the show. Perry Como sang with pure tone and perfect intonation, was considered handsome and cool, and the radio audience loved him. He proceeded to record four-dozen albums for various RCA labels, and become one of the most consistently popular television stars of the '50s and '60s, eventually earning four Emmy Awards. Viewers loved Como's easygoing presence and the beauty of his baritone, not to mention his low key manner and graceful bearing. He sold millions of records, in 1945 launching two simultaneous hits that sold 2 million copies: "Till the End of Time," and the Standard "If I Loved You."

Perry (Pierino) Como was born in Canonsburg, Pennsylvania, and at age eleven became an apprentice in his father's barbershop. He was soon making payments on his own shop, singing songs to anyone who'd listen, shaping his style after his idol, Bing Crosby. At nineteen he went on the road with Freddie Carlone, who headed a regional or "territory" dance band out of Cleveland, Ohio. After several years of seasoning, Como went to New York and the gig with Ted Weems. In the fifty-year career that followed, he sold 50 million records.

Bing Crosby (1903–1977): An adjective badly overworked in describing entertainers is *legend*, but it may be the only one for Harry Lillis Crosby, Jr.

"Bing" grew up in Spokane, Washington, one of seven children. It was a musical family, and this home grounding was augmented by his daily visits to the local music store, where he listened not only to singers, but to the hot music of jazz groups such as the Memphis Five. He claimed his highest times in high school were his gigs as drummer and vocalist with Al Rinker's dance band. Rinker's older sister was the singer Mildred Bailey, and she talked her brother and Bing into joining her in California, to hustle work for themselves in the clubs and saloons. Mildred then got a job in New York with the Paul Whiteman orchestra, and promoted brother Al and his friend Bing to Whiteman's arranger, Matty Malneck, who'd been hoping to put together a vocal trio. He booked the singer/pianist Harry Barris with Al and Bing to become the Rhythm Boys,

Bing doing the lion's share of the solo work. The "legend" was on his way.

With the Whiteman orchestra he apprenticed in network radio just as it was reaching into millions of American homes around 1930. He studied or sensed the profound importance of singing to the microphone. Be it for a radio program, a record session or a live show, he knew instinctively that the microphone was his *instrument*.

The Rhythm Boys took part in the filming of Whiteman's *King of Jazz*, elected to stay in Hollywood, and were soon broadcasting nationally with the Gus Arnheim orchestra. Bing was then offered a lead in Hollywood's first major musical, *The Big Broadcast* (1932). It was a super hit, and Paramount signed him to a long-term contract calling for a series of lighthearted movies with music, wherein he introduced new songs and followed up by recording them. So in 1932, he stood at the nexus of the three massive technological forces that would drive the entertainment industry throughout his career: the radio, the phonograph, and motion pictures.

Radio took him back to New York for a few seasons, still working with Paul Whiteman, but he returned to the West Coast to broadcast what became the *Kraft Music Hall*, one of the longest-running network radio shows in history. People loved Crosby's gentle ad-lib style. (His ad-libs often were due to his lifelong aversion to rehearsals.) He was generous to other performers. Connee Boswell, Ella Fitzgerald, Louis Armstrong, Peggy Lee, and Mary Martin were frequent guests, as was, in the late '30s, a wisecracking comedian by the name of Bob Hope. Their friendly banter and off-the-cuff put-downs led to a movie partnership that would last for twenty-three years and produce the "road" films with Dorothy Lamour. (The first was *The Road to Singapore*, 1940.) His musical films were at their zenith of quality and popularity with Mary Martin in *Birth of the Blues* and Fred Astaire (*Holiday Inn, Blue Skies*) when he was urged by the writer-director Leo McCarey to play the role of a Catholic priest in *Going My Way*. There would be some music, but the script was essentially a drama. Crosby, a church-going, lifelong Catholic, had doubts about his suitability for such a role. He was a performer who drew strict lines between his personal and professional life, never involving himself in political or religious controversy. (He was one of the few celebrities never photographed with a president or presidential candidate.) He finally agreed, and the picture was a major hit in 1944, with Crosby awarded the Oscar for Best Actor.

Bing Crosby all the while was recording, recording, recording—having done so since signing with Brunswick in 1931. When Brunswick boss Jack Kapp founded American Decca in 1934, Crosby went with him on the promise that he could cut anything he wanted—jazz, Standards, country and western, or pop. To each he brought the same laid-back Crosby style, his unbelievably easy delivery masking his fine musicianship. His early recordings reveal a higher, sharper sound than the later, mellow, Crosby baritone of his prime years, or the continuing bass direction in which his voice took him in his late years. He always sang with a touch of jazz, and one fellow performer remarked that Bing Crosby was the "first cool guy of the century." At Decca, since he was making big money in movies and radio, he had agreed to lower fees for his recordings, especially in the early '30s when the record industry was struggling to stay afloat. He remained with the Decca label for years, recording the many Standards created by Paramount's ace songwriting team of Burke and Van Heusen, then producing for the label the biggest-selling single of all time, Irving Berlin's "White Christmas."

Even the circumstances of Bing Crosby's death were in keeping with his lifelong image of a cool and laid-back guy who could handle anything. A legend. On October 14, 1977, in the midst of a strenuous European touring schedule, he took a break to play golf in Madrid, finished a round, headed for the clubhouse, and fell dead of a heart attack. He was seventy-four.

Vic Damone (1928–): Perry Como was a barber in New Jersey and Vic Damone was an electrician in Brooklyn. Yeah, right. But that's when they were teenagers. Then they got their big breaks—a facile cliché about show business usually voiced by people not in show business. Damone was born with a voice that Frank Sinatra called "the best pipes in the business." It was a warm and rich baritone, over which he seemed to be in effortless control. *That* was his big break—that and having parents, especially his piano-playing mother, who encouraged him to use his gift. Growing up in Brooklyn helped, so that one day he could drop by the Arthur Godfrey *Talent Scouts* TV show over in Manhattan, win first place, meet Milton Berle backstage, accept his offer to make a few phone calls, and open a few weeks later at a leading New York nightclub. He was seventeen.

His name was still Vito Farinoli when he was signed by Mercury Records, but by the time his recording of "I Have but One Heart" hit the Top Ten he was Vic Damone, off and running. Unlike many of the popular singers of his time, he had never sung with a band, been in a Broadway show, or established himself as a nightclub star. The source of his success was the recording studio. The hits came thick and fast for a while: "Again," "You're Breaking My Heart," and "On the Street Where You Live," Standards all. He went to Hollywood and made a few movies, but his screen presence never matched his vocal magic. These days his early hits are packaged on CD, and he's out there playing the club and casino circuit, his "set of pipes" as good as ever.

Miles Davis (1926–1991): The majority of performers who have nurtured the Standards over the years are, of course, singers. But the work of the superlative trumpeter Miles Davis, like that of other jazz soloists such as Stan Getz, Lester Young, Coleman Hawkins, and others, clearly illustrates one of the remarkable qualities that define the Standards—their appeal across vocal and instrumental lines. Perhaps, with Davis at least, this has to do with his light, understated style on both trumpet and flugelhorn, a style of almost vocal intensity, breathy and muted. He has probably influenced more young trumpet players than anyone but Louis Armstrong, of whom he has graciously remarked, "Louis played everything before we did."

Miles Davis studied at the Julliard School in New York and was an early entrant into the avant garde bebop movement of the mid-'40s, joining Charlie Parker's band when he was only nineteen. As the word *cool* entered the jazz lexicon, Davis was again out front. His album *Birth of the Cool* is said literally to define the style. Hard bop, the next extension of '40s bebop, was marked by Davis's 1954 release of "Walkin' " and in "Milestones" (1958) he was among the first major players to turn to modal jazz, employing scales and harmonies outside the conventional major and minor scales traditionally employed in American popular music.

A musical revolutionary and a jazz icon, Miles Davis nonetheless found the popular Standards a key element in his performing and recording repertoire. He recorded dozens of Standards throughout his career, and his unique and highly individualistic improvisations within them speaks both to his brilliance as a major jazz talent and to the universal appeal of that great body of American music known as the Popular Standards.

Sammy Davis Jr. (1925–1990): A life in show business and a success in its every discipline—that would describe the life of Sammy Davis, Jr. He was born to the business and was on stage at age three, to become a protean performer—actor, dancer, impersonator, and one of the great vocalists of his time. His powerful and totally versatile voice belied his small stature, and his first recording for Decca was a showstopper, a brilliant sequence of Standards with superb orchestral backing. In 1956 he made his Broadway debut in *Mr. Wonderful* and soon thereafter was acclaimed for his role in the film version of *Porgy and Bess*. His movie credits also include *A Man Called Adam* with

Frank Sinatra and Louis Armstrong, and the Bob Fosse film *Sweet Charity*, often considered his finest performance.

This highly energized, highly visible career marked Davis as one of the first African-Americans to be broadly accepted by all audiences everywhere. His success was not accomplished without controversy and pain, but he paved the way for others to come in all those fields in which he himself had excelled—song and dance and comedy. Sammy Davis, Jr. was one of a kind.

A lifelong smoker, he died of lung cancer in Beverly Hills on May 16, 1990.

Doris Day (1924–): When she was a teenager in Cincinnati and singing on the radio, Doris Von Kappelhoff's big number was "Day After Day" (1939). She took the name, or it took her, (she claimed she hated it), and as Doris Day, took off on a remarkable singing career. Bob Crosby (Bing's brother) hired her to sing with his band in New York, and within a few months, at sixteen, she was with Les Brown's Band of Renown. She recorded big hits with the Brown band, including two in 1945—"My Dreams Are Getting Better All the Time," and the smash, million-seller "Sentimental Journey," now a Standard.

Day's next journey, for work not sentiment, took her to Hollywood, and focused on a career in acting. Some of her films did include music, producing such hits as "Secret Love," from *Calamity Jane* in 1953, which won the Oscar and proved to be the bestselling record of her career. In *Love Me or Leave Me* (1955) she played the role of the 1930s star Ruth Etting, acting and singing in perhaps her most impressive film performance. But more movies with less music followed, and she is perhaps now best remembered as an actress, costarring with Cary Grant and Rock Hudson in bedroom farces like *Pillow Talk* (1959). Doris Day is often overlooked as an important singer of Popular Standards, and is seldom if ever granted praise as one who lent a jazz flavor to her work. Her pop hits labeled her a singer with a "girl next door" voice, but the training of her early years salted her best work with jazz phrasing, and her voice at its best is very much that of a woman in charge of strong alto pipes.

After her movie career and a few outings in TV (which she didn't like), she essentially retired from the business. This admirable woman now devotes most of her time to the cause of animal rights. But Doris Day *is a singer!* And there are scads of great recordings out there to prove it.

Billy Eckstine (1914–1993): "I Apologize," "My Foolish Heart," "Prisoner of Love"—hit records for Billy Eckstine in the late '40s and early '50s—all soon to become Standards largely because of his lush delivery of them. Only a few years earlier he had broken the humiliating code that a Black male could not sing truly romantic love songs, just blues and novelties. Along with Herb Jeffries and Duke Ellington, Eckstine destroyed that barrier once and for all. A popular and successful vocalist, Eckstine was a fine all-around musician and manager, credited with forming the first big dance band to enlarge upon the new bebop style then emerging, stretching the accepted harmonic and improvisational limits in jazz. He had worked with the Earl Hines band in Chicago in 1939 alongside Dizzy Gillespie, Sarah Vaughan, and Charlie Parker, all of whom would became a part of his own band, joining other young newcomers including Miles Davis, Fats Navarro, and Art Blakey.

To the general public, Eckstine's talents seemed limited to his rich baritone voice, ideal for the singing of one romantic ballad after another. And in this role he recorded dozens of the Standards, which were part of his ongoing repertoire. But he was also an accomplished all-around musician who played the trumpet, valve trombone, and guitar. He stayed close to the jazz world, recording with Sarah Vaughan, Count Basie, and Quincy Jones. He is often credited as the key figure to link the jazz vocal styles of his own time to the R&B and rock styles of singers soon to come, such as Sam Cooke and Prince.

He made his final recording in 1986, with Benny Carter.

William Clarence Eckstine died of a heart attack in his home-town of Pittsburgh, Pennsylvania, on March 8, 1993.

Bill Evans (1929–1980): William John Evans was a skilled and thoroughly trained musician who gained wide recognition as a pianist in the 1950s, developing his own unique idiom of modal improvisation on many of the Standards, while respecting the melodic intention of the composers. As a teenager and then in the service, he worked with various musicians including Mundell Lowe, Jerry Wald, and Tony Scott. During 1958 he replaced Red Garland as pianist with the Miles Davis sextet. With his own trio he then continued to record, gaining critical respect and five Grammy awards either as a soloist or with his various trios. His approach to popular Standards was unique, marked by a delicate articulation and voicing, often establishing a romantic mood usually associated with vocal styles. Indeed, he has said it was his desire to "... present a *singing* sound ..." in his playing. His influence was strong on jazz pianists to follow, including Herbie Hancock and Keith Jarrett.

Ella Fitzgerald (1917–1996): It's a good thing for American popular song that the Apollo Theater in Harlem ran weekly amateur nights in the 1930s. First prize didn't amount to much in terms of cash money, but the audience seemed always to contain bandleaders and other New York musicians. Benny Carter was there one night in 1934 when a plucky sixteen-year-old, Ella Fitzgerald, sang a new Hoagy Carmichael tune called "Judy." Carter praised her to bandleader Chick Webb, who considered her too young and inexperienced for a job until she wowed the audience on her tryout night and he changed his mind. The fortunes of the Webb band were soon linked to the rising popularity of this teenage singer, and in 1938 they enjoyed a monster hit record called "A-Tisket A-Tasket."

Chick Webb died in 1939 and the band tapped Ella for their leader, but by 1941 she'd decided she would rather be a free-ranging soloist. During the '40s she recorded with several established acts—the Ink Spots, Louis Jordan, the Delta Rhythm Boys, and with the Norman Granz project *Jazz at the Philharmonic*. Granz himself became her personal manager, and would later play a vital role in the most ambitious undertaking of her career.

Ella Fitzgerald's voice and style were fraught with contradictions. Her sweet and pure voice ranged beyond two octaves, supported by perfect intonation and diction. There was always lilt and humor in her delivery, even on the sad ballads and blues. But Ella could swing, and came to possess a unique jazz style through her mastery of scat singing. When jobbing with the Webb band she felt left out when the players had jam sessions, so she would join in, she said, using her voice as an instrument. Scatting became a key ingredient on recordings and concerts, a quantum departure from her smooth and articulate ballad style. In the beboping 1940s she brought off incredible scat versions, big hits, of "How High the Moon," "Flying Home," and "Lady Be Good."

Norman Granz was the founder of Verve Records, and brought Ella Fitzgerald to the label in 1956 to create, among other things, a landmark series of recordings known as the *Songbook*. During a ten-year period she recorded over two hundred Standards, gleaned from the works of eight of the master songwriters: Rodgers and Hart, Arlen, Berlin, Ellington, the Gershwins, Kern, Mercer, and Porter. The arrangements were handled by top professionals—Billy May, Buddy Bergman, Nelson Riddle, and Paul Weston.

Fitzgerald was one of those singers who kept the Standards alive for the better part of a century by staying alive herself, enjoying an active career that lasted for decades. Although her health and her eyesight began to fail in the 1980s, she rallied time and again, performing until 1994, when she retired to her home in Beverly Hills. She died there on June 14, 1996.

For her fans and for even the toughest critics, it was like the death of an old pal. She had become a household name on the basis of her voice alone. She was never a movie or TV star, and had little of the glamour or mystery surrounding many of her contemporaries, but she was considered by many the finest female jazz singer of the century, known as "The First Lady of Song." "There was no one else in her class," said one critic. Not bad for a little girl born in Newport News, Virginia, who grew up in New York's Riverdale Orphanage and went down one night to the Apollo Theater in Harlem when she was sixteen and scared to death.

Judy Garland (1922–1969): As long as reruns of *The Wizard of Oz* play every year on television, America will remember the teenage girl who played Dorothy, walking up the Yellow Brick Road. The nation fell in love with her, and it seems still is, years after her death. The Standard she sang in that landmark film was "Over the Rainbow," and however many times it's recreated by other artists, the voice of Judy/Dorothy still clings to it.

Judy Garland was born Frances Gumm in Grand Rapids, Minnesota, and at age four was trouping in vaudeville with her two older sisters. She was signed in 1935 by Hollywood's MGM studios, and was soon quite popular as a player in light and fun-filled movies with Mickey Rooney and other teen idols. In *Listen, Darling* (1938), she sang the unforgettable "Zing! Went the Strings of My Heart," another Standard with which she would be identified with for the rest of her life. She won the Academy Award with *Oz* (1939), and starred in other major MGM hits including *Meet Me in St. Louis* (1944) and *Easter Parade* (1948).

The last years of her life were spent primarily on the concert stage, where she became almost a cult figure, increasingly beset by problems of addiction and poor health, admired not only for the never-failing emotional content of her performances, but for the very courage that led her to undertake them.

Erroll Garner (1921–1977): There is no mistaking the Erroll Garner sound. It was totally his own invention, and he apparently found his way into it at such an early age that a wise piano teacher advised him, lest he lose his gift, *not* to learn to read music. Which he never did. He worked out his own fingering at the piano, mastering virtuoso runs and block chords with ease. He worked as a soloist and with trios (bass and drums), his first New York dates with bassist Slam Stewart's trio at the swinging clubs along 52nd Street. In 1947 he backed Charlie "Bird" Parker on the storied "Cool Blues" record sessions, then went out on his own for good.

Garner recorded for many labels, including Columbia and Mercury, and concertized worldwide until illness forced his retirement in 1975. He may have sold more albums than any other jazz pianist, and his astonishing repertoire included hundreds of Popular Standards. It's said he could record twenty sides in a couple of sessions, most of them on the first take, and he never masked his joy at the keyboard, which earned him millions of fans who otherwise did not follow jazz. The James M. Doran biography of Erroll Garner is aptly entitled *The Most Happy Piano*.

Stan Getz (1927–1991): The term "cool jazz" fit no player better than Stan Getz, whose unique tenor saxophone sound led him from his first job at age twenty as one of Woody Herman's Four Brothers sax section, to a long tenure as a leading featured soloist with many backup groups. His repertoire was chock-full of Standards, which he delivered with respect for the melodies and a special talent for improvising upon them.

He was greatly influenced (what tenor man was not?) by Lester Young, and later by the guitarist Charlie Byrd. Their album *Jazz Samba* (1962) included the Bossa Nova piece "Desafinado" by the Brazilian composers Joao Gilberto and Antonio Carlos Jobim, which won for Getz the first of many Grammy awards, and firmly established his career as a soloist. He continued to concertize and record well into the late 1980s, when he was found to have cancer. He died in Malibu, California, in 1991.

Dizzy Gillespie (1917–1993): John Birks Gillespie (they started calling him Dizzy because he was funny and full of life), was one of the pioneers in the movement from swing to bebop in the mid-1940s, working with Charlie Parker and Coleman Hawkins in groundbreaking sessions on pure bop tunes such as "Shaw Nuff" and "Groovin' High." Gillespie, like many of the bop musicians, used the chords and structure of popular Standards as a basis for improvisations that were considered "pretty far out" at the time. Actually, they set new styles and patterns that would influence several generations of jazz musicians to come.

Gillespie grew up in poverty in Cheraw, South Carolina, and by the end of his life had become a world celebrity, not only as a musician but as a teacher and a goodwill ambassador for American music. In his last years he was the leader of the orchestra of the United Nations. In his long career, he recorded hundreds of popular Standards, as did his early partner in bop, Charlie "Bird" Parker.

Benny Goodman (1909–1986): To Goodman goes the credit not only for making "swing" the byword of the late 1930's, but for breaking the color line that had prevailed in jazz. Many of his arrangements were from the hand of the highly respected Fletcher Henderson, and his sidemen included Teddy Wilson on piano, Lionel Hampton on vibes, and guitarist Charlie Christian. Goodman, meanwhile, had become the "King of Swing" through his recordings and his network radio broadcast *Let's Dance*.

Benny Goodman was born and raised in Chicago, the eighth son in an immigrant family of twelve kids. He picked up the clarinet on an instrument loan from the synagogue. Still in his teens, he joined the Ben Pollack band, then founded his own, brought it to New York's Roosevelt Grill, and took the band on the road. By 1936 the band's popularity had reached enormous proportions. He preferred as the years went by to perform with small groups, and his trio and sextet recordings of Standards such as "Body and Soul" and "After You've Gone" are absolute gems. In 1955 he assembled a special band to play the soundtrack for a film, *The Benny Goodman Story*, which featured Steve Allen as Goodman. Perhaps the high point of his career was the Carnegie Hall concert in 1938, which was well-recorded and has been a recognized jazz classic ever since.

Goodman's sidemen and singers through the years were among the best in the business, many of whom went from his tours to solo careers (Peggy Lee) or forming bands of their own (Harry James and Gene Krupa.) He reorganized a Big Band in the 1980s, playing as well as ever until shortly before his death in 1986.

Coleman Hawkins (1904–1969): A native of St. Joseph, Missouri, Coleman Hawkins studied at Washburn College in Topeka, Kansas, before setting out at age eighteen on a long career in music, touring with the blues singer Mamie Smith. His instrument was the tenor saxophone, and it is generally agreed that he alone brought it into maturity as a solo jazz instrument with his rich tone and inspired improvisations. His recording of "Body and Soul" confirmed the piece as a jazz Standard from then on, and stands today as one of the most successful and influential jazz recordings of the century.

Coleman Hawkins remained a key player in the jazz world throughout his life. He toured in Europe early on, recording with the English bandsman Jack Hylton and the French guitar luminary Django Reinhardt. Back in the U.S., he embraced the radical bop style in jazz as it broke through in the mid-'40s, and recorded with bop's first high priests, Dizzy Gillespie and Charlie Parker. He recorded with virtually every leading player in jazz, including the pianists Dick Hyman and Thelonious Monk, the trumpet men Ruby Braff and Buck Clayton, and hundreds of others. Along the way, he recorded his improvisations on most of the American Popular Standards, but he clearly *made* one of them a Standard through his landmark 1939 recording of "Body and Soul."

Billie Holiday (1915–1959): The title of her autobiography and the film based on it is *Lady Sings the Blues*. Actually, she seldom did, at least in the strict and limited form of classic blues. The word is all too often attached to any song about longing or sadness or loss, and Billie Holiday knew plenty about those things, and sang about them. Two of life's darkest and most forbidding subjects—suicide and lynching—were subjects she treated in song: "Gloomy Sunday" (Lewis & Javor/Seress, 1936), and "Strange Fruit" (Lewis Allen, 1939). The former was imported from Hungary, replete with a depressing lyric that supposedly led people to suicide. "Strange Fruit," which Holiday introduced and which was identified with her for many years, describes a lynching, the "strange fruit" the bodies of lynch victims twisting from tree limbs. For years both songs were avoided or banned outright from radio broadcast. These two songs, and the conventional wisdom that Holiday sang nothing but the blues, have distorted comprehension of the superb legacy of recorded Standards she left behind in her brief and tortured life. She sang love songs and a lot of great, up-tempo jazz numbers. What she brought to all of it was an undeniable sense of herself with a voice that somehow imparted an urgency, an involvement with even the blandest material.

Billie Holiday died in a New York hospital in July of 1959, destitute, a longtime victim of heroin addiction, hounded by the police even at her deathbed. The hard times started early, after her birth in Baltimore in 1915. After her father left the family, her mother moved to New York to get work, leaving the baby with relatives, several of whom mistreated her severely. She started working at odd jobs—washing floors, running errands—and once said that she had become a woman by the time she was six. By her early teens she had indeed become beautiful and womanly beyond her years. After an assault by an attempted rapist, the courts consigned *her* to an institution. Her mother managed to get her released after many months, and returned to New York, taking Billie with her. Her singing career began soon after that on a chance audition in a Harlem club, where John Hammond of Columbia Records heard her and booked her first recording session.

Lady Day was the nickname bestowed on her by the great tenor saxophonist Lester Young. (She in turn labeled him "The President" or "Prez" and that stuck, too.) By whatever name, she proved to be a woman of uncommon will and resolve, magically gifted as a jazz singer, who would break ground for those who followed. Musicians, critics, and fans alike were aware that she was unique—the first singer of either race or gender to bring profound personal involvement to the delivery of a song. Before Lady Day, most singers, even in jazz, distanced themselves from the words of the song. They were singing *about* trouble or love or loss, not about their own anguish or joy. Holiday's naked style opened the doors to similar personal expression from Judy Garland, Nina Simone, Dinah Washington—practically all of the singers who outlived her, not to mention an entire generation of folk and rock singers whose every song seems to say "this is me out here, not some songwriter."

But Lady Day seldom sang the blues, she sang the Standards. There were plenty that she probably recorded to placate the people in the front office, but she gave them all her special stamp. One of her early record dates with Teddy Wilson on piano, "What a Little Moonlight Can Do," transformed a so-so pop tune into a jazz tour de force. Her recordings of Standards like "All of Me," "Night and Day," "The Way You Look Tonight," are unmistakable classics. More famous in death than in life, her reincarnation in the Diana Ross film biography (1972) created a new cult of fans that continues to grow. Columbia and Verve Records have remastered practically all of her work, and along with a few other labels, it's possible now to rediscover Billie Holiday from her first record session in 1933 to her last in 1958.

Among the barriers imposed on the career of Billie Holiday was the absurdity known as the New York City "cabaret" card, a holdover from the bad old days of bootleggers and gangsters, whereby entertainers were considered ipso facto to be part of the underworld in one way or another. All entertainers and musicians working in New York cabarets and clubs were fingerprinted, grilled, and issued or denied permits to work. The practice wasn't discontinued until the early 1960s, and was a weapon used against Billie Holiday in her last years. By then she was a sought-after star, but because of past arrests and unfounded suspicions, her card was withheld, and she was prohibited from working in New York's best cabarets and clubs for top money.

Lena Horne (1917–): Three words that characterize the career of this remarkable woman are courage, stamina, and talent. Now, *which* career? Popular/jazz singer? Movie star? Broadway star? She did it all. She was singing at the Cotton Club in Harlem at age sixteen, moved rapidly into featured roles, and before long was touring with the elegant orchestra of Noble Sissle. She was then hired by Charlie Barnet, who, along with Benny Goodman, was determined to break the color line in popular music. Barnet's band played sturdy jazz, and Horne quickly made it her own. Hers was a light soprano voice with almost no imprint of the blues singers who preceded her. Her delivery was saucy but always elegant, her diction flawless.

In 1942 she was signed by MGM, and immediately confronted the cruelty and absurdity of racism, Hollywood style. In many productions she was assigned to musical segments that were edited out when the film was shown to Southern audiences. In two major 1943 films, *Cabin in the Sky* and *Stormy Weather*, she and her costars in the all-Black cast were allowed a bit more freedom from stereotype, but not much. Even with the box office success of these films, the studios continued their apartheid treatment of Horne, injecting her production numbers into films with no plot connection. She was then refused the role of the mulatto woman, Julie, in MGM's filming of *Show Boat*, some said because of her activism in the Screen Actors Guild in its effort to improve conditions for African-American members, or because of her marriage in 1947 to the white arranger/pianist Lennie Hayton. The couple lived for a while in Las Vegas, where she was already a top-money nightclub star, then in New York. Tough times again greeted them, with Horne's name besmirched as a Communist sympathizer during the McCarthy years. Just when her career seemed stymied for good, however, Lena Horne became a star on Broadway in the Harold Arlen/E. Y. Harburg 1957 hit *Jamaica*.

During the 1960s, Horne was increasingly involved with the Civil Rights movement, and in music was busy in the studios, recording many of the Popular Standards for which she is now revered. Then in 1971 tragedy overtook her, with the deaths in one year of her husband, her father, and a son. She went into seclusion until Tony Bennett insisted they team up for Broadway in *Tony and Lena*, a huge success. In 1981 she opened in her own show *The Lady and Her Music*, which ran and ran, was filmed for TV, played London for months, and toured the U.S. for years. Recordings of her music from the show won two Grammys, and in 1984 she was honored at the Kennedy Center for lifetime achievement in the arts.

Dick Hyman (1927–): It's possible that devotees of the Popular Standard, in the course of listening to the great singers, the studio bands, or the jazz combos have heard the piano of Dick Hyman more than any other player of the last fifty years, though they may not have known him by name. Countless studio and concert recordings have relied on Hyman's talent and skill to get things right. He is the compleat pianist, and also a consumate arranger and conductor. He is a composer, a lecturer, a busy director and performer at jazz festivals nationwide. He has scored a number of films, notably those of Woody Allen— playing, composing, conducting, and arranging. Other pianists— Evans, Shearing, Peterson—may have released more solo recordings of the Popular Standards and are perhaps thus better known by name. But it's Hyman's deft and inventive piano that has shone and has held together countless recording sessions. A New Yorker, he studied classical piano with Anton Rovinsky (his uncle) and jazz piano with Teddy Wilson. In recent years, the busy Dick Hyman has scheduled an increasing number of solo piano concerts. Popular Standards? He plays them all.

Peggy Lee (1920–): Norma Deloris Egstrom worked on farms around her hometown of Jamestown, North Dakota, or with her dad at the railroad station. By the time she was fourteen, an offer to sing at the local radio studio looked very good. "It beat shucking grain," she said, and left home. On her next job, in Fargo, the radio people changed Norma Egstrom into Peggy Lee, the name she took with her to Hollywood, and to the Ambassador West Hotel in Chicago. It was 1941. Benny Goodman was in the audience, heard a nervous twenty-year-old Peggy Lee sing, and hired her on the spot. Like many singers of her age and era, Lee credited the subsequent grueling days on a bandstand for endowing her with confidence and teaching her how to swing with the beat. It paid off. The hardworking young woman from North Dakota hit the charts in 1943 with "Why Don't You Do Right?"

Peggy Lee's name could just as well be listed as a composer as a singer. She and her husband, Dave Barbour, were a prolific songwriting team, producing a succession of hits, with Peggy doing the vocals: "I Don't Know Enough About You" (1946), "It's a Good Day" (1947), and the number one hit of 1948, "Mañana (Is Good Enough for Me)," her first single to sell a million. Children in the mid-'50s knew another Peggy Lee, but not by name, through the Disney animated feature *The Lady and the Tramp*, for which she wrote songs and provided voices. In 1955 she and Ella Fitzgerald appeared in *Pete Kelly's Blues*, a classic film about jazz, for which she was nominated for an Academy Award. Her recordings boomed through the '50s and '60s, including another signature piece, "Fever" (1958), and in 1969 the dark oddity "Is That All There Is?" by Lieber and Stoller.

Peggy Lee studied the artists of the past and learned from those of the present. Of her contemporaries, the highest admiration was reserved for Dinah Washington because of her directness and the simplicity of her style. Lee herself was considered the ultimate professional by her peers in the music business, a perfectionist but never a prima donna, who survived personal difficulties that would have felled lesser souls. She was in poor health during much of her life, plagued by diabetes, lung problems, and a severe heart condition. A stroke took her out of action completely in 1998.

Johnny Mathis (1935–): As a teenager John Royce Mathis considered a career in opera, then turned down a college track scholarship and a shot at the Olympics, deciding instead on a singing career, inspired by the likes of Nat Cole and Lena Horne. There's never been a voice like his in the jazz/Popular Standard field, at least not since the days of the countertenors from the early acoustic days of the phonograph. With Mathis it isn't just the high range, however, it's the unique vibrato and superb breath control that make his work immediately recognizable.

Starting young in San Francisco clubs, he was signed by Columbia Records in 1957 and made a debut album of Standards with superb orchestral backing. Switching to new pop tunes— extra-good ones—he scored two big hit singles later that year, in "Chances Are" and "It's Not for Me to Say." From then on, scattering singles along the way, Mathis, like Sinatra and others of the '50s and '60s, concentrated on the growing market for long-playing (LP) albums, and recorded hundred of Popular Standards, mainly for Columbia.

Carmen McRae (1920–1994): A fine pianist who could work a room solo with only piano and voice, Carmen McRae developed a jazz vocal style unlike any of her contemporaries such as Ella Fitzgerald and Sarah Vaughan. Her voice may have lacked the cut-through power of those two, but McRae's sense of beat and her superb diction lent her strict readings of popular Standards a special urgency, resting on total musicality. She was influenced in her early career by Billie Holiday, and by the surge of bebop in the '40s, but limited her improvisations in recordings of the Standards more than Vaughan or Fitzgerald. She was profitably busy during most of her career, recorded many albums with studio bands on Decca, Columbia, and Atlantic, including brilliant tributes to Vaughan, and to pianist Thelonious Monk. A constant smoker all her life, she was plagued by emphysema and forced into retirement in 1991.

Charlie Parker (1920–1955): Kansas City native alto man "Bird" Parker is considered, along with trumpeter Dizzy Gillespie and pianist Bud Powell, the prime mover in the bebop invasion of jazz in the 1940s. He had considerable Big Band experience, but preferred working in small groups, where his (at the time) radically inventive improvisations had room to roam. Bop's erratic and atonal improvisations might seem ill-paired with the melodic and richly harmonic materials in the Standard repertoire, but Parker recorded a great number of them, some in beautifully liquid tones. He surprised everyone by recording, after 1950, a healthy number of Standards backed by string and woodwind ensembles, the first jazz figure to pioneer a "with strings" sound in jazz.

Parker suffered from a series of illnesses and emotional difficulties, and died of a heart attack in 1955. In 1988 moviemaker and jazz aficionado Clint Eastwood paid tribute to Parker with the film biography *Bird*.

Oscar Peterson (1925–): A major stroke in 1993 took Oscar Peterson out of action for a couple of years, but he's been back to concerts and record sessions since then, and if the illness slowed his majestic left hand down a bit, it would take a careful student of his work to notice. Peterson is usually compared to no other jazz pianist except Art Tatum in the immense range of his technique and his harmonic sense. Like most jazz musicians, Peterson started young: piano lessons at six, his own radio show in his hometown of Montreal at fourteen, recording for Victor with his trio from 1945 to 1949. Impresario Norman Granz found out about Peterson that year and signed him for many outings with his *Jazz at the Philharmonic* concerts and to his Verve record label, where Peterson would record an astonishing eighty-four albums, all with his various trios. In 1968 he made his first solo piano recordings for MPS, and has since recorded also for Mercury and Telarc. It's hard to find a Popular Standard that Oscar Peterson *didn't* record somewhere in a remarkable career now entering its sixth decade.

George Shearing (1919–): All jazz musicians seem to start young, but George Shearing, blind from birth, sat down at the piano at age three and is still there in one of the longest and most illustrious careers in music. Shearing was born in London, and after becoming quite well-known there, especially in his work with the superb jazz violinist Stephane Grappelli, came to the U.S. at the urging of his countryman, the jazz historian and composer Leonard Feather. Jobbing around in New York, he immersed himself in the language of bop, then formed in 1949 the first of his famous quintets, which were to break new ground in jazz, and sell millions of singles and LPs for MGM and Capitol. The Shearing sound in those years was a five-way mix of piano, guitar, bass, drums, and vibes (vibraphone.) Marjorie Hyams was his first vibes player—a highly visible breakthrough in the role of women in jazz. Shearing employed "locked hands" block chords on the keyboard, in long unison passages with guitar and vibes, plus a swinging rhythm section. One of their biggest hits was the Popular Standard composed by Shearing, "Lullaby of Birdland." (1952).

George Shearing is now in his seventh decade of performing, and can look back on an immense body of work that included recordings with Peggy Lee and Nancy Wilson, Mel Tormé, the French horn player Barry Tuckwell, and fellow pianists Hank Jones and Marian McPartland. His solo albums since 1979 on the Concord label have continued his lifelong exploration of the Popular Standards. Hundreds of them.

Dinah Shore (1917–1994): Frances Rose Shore left her hometown of Winchester, Tennessee, having graduated from Vanderbilt University, and went to work for a radio station in New York. She sang on several shows around town and suddenly found herself with a hit record in 1941, "Yes, My Darling Daughter." In the recording career that followed, she graced an immense number of popular Standards with that homey, slightly Southern but always musical voice. Her recordings of "I'll Walk Alone" and "Blues in the Night" are just a couple of the many Standards she released during this period. Her warmth and crisp intelligence then led to equal success in radio, television, and motion pictures, and her long-running TV variety show (1951–1963) kept her in the public eye after her singing career began to taper off. She was also an ideal talk show host (1970–1984). A crack golfer herself, she established the Dinah Shore Classic, a professional tournament now in its third decade.

Frank Sinatra (1915–1998): "The wheel of fortune goes 'round and 'round and where she stops nobody knows." With that phrase Americans were welcomed once a week to *Major Bowes and His Original Amateur Hour*, the long-running nationwide talent contest on network radio. It was the top-rated show in those days, grossing a million dollars a year from advertising revenues and the national tours of the winning acts. For one of the 1935 winners the wheel of fortune kept on turning until he died in 1998. Working and winning under the name Frankie Trent got him out of Hoboken, New Jersey, and on the road with a *Major Bowes* unit. But after a few months he quit. There was no future, he decided, in being an amateur. He wanted to turn professional.

As Frank (Francis Albert) Sinatra, it didn't take him long. After a year or so working club dates in New Jersey, he was signed in 1939 by the Harry James band, then Tommy Dorsey, with whom he recorded over eighty songs, including "I'll Never Smile Again," which became a number one hit, then a solid Standard. When the trade magazines voted him Outstanding

Male Vocalist, he decided it was time to get out of the band business and go it alone.

The Sinatra career from here on can be tracked by surveying the companies for whom he recorded. The Dorsey singles had been on RCA-Victor. Then in 1943 he began a long association with Columbia Records, where he recorded dozens of ballads backed by the lush orchestrations of Axel Stordahl, and occasionally by small jazz combos such as the Metronome All Stars. His work toward the end of his Columbia years, however, became increasingly demeaning, with producer Mitch Miller urging a variety of pop ditties on him. Sinatra struggled with material like "Bam Bam Baby," and "One Finger Melody." His career was faltering anyway, what with new singers and new styles coming on. But the wheel of fortune turned again—this time toward Hollywood and a new career as a serious actor. He landed the part of Maggio in the film *From Here to Eternity* and won an Academy Award.

It was 1953, the year he signed his third major recording contract, this time with Capitol Records. The songwriter Johnny Mercer was one of the owners, and he told Sinatra to pick his own material and to work with arranger-conductor Nelson Riddle. This was a new Sinatra now, pushing forty, seasoned, his jazz-tinged delivery spurred by Riddle's swinging charts. He was in peak control not only of his repertoire but his voice, and his years with Capitol generated the albums dearest to the hearts of Sinatra fans, including *In the Wee Small Hours of the Morning* and *Songs for Swingin' Lovers*.

The next turn of Sinatra's wheel of fortune, again spun by the record business, was a major one and a groundbreaker. By 1961, the old entrenched labels, even energetic Capitol, were in turmoil. The advent of rock music and other changes in the nation's taste and buying habits had everybody guessing. Frank Sinatra's solution was a radical one. He started his own record company. He would record over fifty albums on this new label, Reprise. He released *Sinatra and Basie*, arranged by Neal Hefti. He paired again with Nelson Riddle for an album of Standards by Richard Rodgers, then did a couple of albums with bossa nova master Antonio Jobim. In 1967 he recorded a landmark LP with Duke Ellington, and it was on Reprise in 1969 that he cut "My Way," which would be his motto as a man and a performer for the rest of his life.

After a brief "retirement" in 1971, Frank Sinatra of course returned to work full-time in 1973. He had twenty more fully productive years until he finally quit for keeps in 1995. The wheel of fortune finally stopped turning on May 14, 1998, for the man who has influenced generations of singers, and will influence generations to come. Who were *his* influences? He told anyone who asked that he idolized above all others Billie Holiday. He was convinced that every popular singer had been touched in some way by her presence—her phrasing and her diction, but above all her gift of making a song her own, convincing an audience that it was important, a part of her. He also had great respect for Ethel Waters, her feeling for the blues, and the great warmth that she projected.

Frank Sinatra was possibly the biggest star in a century that invented stardom. In terms of richness or power, his universally known voice lacked some of the elements of his contemporaries. Como sang prettier, Crosby easier, Bennett with greater power. But Sinatra had all the skills of showmanship to go with his plenty excellent voice, his sure sense of jazz, his acumen in selecting material, and his determination to work with only the finest musicians of his time. He recorded over 4000 songs, including 156 hit singles, between 1943 and 1975. Add to that the 50 hit albums from 1946 to 1981, including 13 in the top five. Sinatra's work literally defines the genre known as Popular Standards. He sang the songs of the masters, works of unparalled craftsmanship, with literate lyrics and worldly views of life and love that transcend the self-pity and indulgence that characterize many other types of popular music. For his recordings he employed the best musical support the business had to offer—the giants of jazz, superb studio musicians, and top arranger-conductors who reveled in the challenges of harmony and structure that mark both the Sinatra style and the Popular Standards he cherished.

Sinatra will be remembered as a quiet force in the melding of race and ethnicity in the business of popular music. He was the son of a working-class Italian family, and knew what it was like to be called a dago or a wop or worse. He sought the best musicians of whatever race or background, insisting that performers be accepted on the basis of talent alone. He unfailingly credited on stage and in print the songwriters and arrangers with whom he worked. He observed toward the end of his life that the entertainment world as a whole had always been ahead of the rest of the country in the matter of equal and decent treatment for all.

Maxine Sullivan (1911–1987): The Scottish folk song "Loch Lomond" would seem an unlikely song to launch the singing career of a Black woman from Homestead, Pennsylvania, but that's the tune that did it for Marietta Williams. She had changed her name to Maxine Sullivan and was singing at the Onyx Club in New York when the inventive young pianist/arranger Claude Thornhill arranged the recording session that would produce the hit. Sullivan recorded some more swinging arrangements of folk tunes, got a part in the movie *Going Places* with Louis Armstrong and another in the Broadway show *Swingin' the Dream*. She performed with the John Kirby sextet for a few years, then dropped out of the business and became a trained nurse. Because her sweet and swinging delivery had influenced so many singers that followed her, she was coaxed back into music in the late '60s, did some festivals, and began again to record. She managed in this long if interrupted career to create a fabulous legacy of popular Standards, mainly recorded with small bands, including the World's Greatest Jazz Band, and a mainstream group led by Scott Hamilton.

Art Tatum (1910–1956): It's difficult to find a jazz pianist of any age or persuasion who does not reply "Art Tatum" when asked to name her/his idol and primary influence. When Tatum came to New York's 42nd Street out of Toledo, Ohio, with his awesome technique (but extremely light touch), his radical harmonic and tonal improvisations, all of it sitting atop the unflagging rhythm instrument that was his left hand, other pianists considered leaving town. "Fats" Waller deemed him, quite literally, "God."

Tatum was legally blind—no sight in one eye and a small percentage in the other. His health was poor, and it was uremia that would end his life at age forty-six. Fortunately, mainly through the efforts of the jazz producer/manager Norman Granz, Tatum's mastery is well-documented on record. His legacy consists almost solely of his effusions of the popular Standards. There was no one like him.

Mel Tormé (1925–1999): Harry Mills (of the Mills Brothers) and Patti Andrews (of the Andrews Sisters) were his greatest influences—pretty good models to have if one of your early ventures would be the Mel-Tones, Tormé's vocal group, formed when he was eighteen and soon recording with the Artie Shaw orchestra. Seasoned by working within this tightly knit vocal group, he then broke away to spend the rest of his musical life as a soloist. From those days on, Tormé would be known as a "singer's singer," as accomplished a musician as he was a performer—a superb jazz drummer, a pretty good piano player, and one of the few vocalists who could write his own orchestrations.

Along with Sinatra, Fitzgerald, Armstrong, Bennett, and Crosby, Mel Tormé seems to have recorded *every* Popular Standard. Maybe not, but he was working on it. And he hadn't begun to explore the Standard canon fully until into midlife, probably because he had been too busy in a career that began at age four, singing once a week with the Coon-Sanders Band at the Blackhawk Hotel in Chicago. That's where he was born and raised, the child of Russian Jewish immigrants William and Sarah Sopkin Torma, whose name was altered to Tormé at Ellis Island. Like many other entertainers of his generation, he credited his mother with exposing him to music at a very early age. She had a job during the Depression playing the piano at Woolworth's, demonstrating sheet music for the curious listeners. Then too, she saw to it that the radio was always on at the Tormé's, and by the time he was four or five, little Mel knew dozens of songs.

He grew up studying, writing, and singing constantly. At age fifteen he sold a song to the Harry James orchestra, the first of 250 he would compose in his amazingly productive life, including the Standards "Born to Be Blue," (1947) and in 1946 "The Christmas Song" ("Chestnuts roasting on an open fire ..."). At sixteen he was playing drums and writing charts for a touring band led by Chico Marx, the piano-playing Marx Brother. Then came the Mel-Tones, based in Hollywood, with recording deals on Decca and Capitol. By the time he was twenty-one, Mel Tormé had become a full-fledged idol of the bobby-sox generation. It was at this time that disc jockeys began calling him "The Velvet Fog" because of a pleasant burr in his voice, which he claimed was due to a botched tonsillectomy when he was a kid.

In a career that literally spanned seven decades, Mel Tormé experienced some of the unavoidable ups and downs of the entertainment business. Like many others of his generation, his recording sales slumped with the advent of rock in the '60s, and his career faltered for a time. But he came back strong, always taking pride in his reputation as a professional—a craftsman who knew the ropes. Tormé was one of the few ballad singers who, like Ella Fitzgerald, could nail the words and the melody of a song right off the page, then turn that voice loose like a musical instrument and improvise—*scat*—leaving words and music to fend for themselves. Toward the end of his career, he claimed to know five thousand songs, but said he tried never to perform any song the same way twice. Then, he said, it wouldn't be jazz, and jazz informed his music and his life.

He suffered a stroke in 1996 while recording an album trib-

ute to Ella Fitzgerald, and made only a handful of public performances before his death in June of 1999.

Sarah Vaughan (1924–1990): Critics and fans called her "The Di-
vine One," but the musicians who worked with her preferred
the down-to-earth nickname "Sassy" Vaughan. Her voice was
big and wide-ranging—four octaves when needed, and she
could explore that range from the low and smoky bottom to
the soaring soprano heights. Her superb musicianship and near-
perfect pitch freed her to use that voice as she pleased—warm
and intimate one moment, or clarion clear the next, phrasing
her notes ad-lib, like a horn player.

Her studies on piano and organ as a child endowed her with
harmonic insight. She was also, as a kid, singing in the choir
at Mt. Zion Baptist Church in Newark, New Jersey. One day
when she was about eighteen years old she went over to New
York City and up to Harlem, where she won first place in the
amateur-night contest at the Apollo Theater. The tough, sophisticated audience that night included a young and upcoming
African-American singer named Billy Eckstine, who was working with the Earl Hines Orchestra at the time. He urged "Fatha" Hines to put Vaughan on the payroll, and the rest, as they
say, is history.

Her style and repertory matured in the yeasty years of hot
jazz and cool bop that marked the mid-'40s. She took it all in
and made it her own, recording Standards with lush orchestral
settings one day, and small-group jazz sessions the next with
top jazz players like Cannonball Adderley, Clifford Brown, and
Count Basie. While recording for the Mercury label she actually
had two separate contracts—one for jazz and the other for, as
she said, "commercial things." She had never wanted to be
classified solely as a jazz artist, and told one interviewer "...
[my] heart really lies with the pretty ballads."

On her own as a soloist soon after the early apprenticeship
with Hines and Eckstine, Sarah Vaughan by the late '40s was

recording popular romantic singles such as "It's You or No One" and the soon-to-be Standard "Tenderly," chalking up twenty hit singles in the next decade. Vaughan was successfully building a huge and loyal middle-of-the-road or "commercial" following, and at the same time recording plenty of jazz dates in the company of her favorite players—sought-after pros such as guitarist Mundell Lowe, bassist George Duvivier, and on piano, Jimmy Jones.

By 1950 her recordings had vaulted her into international stardom, and she toured widely in Europe and the U.S.A. Even in the face of the rock explosion, Vaughan stayed hot during the '60s with strong-beat tunes like "One Mint Julep." She finally took a five-year hiatus from the recording studios, but came back strong with masterpieces such as her 1979 recording with Count Basie and Oscar Peterson of a Duke Ellington Songbook. In 1989 she was awarded a special Grammy for Lifetime Achievement in music.

It came just in time. She was diagnosed with cancer soon after receiving that honor, and she died in Los Angeles, California on April 30, 1990.

Dinah Washington (1924–1963): A performer who proudly wore the sobriquet "Queen of the Blues," Dinah Washington was also completely at home with gospel, jazz, country, and Popular Standards, and recorded prolifically in each genre. Hers was a strong, somewhat high-pitched voice, delivered with crisp diction and a unique snap at the end of a phrase to drive it home. Some critics credit her with introducing the fluid phrasing of gospel (the bending of a note, or *melisma*) into mainstream popular music even before the master of the style, Ray Charles, was doing so. In any case, no one ever mistakes Dinah Washington for other singers of her age and time. Her style was all her own, free of sentimentality and pretense. She imitated no one.

Ruth Lee Jones was her name when she was born in Tuscaloosa, Alabama. Her family moved to Chicago when she was three, and she grew up with music under the guidance of her mother, Alice Williams Jones, a pianist and church choir director. By age sixteen she was touring as pianist and vocalist with the first female gospel group, the Sallie Martin Colored Ladies Quartet. At seventeen she discovered nightclub life and began singing in Chicago clubs, including the Downbeat Room, where she worked with "Fats" Waller. Bandleader Lionel Hampton heard her, hired her, changed her name to Dinah Washington (or so he claimed), and took her on tour for the next three years.

She did her first recording session in 1943 with six sidemen of the Hampton band. One of the sides was "Evil Gal Blues," which not only became a minor hit, but defined Dinah Washington's stance from then on in the dog-eat-dog music business: "I'm an evil gal, don't you bother with me . . ." By the time she left the band for a solo career, she was already a rhythm and blues star but was also recording pure jazz sessions with some of the best musicians in the game—Clifford Brown, Clark Terry, and Ben Webster.

National recognition came, however, with the release of a popular ballad (soon a Standard), "What a Diff'rence a Day Makes" (1959). From then on, she recorded constantly for Mercury and Roulette, sometimes with elite jazz ensembles, sometimes backed by lush orchestrations of minimal jazz/R&B seasoning. She caught some bad notices for submerging the music of her roots to the pressures of commercial success. She didn't care. She was building a recorded legacy, doing it her own way, increasingly known to be a performer who took no prisoners. She was street smart and street tough—a woman who, if threatened, fought back, literally and physically. It's said she carried a handgun in her purse and knew how to use it. She loved the life she led, and all the trimmings of nightlife and fame. She would work only with the best musicians of both races, singing the songs that pleased her, no matter the style or source. And she was remarkably prolific, recording over five hundred sides on various labels between 1943 and 1961.

Toward the end of her life she accomplished a lifelong ambition. She had always dreamed of owning a restaurant, so in 1962 she opened a classy one (in Detroit), and ran it personally, showing up every night behind the cash register. She didn't give up recording, however, and in 1963, the last year of her life, released a remarkable eight albums. She was thirty-nine years old.

Thanks in part to Clint Eastwood's use of her voice on the soundtrack of his film *The Bridges of Madison County*, her musical legacy, in no small part a bounty of Popular Standards, has found new life and reached a new generation.

Ethel Waters (1896–1977): One of the first African-American singers to record commercially, Ethel Waters (born Ethel Howard in Chester, Pennsylvania) was often labeled a blues singer in those early days, but actually was possessed of a style and voice that anticipated the pop/jazz singers that would follow her ten to twenty years later. Billie Holiday, Mildred Bailey, Lena Horne, and Bobby Short are just a few of the stars who emulated her perfect intonation, superb diction, and formal attention to the words of songs. Because she "sounded White," she was able to perform on Southern radio stations and theaters in the 1920s. Her role was in many ways a mirror image of the desire of many White performers—Bing Crosby, Mildred Bailey—to borrow style from the Black singers of the period.

Waters starred in New York's nightclubs and theaters, introducing songs that would become Standards, such as "Dinah," "Am I Blue," and the Arlen-Koehler masterpiece, "Stormy Weather." Highlights of her film career include *Cabin in the Sky* (1943), in which she introduced the Standard "Taking a Chance on Love." In Hollywood, she then turned to nonsinging dramatic roles, constantly fighting against stereotype, a pioneer in assaulting those racist barriers when and where she could. Her last years were spent on tours with the evangelist Billy Graham, and the jazz and theater critics lost sight of her. Waters's majestic voice and presence were widely seen and heard, however, in hundreds of live and televised events. Hers was a great and meaningful life.

Margaret Whiting (1924–): At sixteen she was singing on the radio from Hollywood under contract to NBC. She was still in high school when New York called. It was *Your Hit Parade*, the most popular program on the radio networks. They fired her after two weeks. George Washington Hill, the cranky CEO of the show's sponsor, Lucky Strike Tobacco, said that Miss Whiting didn't always sing on the beat. (Good for her, as it turned out. She was developing her style.)

Not to worry. She had known about the ups and downs of show business before she could walk. Her father was the composer Richard Whiting, who had collaborated with many of the best lyricists in the business, including Johnny Mercer. When Mercer and two associates founded Capitol Records in 1943, "The Kid," as he called her, was invited to record for the new label. She sang Harold Arlen's "That Old Black Magic," and her version of "My Ideal," a Standard composed by her father. Two hits. Then in 1944 "Moonlight in Vermont," backed by an all-star orchestra under trumpet man Billy Butterfield, became her first million seller. She was twenty.

Margaret Whiting did not live the dues-paying life of a dance band vocalist, as did most of her peers of the time. It proved a happy omission, allowing her to develop a new posture as a singer, breaking away from the accepted dance band pattern of one quick vocal chorus. From the earliest recordings, studio arrangements were designed to feature *her*, not the orchestra, a pattern which very soon became standard for all the leading vocalists of the time.

Her Capitol recordings had preceded her the world over, and when America went to war in 1941, Margaret Whiting was soon touring the army camps and air bases in the company of stars like Bob Hope, Bing Crosby, and Red Skelton, and by war's end her career was booming with hit songs, many of them Standards-to-be, including "It Might As Well Be Spring," and

"Come Rain or Shine." She was on the Capitol label for seventeen years, producing thirteen gold records.

As the '50s ended and rock music rocked the music business, Whiting went in a different direction and teamed up with country star Jimmy Wakely for a big hit called "Slippin' Around." She could literally do anything she wanted to with that voice— a strong, true, totally disciplined mid-range voice that one critic likened to a trumpet. She settled into a long and productive period of recording for various labels a solid succession of Popular Standards, played the clubs and one-nighters, and toured with road companies of musicals like *Call Me Madam* and *Gypsy*. Margaret Whiting is singing today in great voice, with total admiration from her legions of fans. Like the title of her father's final major hit (with words of course by Johnny Mercer), she is just "Too Marvelous for Words."

Teddy Wilson (1912–1986): Theodore Wilson from Austin, Texas, knew every Standard in the book and then some, and recorded them by the dozens—with Benny Goodman units, with studio groups, and in solos. Wilson was classically trained, with a relaxed, sophisticated style and uncanny chord sense. He and Lionel Hampton, with the Benny Goodman band and ensembles, broke down for good the remaining blockades of race in the world of jazz. Wilson had accompanied and recorded with Billie Holiday, and for a short time fronted his own band. He was known also as an accomplished arranger and teacher, and for many years lectured at the Julliard School in New York.

Lester Young (1905–1959): "Prez" to fellow musicians (he was "The President"), Young wrought profound change to the playing of tenor sax, moving away from the heavy, sensuous tone toward a lighter, cool sound, which would indeed be a factor in moving jazz after 1950 or so, in the direction of "cool." Young is important to American music not only for the power of his example to young players coming up, but because he managed to do a lot of recording, in spite of increasingly poor health and emotional anguish that fellow players attributed to racist encounters he dealt with in the military. He had played with some of the pivotal big bands in the '30s, including those of Fletcher Henderson and Count Basie. He worked with Billie Holiday, and later with pianists Teddy Wilson and Oscar Peterson. They took plenty of Standards into the studio; friends of jazz and fans of Prez only wish there could have been more.

SIX

The Standards

"They're writing songs of love…"
—*George and Ira Gershwin, 1930*

The Golden Age of American popular music blessed the world with hundreds of Standards. Below are the stories of exactly one hundred of these songs. The idea here is to introduce the genre at its best, but with absolutely no implication that there couldn't be another one hundred, and another, that wouldn't do the job every bit as well. One of the rewards of the world of Standards is the search for new and old treasures. This roll of songs, meanwhile, will provide a good place to begin, to experience the charm and beauty of the known and to contemplate the promise of the unknown. The songs have been carefully chosen to represent a healthy cross-section of the myriad Popular Standards out there. At the same time, in themselves, they offer one hundred gratifying and diverse listening experiences. (If the song descriptions sometimes get a bit technical, it may be useful to refer to "Popular Standards Deconstructed" and/or "The Language of Popular Standards.") Headings for each entry are arranged: Title; Lyricist/ Composer; Year of Publication.

Granting that a sampler like the one that follows must be partially subjective (we all have our favorites), the essential Popular Standards from everybody's roster have been conscientiously included. No self-respecting list would be complete without "Star Dust," "Night and Day," "Body and Soul" or "I Got Rhythm," for instance. But an ongoing charm of exploring the world of the Popular Standard is the discovery of lesser-known gems. Accordingly, a few of them are sprinkled through the list, suggesting attention to the simple beauty of the Blake/ Razaf ballad "Memories of You," the dazzling inventiveness of Irving Berlin's "Cheek to Cheek," or the startling conceit of "Love for Sale" by Cole Porter.

A flock of recordings is casually cited for each of the following songs, partly as a testimony to their wide appeal to performers in multiple times and styles, but also to provide clues to future treasure hunts. Some are long out of print, but many now reside in reissues. Others may be discovered in old record shops where vinyl is still spoken, in libraries, and among collectors and dealers. Most, however, can still be found at your friendly CD emporium.

"After You've Gone" (Henry Creamer/Turner Layton, 1918): This is one of the first meaningful torch songs, and as such, one of the earliest Popular Standards. 1918 is *early* for a lyric as dark and ironic as this one—a quantum leap from the pollyannish sentiments of most Tin Pan Alley love songs of the time. Al Jolson and Sophie Tucker sobbed it on stage perennially in the '20s, but it took Mildred Bailey, and then Judy Garland to put content over style and really explore the emotional power in the words. "After You've Gone" has had a parallel existence as a prime jazz Standard, springing perhaps from the stunning Benny Goodman quartet treatment in the late '30s. It's been recorded by jazz icons from Roy Eldridge to Art Tatum, and is alive and well today in the hands of younger musicians like Wynton Marsalis and Harry Connick, Jr.

"Ain't Misbehavin' " (Andy Razaf/Thomas "Fats" Waller and Harry Brooks, 1929): Following its first (of many) Broadway exposures, this song quickly established Standard status with recordings by Fats Waller himself and by Ruth Etting. It was then featured in several films, including *Stormy Weather* (1943) and *The Strip* (1951) with Louis Armstrong and Mickey Rooney. So it was already a Standard when the Broadway revue *Ain't Misbehavin'* (1978) jump-started it for a new generation. Artists of every persuasion have recorded it over the years, both vocally and instrumentally. How's this for a mixed-bag sampler: Hank Williams, Jr., Billie Holiday, Leon Redbone, Louis Armstrong, Ray Charles, Dave Brubeck, Judy Carmichael, and Kenny Burrell.

"All the Things You Are" (Oscar Hammerstein II/Jerome Kern, 1939): *Very Warm for May* was Jerome Kern's last Broadway effort. It was a commercial failure, but it birthed this superb Standard, a song of unconventional ABCD structure with four key changes inside its thirty-two-measures, and a twelve-note range likely to mortify most singers. Kern himself believed it too complex to be popular, but it jumped right on *Your Hit Parade* and established itself as a Standard. Following some early big-voice deliveries on film by Tony Martin and Mario Lanza, it's been sung by folks from Barbra Streisand to Willie Nelson to Placido Domingo. It has also flourished as a jazz Standard. Check out Miles Davis, Howard Alden, Pat Metheny, Paul Desmond, and especially Andre Previn.

"Always" (Irving Berlin, 1925): Recordings of this prime Standard are so abundant they hardly need enumerating, but two of the most pleasant and surprising are those of country stars Patsy Cline and Kenny Rogers. The song was originally intended for the Marx Brothers Broadway howler *The Coconuts*, but was cut from the show. Published later as a single, it became Berlin's wedding gift to Ellin Mackay. Once again the composer chose easy-going waltz time and simple words. But this is not a simple song. Berlin never repeats himself, but offers four distinct phrases in the form ABCD. The B-theme leaps into a new key (up a major third) and continues to climb throughout the eight measures of the C-theme, before coming gently home to the keynote in the conclusion, with a lyric that is surely one of the sweetest expressions of true love in any song, in any language: "...not for just an hour, not for just a day, not for just a year..."

"April in Paris" (E. Y. Harburg/Vernon Duke, 1932): *Walk a Little Faster* was the first complete Broadway score for the gifted Vernon Duke—a revue, mostly for laughs, with Beatrice Lillie and funnyman Bobby Clark heading the cast. At the last minute a romantic scene was called for, and "April in Paris" was hastily composed—a hit in the Boston tryout, but brushed off, however, by the New York critics. Blues singer Marian Chase championed it on club dates and recordings, and it caught on. In 1953 it became the title of a Doris Day film, and a hit record for her at Columbia. Clooney, Sinatra, Fitzgerald—our ever-faithful Standard bearers—recorded it, and it has made the rounds in jazz as well: the Sauter-Finegan Orchestra, Coleman Hawkins, Thelonious Monk, and on three occasions, the Count Basie Orchestra. Recent recordings by trumpeter Wynton Marsalis and singer Dawn Upshaw have kept this Standard high.

"As Time Goes By" (Herman Hupfeld, 1931): This is a fine song that took a strange route to Standard country. Rudy Vallee gave it some record and radio time, but no one was listening until the intrigues of World War II brought Humphrey Bogart and piano man Dooley Wilson to Rick's nightclub in the film *Casablanca*. Suddenly everybody was listening to the song, and it's been one of the "usual suspects" ever since. Recordings since then? For openers there's Jimmy Durante's classic version, plus Harry Nilsson, Carly Simon, Rosemary Clooney—and lots more.

"Autumn in New York" (Vernon Duke, 1935): You can be fairly sure a song is a Standard when it turns up in new clothes on the soundtrack of a nonmusical movie. Harry Connick, Jr., with arrangements by Mark Shaiman, so employed this fine Standard for that fine film *When Harry Met Sally* (1989), starring Billy Crystal and Meg Ryan. Its busy history until then had included both vocal (Billie Holiday, Lena Horne) and jazz versions (Modern Jazz Quartet, Kenny Barron, Bud Powell).

"Basin Street Blues" (Spencer Williams, 1928): Louis Armstrong practically *owned* this Standard. He introduced it on a Vocalion 78, which was reissued several times in the following decades. He then recorded other versions and performed it in three movies, including *The Glenn Miller Story* (1954). It has prevailed since primarily in jazz settings, with trumpeters Roy Eldridge and Miles Davis, pianists Dave McKenna and Marian McPartland. Ella Fitzgerald and the Mills Brothers have sung it; so has Harry Connick, Jr. Basin Street's in his hometown, you know: "...New Orleans, the land of dreams..."

"Begin the Beguine" (Cole Porter, 1935): Sometimes it takes awhile for a song to catch on with the public, even if it's Cole Porter. With "Begin the Beguine" it's no wonder. The song is a challenge, but a rewarding one, for both the musician and the singer. Vocally, it spans three steps beyond the octave. This is a long piece, with a lot of words. Many other Standards exceed the customary thirty-two measures, but here is Porter with one hundred and eight measures (in a structure that is something like AA¹BA²CC¹Tag), and a chord progression moving in and out of several modes and keys. Not much happened following its introduction in the Broadway musical *Jubilee* until the Artie Shaw orchestra recorded the song in 1938, and sold over 2 million copies. It's been a Standard ever since, featured in many films, including the Porter biography *Night and Day* (1946) The Big Bands of Les Elgart, Stan Kenton and Charlie Spivak recorded it; vocals encompass the varied styles of Sammy Davis, Jr. and the Andrews Sisters, the Flamingos, and Johnny Mathis.

"The Birth of the Blues" (B. G. DeSylva and Lew Brown;/Ray Henderson, 1926): DeSylva, Brown, and Henderson worked together so well and so often they're sometimes referred to in catalogs simply as DBH. Their "Birth of the Blues" has attracted heavy-hitting singers like Bing Crosby, Ray Charles, Sammy Davis, Jr., and the Hi-Lo's. It's had its share of pure instrumental outings too, with Al Hirt, Gerry Mulligan, and Flip Phillips. A delightful variation was recorded on dual guitars by dual legends Les Paul and Chet Atkins, as "Chester and Lester."

"Blue Skies" (Irving Berlin, 1927): Written for Broadway star Belle Baker, "Blue Skies" was interpolated overnight in a floundering musical called *Betsy*. It was the hit of the show, and topped sheet music sales for a whole year. It then found a place in movie history, first with Al Jolson in the seminal film musical, *The Jazz Singer*, then Eddie Cantor in 1929, Ethel Merman and Alice Faye in 1938, and Bing Crosby twice—first as the title song of a 1946 film, and again in 1954's *White Christmas*. Jazz musicians love "Blue Skies," with its wide-open spaces for improvisation over routine chords that move from minor to major and back again. It was a Big Band favorite, recorded by Glenn Miller, Tommy Dorsey, Count Basie, and Benny Goodman. Small jazz ensembles favor it as well, inspired by the likes of Ben Webster, John Kirby, and Red Norvo. Vocally, Frank Sinatra and Ella Fitzgerald did it, of course. Willie Nelson's hit version in 1978 brought it back, although it had never really been away. It has since cut across all musical lines, recorded by Riders in the Sky, Tom Waits, Dr. John, Michael Jackson, and Crosby, Stills, and Nash.

"Body and Soul" (Edward Heyman and Robert Sour and Frank Eyton/John Green, 1930): The pedigree for this Standard begins with the British Broadcasting Company and the voice of the star, Gertrude Lawrence. One of her accompanists, the Harvard-educated New Yorker Johnny Green, composed the music. An immediate hit in England, the song was then picked up for the Broadway revue *Three's a Crowd*, and its star Libby Holman was identified in the U.S. with the song. To the jazz world the defining moment came in 1939 with Coleman fit Hawkins's now-classic improvisation on tenor sax. Since then "Body and Soul" has become a prototypical Standard for the jazz musician—a challenging piece harmonically, although framed in a surprisingly simple AABA matrix. Singers have been somewhat wary of this Standard, perhaps because of its wide range and odd harmonies, but it was always a staple for Joe Williams, and part of a recording session for Diana Krall.

"But Not for Me" (Ira Gershwin/George Gershwin, 1930): This disarming little Gershwin song has always touched the hearts of unrequited lovers: "... although I can't dismiss the mem'ry of her kiss, I know it's not for me." Musically, the song couldn't be simpler—a tight ABAB[1] structure within a singable range. It's been on the Standard track since its 1930 Broadway debut in *Girl Crazy*, care of Ginger Rogers, who sang it again in the film version. In the 1943 *Girl Crazy* remake Judy Garland sang it, then recorded it, thus assuring it a Standard imprimatur. Surprisingly, for a song that seems to owe its long life to its lyric, the melody of "But Not for Me" has flourished in great variety as well. An early treatment was Bobby Hackett's supple trumpet solo on some early ten-inch LPs made with the Jackie Gleason Orchestra, now reissued. Barbara Carroll, Red Garland, and Toronto's John Arpin are among the many pianists who have explored it, as has Marcus Roberts, in a free and swinging hard bop approach.

"Can't We Be Friends?" (Paul James/Kay Swift, 1929): This theater song was introduced to New York audiences in *The Little Show* by Libby Holman. Some seasoned pros (when young) like Mildred Bailey and Betty Carter recognized and recorded it. Meanwhile it had already crossed over cleanly into the jazz books of Roy Eldridge and Lester Young, among others. It has had special appeal to pianists of wide variety—Art Tatum, George Shearing, and the polished cabaret star Peter Mintun—and received renewed attention when Linda Ronstadt included it on her elegant *Lush Life* album with the Nelson Riddle Orchestra.

"Cheek to Cheek" (Irving Berlin, 1935): The couple we'll always remember dancing cheek to cheek are of course Fred Astaire and Ginger Rogers in the film *Top Hat*. Astaire's reedy but always appealing vocal is recalled as well, on a dozen CD reissues. Not that Astaire's imprint scared off Peggy Lee, Steve Lawrence, Tony Bennett, or Doris Day—a few of the standout singers who've done the song their way. It's been an easy jazz crossover, too, for Phil Woods, Joe Pass, Pete Fountain, and the pianists Erroll Garner, Dick Hyman, and Oscar Peterson. "Cheek to Cheek" is anything but an ordinary thirty-two-bar tune, Standard or not. It's a seventy-two-bar masterpiece in the form AABBCA. The startling C theme jumps without warning into the minor of the key, then leads smartly back to the major to reprise the familiar statement of the A theme, "Heaven, I'm in heaven . . ." Irving Berlin at his heavenly best.

"Come Rain or Come Shine" (Johnny Mercer/Harold Arlen, 1946): This is one of the finest of the many Mercer-Arlen collaborations, which include "Blues in the Night" and "That Old Black Magic." The chords and melody line are essential Arlen, combining elements of Black and Jewish heritage with a sure theatrical touch. It's not an easy song for either the singer or the instrumentalist, with its shifting harmonies and tonality, and it moved slowly upward in the Standard canon. Early recordings include those by Maxine Sullivan, Dick Haymes, and a very young Margaret Whiting. Nowadays it's out there for the asking—vocally by many of the newer names in the business such as Ann Hampton Callaway, Al Jarreau, and Kenny Rankin, and by the older crowd as well—Dinah Washington and Dinah Shore, Barbra Streisand, and Barbara Lea. It can always be found in fine jazz fettle, too. Check out Dexter Gordon, Bill Evans, Art Blakey, and David Sanborn.

"Dancing in the Dark" (Howard Dietz/Arthur Schwartz, 1931): Introduced in the Broadway revue *The Band Wagon*, "Dancing in the Dark" jumped right on the Standards bandwagon and has stayed there ever since. Theater critics agreed that the show itself was a breakthrough in the revue format because of the inspired new elements of glamour and satire in sketches and book by George S. Kaufman. Both the song and the show played a vital role in the career of Fred Astaire. The show was the last in which Astaire played opposite his sister Adele. But with Cyd Charisse as his partner, he danced to the song again in the movie version of *The Band Wagon* (1953). On its own, the song has crossed all styles and settings, recorded by the orchestras of Guy Lombardo and Duke Ellington, by jazz giants Miles Davis, Zoot Sims, and Cannonball Adderley, and vocally? Well, there's Barry Manilow, Tormé, Sinatra, Bennett. . . .

"Don't Blame Me" (Dorothy Fields/Jimmy McHugh, 1933): There are literally hundreds of recordings of this Standard, with and without words, not to mention the amazing variety of styles and dates they represent. A random cross-section: Ethel Waters, The Platters, Andre Previn, Joni James, Mary Lou Williams, John Coltrane, Patti Page, McCoy Tyner, Johnny Hodges, and Sarah Vaughan. Woe to the club-date musicians who haven't memorized its mundane AABA melody, and don't know that its standard key is C, with the release going to F. They'll soon be looking for other work.

"Embraceable You" (Ira Gershwin/George Gershwin, 1930): There are at least five hundred separate recordings of this Standard, from a recent Judy Collins back to a classic Louis Prima, with Nat Cole and Johnny Mathis along the way, and tenor sax man

Al Cohn's jazz version. Recordings aside, there are few Standards that can equal the film history of "Embraceable You." But first, it had a glorious start on Broadway in *Girl Crazy* with Ginger Rogers. Glorious because the pit band, led by Red Nichols, included Benny Goodman, Glenn Miller, Jack Teagarden, Jimmy Dorsey, and Gene Krupa (wow). There were several film versions of the show, including Judy Garland's headliner in 1943. The song was used again in the George Gershwin film bio *Rhapsody in Blue* in 1945, and with Leslie Caron in *An American in Paris*, 1951. Liberace performed it in *Sincerely Yours*, 1955. The definitive Standard.

"Everybody Loves My Baby" (Spencer Williams and Jack Palmer, 1924): Jazz musicians tend to think of this Standard in tandem with the Palmer/Williams follow-up in 1926—"I Found a New Baby." Both are "trad" jazz Standards, widely played by the jazz ensembles of the '20s, and most others since. Clarence Williams Blue Five, featuring a young Louis Armstrong, helped to launch this one, and it's almost as if Palmer and Williams then said to each other after it became a hit, "Hey, let's find a *new* 'baby,' " and so they did. They even used the same chord progression in the main theme of both, starting in a minor key and moving to its relative major at the end of eight bars (both are basic AABA tunes). "Everybody Loves My Baby" has had more vocal attention than the sequel, capped by Doris Day's soundtrack version as Ruth Etting in the 1955 film *Love Me or Leave Me*. It was also stock-in-trade for Dinah Washington and the timeless veteran Alberta Hunter.

"Exactly Like You" (Dorothy Fields/Jimmy McHugh, 1930): "... Now I know why mother taught me to be true..." Not many lyricists in 1930 would dream up a line so homey and yet just right, to be the final rhyme with "Exactly Like You." Dorothy Fields had the knack, and seemed to toss off effortlessly such easy-to-sing lines in her many hit songs, a number of which were written with Jimmy McHugh. "Exactly Like You" is a song of love without pain, an uptempo, upbeat AABA pop tune that became a Standard because everybody simply *digs* it. Singers love Field's plainspoken lyrics, despite the wide range of McHugh's tune (Sinatra, Nat Cole, and nowadays, Rebecca Kilgore). Jazz musicians of every ilk love the way the tune seems to swing all by itself. It has found favor with both John Coltrane and the Preservation Hall Jazz Band, and Louis Armstrong's version remains a big seller of this A-1 Standard, which began life on Broadway in Lew Leslie's *International Revue*.

"Fascinating Rhythm" (Ira Gershwin/George Gershwin, 1924): This many-noted Standard may well have started out as one of George Gershwin's teenage forays into ragtime, but his big brother Ira found a way to set words to its busy notes, and the song was on its way. Its fascination has remained, with musicians as diverse as flutist Jean-Pierre Rampal and pianist Dave Grusin exploring its notes, and singers Maureen McGovern and Michael Feinstein its words. Antonio Carlos Jobim has recorded it, and it's in the Carpenters 1977 album *Live at the Palladium*. The first hit record was issued back there in 1924 by Cliff "Ukelele Ike" Edwards, who performed it in the company of Fred and Adele Astaire in the musical *Lady, Be Good*.

"Fine and Dandy" (Paul James/Kay Swift, 1930): The rousing title song of a funny Broadway hit, this is a song that's upbeat and quick, with a neat harmonic shift in its center and a nifty closing tag. Kay Swift was a major Broadway composer, a Julliard-trained pianist and arranger. Her lyricist in this and other theater songs was her first husband, the financier and author James P. Warburg, who used his middle and first names as a pseudonym. "Fine and Dandy" is a real showbiz tune, often used without words to ring curtains up and down all over America. But its appeal across musical lines is remarkable, recorded on piano by Teddy Wilson, Art Tatum, and Marian McPartland;

as jazz by Milt Jackson, Chet Baker, and Johnny Hodges; and vocally, take your pick from Tormé or Gormé, Streisand, Doris Day, or Louis Armstrong. And there are dozens more.

"Fly Me to the Moon [In Other Words]" (Bart Howard; 1954): This may be the shortest Standard of all. Its two sixteen-measure phrases are almost identical, (AA), so it is essentially one brief song—but what a song. Frank Sinatra's recording is especially memorable, not to forget those of Sarah Vaughan, Julie London, and Keely Smith. Pianists have taken to the tune's urge to swing: the rhythm trios of Dave Grusin and Cedar Walton stand out. Felicia Saunders made the first recording under the song's original title "In Other Words," as introduced in cabaret by Mabel Mercer, with music by her pianist Bart Howard. As it caught on, it was increasingly dubbed "Fly Me to the Moon," the first few words in the lyric. Never mind that the original title occurs four times in the brief lyric, the new title stuck, and the publishers finally changed it officially.

"A Foggy Day (in London Town)" (Ira Gershwin/George Gershwin, 1937): Fred Astaire, front and center with the Gershwin brothers, introduced this evocative ballad in their 1937 film *A Damsel in Distress*. (George Burns and Gracie Allen had supporting roles.) Astaire recorded it half a dozen times, leading the way for other singers who are now equally identified with it: Frank Sinatra, Mel Tormé, and Ella Fitzgerald. The original version opens with a good verse, seldom sung, and the chorus then proceeds in an ABAC form, with a few nice surprises.

"Fools Rush In" (Johnny Mercer/Rube Bloom, 1940): Lyricist Johnny Mercer worked one of his miracles here, again adding exactly the right words to a melody already published by the busy pianist/arranger Rube Bloom, and turning it into a hit. From initial recordings by the Glenn Miller Orchestia and singers Mildred Bailey and Dick Haymes, "Fools Rush In" was hit material in 1960 for Brooke Benton and in 1963 for Ricky Nelson. The mainline singers Eckstine, Tormé, and Peggy Lee have done their characteristic versions, and so have some doo-woppers like Dion and the Belmonts, and Frankie Lymon and the Teenagers.

"Forty-Second Street" (Al Dubin/Harry Warren, 1932): A swinging two-piano session by Dick Hyman and Derek Smith is a good introduction to this Standard, with other great jazz trips by Jimmy Giuffre (sax) or Warren Vache (trumpet). It's been recorded less often by singers, but the ever-inventive Mel Tormé got the job done in style. "Forty-Second Street" belongs to New York, although Dubin and Warren composed it in California for the film musical with the same title, with Dick Powell and Ruby Keeler. It came home to New York in 1980, this time titling the Broadway version of the stagestruck chorus girl who gets "her big chance" in show business. The spectacular renewal of the famous New York street itself has given the song yet another lease on life.

"Georgia on My Mind" (Stuart Gorrell/Hoagy Carmichael, 1930): "... just an old sweet song keeps Georgia on my mind ..." That old sweet song has won two Grammys in its long career—for Ray Charles in 1960 and Willie Nelson in 1978. Carmichael himself made some of the earliest recordings, and a Mildred Bailey hit single kept the song alive for years. The song's pattern is solid AABA, with a bridge that falls twice into a minor key and then returns to the major for the final A-theme. It's always been an irresistible fabric for improvisation to pianists, from Floyd Cramer to Oscar Peterson. Vocally, with Ray Charles and Willie Nelson setting the pace, singers from every discipline have been drawn to it, from Frankie Laine and James Brown to Gladys Knight and Michael Bolton.

"Give Me the Simple Life" (Harry Ruby/Rube Bloom, 1945): There's an unusually happy marriage of melody and lyric in this Standard, introduced in the movie *Wake Up and Dream*. The words are saucy and impertinent, and the music—there's no other way to put it—*swings*. Maybe because Rube Bloom was a pianist himself, the tune has been swung ever since by pianists like Marian McPartland, Billy Taylor, and Ralph Sharon. The Four Freshmen recorded it, with words of course, as have Rosie Clooney, June Christy, and Ella Fitzgerald. And Mel Tormé. And a classy, *swinging*, Page Cavanaugh.

"Here's That Rainy Day" (Johnny Burke/Jimmy Van Heusen, 1953): The Broadway musical *Carnival in Flanders*, in which Dolores Gray introduced this song, faded fast, and it took awhile for the song to get back into action. This is a torch song, and singers can get burned by it. It almost seems that Van Heusen was challenging them with harmonies odd and difficult, changing tonality three times in the first four measures, requiring them to hear vagrant intervals outside the expected chords. But it's such a good song, and no Standard has ever intimidated the great singers who have embraced "Rainy Day" with all its sad echoes of lost love: Ella Fitzgerald and Peggy Lee, Joe Williams, and Sammy Davis, Jr., in one of his finest tracks.

"Honeysuckle Rose" (Andy Razaf/Thomas "Fats" Waller, 1929): The life of this Standard by Waller and Razaf is a rich one, lived variously in the worlds of theater, jazz, and film. And country, too, if you include Willie Nelson's hit record in 1980, and his more recent exploration on guitar alone. Every jazz musician knows its AABA structure and sizzling tempo. Pianists romp with it: Tatum, Previn, Earl Hines, Teddy Wilson, and Judy Carmichael; it's been in the book of most Big Bands, too, including those of Basie, Ellington, and Goodman. Razaf's adroit lyric isn't trotted out as often as Waller's riffy melody, but Joe Williams and Sarah Vaughan had no trouble with it. Along with other Waller specialties "Honeysuckle Rose" was reborn on Broadway in 1978 in the revue *Ain't Misbehavin'*. It has had a film career as well, one highlight of which was Lena

Horne's 1943 performance in *As Thousands Cheer*, another in a movie with Ricky Nelson in 1981 called—*Honeysuckle Rose*.

"How Deep Is the Ocean?" (Irving Berlin, 1932): Some of Irving Berlin's best ballads ask questions: "What'll I Do?" "How About You?" "How Deep is the Ocean?" There is no question, however, regarding the credentials of this one as a Standard. Like so many Berlin ballads, it keeps reestablishing itself, as all true Standards must. Young performers discover it and sing it: Harry Connick, Jr., Susannah McCorkle. And play it: saxophonist Joshua Redman, thus continuing its life in jazz begun by players like Chick Corea, John Coltrane, and Miles Davis. The homely, easygoing lyric, meanwhile, has attracted over the years the good offices of Sinatra, Nat Cole, Ethel Merman, and Julie Andrews, to name a few. In 1932 the song went directly into the noisy popular music marketplace of Tin Pan Alley, not blessed by earlier exposure in a theater or film score. It did get on camera later, with Bing Crosby in *Blue Skies* (1946) and Frank Sinatra in *Meet Danny Wilson* (1952).

"How High the Moon" (Nancy Hamilton/Morgan Lewis, 1940): Hamilton and Lewis may not be among the famous names attached to most Popular Standards, but both were career professionals in music and theater, and created this song for the Broadway revue *Two for the Show*. Since then just about everybody in the business has recorded "How High the Moon": Billy Taylor, Ellington, Basie, Anita O'Day, Mel Tormé, and Nat Cole. Instrumental versions outnumber vocals, probably because of the song's challenging chord progression, which moves through three tonalities inside a sixteen-measure melody, then repeats itself to fill out the expected thirty-two measures. It simply demands improvisation from the jazz musician, and has inspired volumes of it from the bop generation on. Not that it doesn't suffice vocally. The first hit was sung by Helen Forrest with the Benny Goodman orchestra. Then came the remarkable hit version by Les Paul and Mary Ford in 1951.

"I Can't Get Started with You" (Ira Gershwin/Vernon Duke, 1936): How Ira Gershwin found time, fresh from collaborating on the massive score for *Porgy and Bess* in 1935, to pair off with Vernon Duke for this lighthearted Standard is anybody's guess. But the versatile Ira dashed off a lyric that fit Vernon Duke's dapper melody like a glove—topical and slangy—". . . I got a house and showplace, but I can't get no place with you . . ." The melody feels more like Tin Pan Alley than Broadway, set in the routine AABA form, albeit with a bridge more adventurous than most. The melody led first to success, with a hit record on trumpet by bandleader Bunny Berigan, and while he also assayed a casual vocal chorus, it took singers the likes of Billie Holiday, Ella Fitzgerald, and Dinah Washington to imprint "Standard" on this one. Not that it has ever been neglected by jazz folks. *Sans* lyric it has been improvised upon by Erroll Garner, Dizzy Gillespie, Sonny Rollins, and Doc Severinsen.

"I Can't Give You Anything but Love" (Dorothy Fields/Jimmy McHugh, 1928): What a long life this jolly Standard has led! Broadway hasn't been able to give it anything but love for years. Fifty years after its introduction in *Blackbirds of 1928*, it found a place in the 1978 tribute to "Fats" Waller—*Ain't Misbehavin'* (Waller didn't write it, but he often performed it). Ann Miller and Mickey Rooney dueted the song in the Broadway hit *Sugar Babies*. Meanwhile, it's been recorded and performed countless times—by Ella and Frank and Louis, of course. But don't overlook Doris Day. Or Bobby Short.

"I Don't Stand a Ghost of a Chance" (Bing Crosby and Ned Washington/Victor Young; 1933): Three great names in American music are immediately associated with this Standard: Bing Crosby, who had a hand in creating it and was the first to record it (on Brunswick), Leon (Chu) Berry, the tenor sax genius for whom it was a major hit with the Cab Calloway orchestra, and trumpeter Bobby Hackett, for whom it was both a favorite and a bestselling record. It is an uncomplicated AABA thirty-two-bar pop tune, but something about it has attracted all sorts of musicians and singers and brought it into the Standard canon. Art Tatum, and the revered teacher/pianist Lennie Tristano have recorded it, and Diana Krall, in a vocal tradition begun by Lee Wiley and Billie Holiday, sings it in her current album *Love Scenes*.

"I Found a New Baby" (Spencer Williams and Jack Palmer, 1926): Every jazz musician knows this funky Standard by heart. It may not be sung as often as its companion piece by Palmer and Williams, "Everybody Loves My Baby," but you can be sure it'll be played once a night by every one of those myriad young "trad" groups fueling the jazz festivals the world over these days. Early recordings by Fletcher Henderson and McKinney's Cotton Pickers launched the tune; the Dukes of Dixieland, and the hot bands of Lu Watters, Max Collie and dozens of others have kept it afloat. It's had a special appeal to stride pianists, too, including Dick Wellstood, Cliff Jackson, Judy Carmichael, and Ralph Sutton.

"I Get a Kick Out of You" (Cole Porter, 1934): Not many songwriters in 1934 were mentioning cocaine, but leave it to Cole Porter to pronounce it a bore, in this excellent lyric from the Broadway show *Anything Goes*. Ethel Merman and William Gaxton performed it there, and dismissed the deadly kick of cocaine, rhyming "... one SNIFF would *bore* me ter-RIF-ically too ..." The song has been recorded by almost everybody in the business since then—Sinatra, Ella, Louis, not to mention Nancy Wilson, the Ames Brothers, John Gary, and Tom Jones. Jazz musicians go for it—they love most anything of Porter's—those long melody lines and the beat, often Latin-tinged, that is so often implicit in his theater songs. It's had quite a movie career, too. Billy Daniels sang it in *Sunny Side of the Street* (1951); it was featured in the 1975 film *At Long Last Love*, and it is prominent on the soundtrack of Kenneth Branagh's new look at William Shakespeare's *Love's Labour's Lost* (2000).

"I Got It Bad (and That Ain't Good)" (Paul Webster/Duke Ellington, 1941): The alto saxophone of Johnny Hodges and the smoky voice of Nina Simone are forever linked to this Standard. In its first measure, the melodic leap of a major nineteenth seems made for Hodges's sliding, weeping alto sax, featured in Ellington's inceptive recording. Simone's later recording, meanwhile, found new life on the soundtrack of the Coen brothers film *The Big Lebowski* (1998). While the song has been explored instrumentally by Keith Jarrett, Peter Nero, and Andre Previn on piano, plus Basie and Armstrong versions, women have dominated vocally, and the line begins with the legends Helen Hume, Ernestine Anderson, and Billie Holiday, and leads straight to Cher. Maybe that's because the lyric seems gender-strictured: "...never treats me sweet and gentle, the way *he* should..." Tony Bennett, however, wasn't about to let anything keep this Standard off his 1999 birthday celebration CD of Ellington. He just changed *him* and *he* to *her* and *she*. Not a problem.

"I Got Rhythm" (Ira Gershwin/George Gershwin, 1930): You'd better believe this Standard was born to be *sung*. It was Ethel Merman's song in the musical *Girl Crazy*, her Broadway debut. She owned it for a time, although other singers have also nailed it: Garland and Horne, Bobby Darin, and Leslie Uggams. "I Got Rhythm," however, had another destiny. It has become a *sine qua non* for jazz musicians, who must know intuitively its changes and its plain AABA architecture, a matrix for improvisation as essential as the twelve-bar blues. Players of every persuasion have seized upon the bare bones of "I Got Rhythm" and built chorus after chorus of their own invention. Dozens of new spin-offs are composed in the process. It would be easier to tally the players who have *not* recorded it, but here's a glimpse of the range: violinists Joe Venuti and Stephan Grappelli; guitarists Django Reinhardt and John Pizzarelli; pianists Fats Waller, Roger Williams, Teddy Wilson, and Erroll Garner; Larry Adler on harmonica. And everybody else.

"I Know That You Know" (Anne Caldwell/Vincent Youmans, 1926): When a tune has been recorded by trumpet man Bunk Johnson (1879–1949) and also by guitarist/singer John Pizzarelli (b. 1960), you can be pretty sure it's a Standard. This is a show tune from *Oh, Please* (1926), outfitted with a solid verse and pretty good lyrics, but hardly anybody uses them. It's a tune more interesting to play than to sing, and while Doris Day, and tenor Robert White, have sung it, the list of jazz musicians who've *played* this Standard reads like the Hall of Fame. Piano players from James P. Johnson to bopper Bud Powell to Art Tatum; Lionel Hampton and Red Norvo on vibes, and Coleman Hawkins and Stan Getz on tenor sax. It's a tune with wide open spaces between the notes—lots of elbow room for improvisation.

"If I Had You" (Ted Shapiro, Jimmy Campbell and Reginald Connelly, 1928): Rudy Vallee, "The Vagabond Lover" did the first recording of this Standard in the U.S., but before that it was a hit in England. Once on this side of the Atlantic it rapidly became a Standard for both singers and jazz musicians. Pianists love to improvise on its easy (but gently swinging) thirty-two measures, and singers keep coming back to the dreamy list of tasks for a storybook lover, who would "... cross the burning desert ... sail the mighty ocean wide ..." It's a perfect vehicle for the declaration of true love, duly enunciated on record by The Platters, Jimmy Durante, and Tiny Tim, and if these artists seem less than ideal romantics, add the recent outings by Diana Krall and Betty Buckley. "If I Had You" in the movies crosses time from Dan Dailey's version in *You Were Meant for Me* (1948) to a 1999 soundtrack appearance in Stanley Kubrick's *Eyes Wide Shut.*

"If I Should Lose You" (Leo Robin/Ralph Rainger, 1935): For many years this song lived a secret life. Certain singers and musicians caught wind of its expressive lyric ("... and I would wander around, hating the sound of rain ..."), or the tense dissonances where the melody meets the chords. You could say it was a Standard-in-waiting, introduced in the 1935 film *Rose of the Rancho*, starring John Boles and Gladys Swarthout, whose big legit voices could not have signaled the future attention the song would receive from musicians and singers steeped in jazz. But Charlie "Bird" Parker picked it for his groundbreaking album of jazz saxophone with full string orchestra, and George Shearing began to play it. Some powerful singers found it— Peggy Lee, Aretha Franklin, and Nina Simone. Its secret life over, the song is now cherished by such contemporary artists as pianists Geri Allen and Keith Jarrett, and the promising young singer Melissa Walker.

"I'll Be Around" (Alec Wilder, 1943): This Standard was probably also the biggest hit for songwriter/composer/critic/radio host Alec Wilder. His book *American Popular Song: The Great Innovators 1900–1950*, with James T. Maher (Oxford, 1972), has informed and molded opinion and taste on the subject for years. Wilder was also a prolific composer of songs and chamber music. With "I'll Be Around" Wilder created, simply, a first-rate popular song, structured in keeping with the practices of its day (AABA), and possessed of a quietly poetic lyric that pledges true love through a totally commonplace expression—"I'll be around." Over the years, perhaps because of its accessibility, the song has been revisited both vocally and instrumentally by a surprising diversity of artists. With words: Carly Simon, Eileen Farrell, and most of the usual Standard bearers; without words: Scott Hamilton and Ruby Braff, pianists Marian McPartland and Hank Jones.

"I'll Be Seeing You" (Irving Kahal/Sammy Fain, 1938): The important date for this song is not 1938, when it was introduced in a forgotten musical, but 1943, when it swept the country during World War II. Hit singles by Frank Sinatra and Frances Langford made it the leading heart song for couples separated by wartime service. It emerged from this heightened recognition to become a Standard, with a flood of recordings ever since. Willie Nelson, Barry Manilow, and Neil Sedaka have sung it, as have Carmen McRae, Judy Collins, and Johnny Mathis. And there are lots of people who recall it not from the war, but from hearing it as Liberace's closing theme for many years.

"I'll Get By" (Roy Turk/Fred Ahlert, 1928): The odd and awkward intervals in the melody of "I'll Get By" have not fazed the dozens of singers who've made it a Standard, from classic Billie Holiday to country Willie Nelson. Sophisticates Michael Feinstein and Peggy Lee ease into the simple lyric about steadfast love (". . . though there be rain and darkness, too . . ."), and those intervals and the chords behind them in this brief twenty-eight-measure tune have provided a jazz framework for Johnny Hodges, John Coltrane, and pianists John Bunch and Earl Hines.

"I'll String Along with You" (Al Dubin/Harry Warren, 1934): The singer/pianist Diana Krall is among the young singers who have refreshed this longtime Standard, a favorite of such earlier stars as Doris Day, Dean Martin, and Louis Armstrong. The song was introduced in the Hollywood film musical *Twenty Million Sweethearts*.

"I'll Take Romance" (Oscar Hammerstein/Ben Oakland, 1937): This Standard is full of surprises. It has the sound and texture of a major theatrical number, probably because of Hammerstein's presence as lyricist. Composed as the title song for a film, it flows in Viennese like waltz time, fully developed in seventy measures. The chord changes are rich, with the release moving through two new keys before returning to the tonic. It's those changes that have appealed to jazz musicians, who build on them in 4/4 rather than 3/4 (Art Farmer and Sonny Rollins). Most of the vocal performances are also swung in four, including those of Ernestine Anderson (with pianist George Shearing), Eydie Gorme, and June Christy. It's a fine song, and as times changed, its *time* changed.

"Imagination" (Johnny Burke/Jimmy Van Heusen, 1940): Standards come in all sizes and degrees of complexity. This one is small and simple, but its very simplicity has attracted some very sophisticated artists. Joe Williams, Lena Horne, and Carmen McRae have recorded it, but then so have folks like Pat Boone and Kate Smith. Its appeal seems to stem from its guileless, almost childlike poetry, in which your imagination "... starts you asking a daisy what to do ..." Van Heusen's music has cast its own spell, however, and the jazz masters have found it and kept it, from Clark Terry and Benny Carter to pianists Hank Jones, Teddy Wilson, and Dave Brubeck. Setting "imagination" to music, by the way, has occurred to many others. The score of a Broadway show in 1928 called *Here's Howe* contains a totally different tune, and the British rock star Elvis Costello recorded his own "Imagination (Is a Powerful Deceiver)."

"I'm in the Mood for Love" (Dorothy Fields/Jimmy McHugh, 1935): There's no argument a song is a Standard when it's been recorded by everybody from Spike Jones and the City Slickers to pianist Roger Williams, the McQuire Sisters, Liberace, the Flamingos (Doo-Wop), The Chimes (contemporary), and Fats Domino, who had a hit with it back in the days before rock-and-roll became just rock (1956). It had been introduced in the movie *Every Night at Eight* by Frances Langford, had then turned up in many other films and on more than five hundred recordings: Les Paul and Louis Armstrong, Julie London and Joni James, Charlie Parker and Oscar Peterson—everybody.

"I Only Have Eyes for You" (Al Dubin/Harry Warren, 1934): This tune was sung in the film *Dames* by Dick Powell, a clean-cut guy with a tenor voice that served him well in pictures during the '30s and '40s until it dropped into the bass register, allowing him happily to play tough, private-eye types the rest of his life. The song itself had a movie career of its own: 1949's *Jolson Sings Again* and two 1950 films, *Young Man with a Horn and Tea for Two*. It was a solid Standard well before Art Garfunkel recorded it on his bestselling album *Breakaway* (1975). Other recordings run the gamut of style from Doo-Wop (the Flamingos) to Kenny Rogers, Doris Day, Diane Schuur, and Andre Previn.

"It Had to Be You" (Gus Kahn/Isham Jones, 1924): A series of reincarnations has kept this rather mundane ABAC tune in good Standard standing ever since it was first recorded (acoustically) by the veteran pair Billy Murray and Aileen Stanley in its first year. An array of styles were then brought to it as the years passed, by Cliff Edwards, (famous as "Ukelele Ike"), Ray Charles, Sylvia Syms, and Harry Nilsson. It was versatile enough to accommodate the rich and homey voice of Kate Smith and the edgy jazz delivery of Anita O'Day. John Travolta recorded it in 1976, and since then, Harry Connick, Jr., Kenny Rogers, and Ann Hampton Callaway have followed up. Danny Thomas attended to one of its reincarnations in the 1951 film *I'll See You in My Dreams*, and put it back on the *Hit Parade* for twelve weeks.

"It's Only a Paper Moon" (Billy Rose and E. Y. Harburg/Harold Arlen, 1933): The film career of this imaginative Standard began in 1933 (*Take a Chance*), but that's pretty far back in movie history, so how about 1973's *Paper Moon*, with Tatum O'Neal and her daddy Ryan, or *Funny Lady* with Barbra Streisand (1975). People love this no-nonsense thirty-two bar AABA gem, whose words and music are in perfect sync—which should come as no surprise because, don't forget, in a few more years Arlen and Harburg are going to write "Over the Rainbow" for Judy Garland. Since then Judy also recorded "Paper Moon," and so did John Kirby, Django Reinhardt, Dion and The Belmonts, Marian McPartland, Les Paul, Count Basie—well, almost everybody. The veteran actor/singer James Darren is among the artists most recently to have revisited the paper moon, the cardboard sea, and the muslin tree.

"I've Got a Crush on You" (Ira Gershwin/George Gershwin, 1930): "The world will pardon my mush ..."—a daring rhyme with "crush," but the ballad singers who've performed the song seem to deliver the lyric without a blush. The song is one of those that changed direction after its introduction in a Broadway musical (*Treasure Girl* 1928, and then *Strike Up the Band*, 1930). Originally it was, at Gershwin's direction, an up-tempo novelty, where the mush-crush rhyme seemed sweetly silly. Then singer Lee Wiley, her roots deep in jazz, slowed it down, adding a sense of longing to its clear declaration of "I love you," and from then on, it was on everybody's ballad list. Linda Ronstadt picked it for her first venture into the Standards, with Nelson Riddle's orchestra. Jazz soloists on guitar (Howard Alden), piano (Joe Bushkin), and trumpet (Harry "Sweets" Edison) have observed Lee Wiley's lower speed limit, as have many other singers, including Barbara Lea and Bobby Short. It's another of the Standards, by the way, gracing the soundtrack of Kenneth Branagh's filming of Shakespeare's *Love's Labour's Lost* (2000).

"I've Got the World on a String" (Ted Koehler/Harold Arlen, 1933): Harold Arlen and his partner Ted Koehler wrote a number of hits for Harlem's Cotton Club in the early '30s—solid, catchy tunes in the straightforward AABA pattern, with none of the darker harmonies and extended lines that Arlen would compose later on. The very simplicity of the music has invited improvised flights by pianists (Tatum, Peterson, Joanne Brackeen) and jazz greats (Flip Phillips, Benny Carter, Roy Eldridge), and the carefree words of a host of singers (Bobby Short, Leslie Uggams, Tony Bennett). New sessions with contemporaries Steve Tyrell and the Jay Leonhart quartet are keeping this Standard high.

"I've Got You Under My Skin" (Cole Porter, 1936): Another Cole Porter work, taken up by a variety of vocalists and jazz musicians: Louis Prima and Keely Smith for openers, and the orchestras of Woody Herman, Stan Kenton, and a major recording by Xavier Cugat, testimony again to the subtle Latin inflections in many Cole Porter Standards. The Four Seasons had a Top 10 record of this song in 1966, Neil Diamond has recorded it, and it's in the repertory of some of the best jazz pianists in the neighborhood, including Bud Powell, Oscar Peterson, and George Shearing. It started life in the movies. Virginia Bruce sang it in *Born to Dance* (1936), and it's gotten under everybody's skin ever since.

"Just One of Those Things" (Cole Porter, 1935): Call it cynicism, Depression Era sophistication, Cole Porter's own view of romance—this Standard delivers a "good-bye to love" lyric typical of Porter, but not so typical of the love songs of his time. "... our love affair was too hot not to cool down ..." so get over it, says the lyric, but it was great fun while it lasted. The song became a strong Porter Standard soon after its introduction in his Broadway musical *Jubilee* (1935). Musically it is another deftly harmonized Porter gem, sixty-four measures long, with an internal change of key (down a step) at the release. Singers cherish it, it's a jazz favorite, and the movies have drawn on it in film after film: Lena Horne in *Panama Hattie* (1942), Peggy Lee in *The Jazz Singer* (1953), Madeline Kahn in *At Long Last Love* (1975). Many others.

"Love for Sale" (Cole Porter, 1930): The vocal ensemble Manhattan Transfer has recorded this Porter song, unaware perhaps, that it was banned from radio broadcast in the '30s because its lyric speaks in the voice of a prostitute offering her "wares." Oddly enough, the rash of recordings since then have been mainly instrumental, but certainly not because, in today's unbuttoned times, the lyrics remain embarrassing. It's just that jazz musicians are intoxicated by the shifting tonality and moody chord changes of the piece, prowled by pianists (Ahmad Jamal, Ramsey Lewis, Art Tatum), trumpet men (Doc Severinsen, Ruby Braff, Dizzy Gillespie), and large bands (Stan Kenton, Ray Anthony). The lack of vocal recordings is of course due in part to the fact that the lyric is gender blocked. It is a woman singing, and except on recordings by Anita O'Day, Della Reese, Dinah Washington and a few others, the words are seldom heard. The earlier recordings, by the way—the ones nobody heard on the radio—were made by the Fred Waring Orchestra, with a vocal by the Three Girl Friends, who had introduced the song in the Broadway musical *The New Yorker*. Libby Holman, a major star of the day, also defied the bluenoses with a hit record.

"Love Is Here to Stay" (Ira Gershwin/George Gershwin, 1938): This song was the last composed by George Gershwin before his death on July 11, 1937. It has proven to be one of the most widely recorded songs by the Gershwins, and was originally entitled *"Our* Love Is Here to Stay." Publishers and record companies officially dropped the "our," resulting in considerable confusion, since the orchestra leader Gordon Jenkins also composed a song with the shorter title, and much later, so did rock star Lou Reed. The Gershwins wrote their version for the film *Goldwyn Follies* (Gene Kelly sang it), and recordings for a while thereafter—by Eddie Howard, Vic Damone, Les Brown, and the Jackie Gleason orchestra—used the full title. But whatever its name, this bone simple ABAC Standard has been lovingly recorded by Placido Domingo and Kenny Rankin and Kenny Rogers and Susannah McCorkle and Barbara Lea and Louis Armstrong, and Ella, Dinah, Billie . . .

"Love Me or Leave Me" (Gus Kahn/Walter Donaldson, 1928): Is it the unusual chord progression or the blunt lyric that has made this song so ubiquitous? " . . . I'd rather be lonely than happy with somebody else . . ." is one of the lines attached to the melody as it jumps from its initial minor key into the relative major with nary a passing chord to warn the ear. But it works, and jazz musicians have improvised endlessly on this tight AABA Standard. The Soprano Summit (that's Bob Wilbur and Kenny Davern on soprano saxes) have owned it, ditto everybody from

Jack Teagarden to Dan Barrett on trombone, and Benny Goodman with a classic clarinet. Stride pianists especially cotton to it, Ralph Sutton and Johnny Guarnieri among them. And singers? Both Lena Horne and Sammy Davis, Jr. generated hit records after Doris Day brought it back resoundingly in the film that told the story of the woman who introduced it in 1928 on Broadway, Ruth Etting. Etting had starred with Eddie Cantor in the fun-filled *Whoopee*, but the laughs had faded by the time Day sang it in the touching Etting film biography *Love Me or Leave Me* (1955).

"Lover" (Larry Hart/Richard Rodgers, 1933): A good song finds a lot of levels. This one started out as a somewhat formal waltz for the somewhat formal soprano of movie fame, Jeanette Mac-Donald, in *Love Me Tonight* (1932). It almost immediately started to molt the composer's 3/4 time signature and become a 4/4 jump tune in the jazz world. Stan Kenton, John Coltrane, and Roland Kirk, and the pianists Mary Lou Williams and Billy Taylor, are just a few artists who changed it into anything but a somewhat formal waltz. Today it is also remembered as one of Les Paul's wildly successful multitrack guitar recordings with Mary Ford (1948), or in Peggy Lee's hot million-seller for Capitol in 1952. She sang it 6/8, not 3/4, proving that a great song can change its time with the changing times.

"Lover Come Back to Me" (Oscar Hammerstein/Sigmund Romberg, 1928): Sigmund Romberg would be amazed. No jazz master he, but possibly the last in the line of Vienna-inspired masters of operetta, composing for voices like those of Jeanette MacDonald, Kathryn Grayson, and even a grand opera personage like Dorothy Kirsten (all recorded this Standard). So did Frankie Lyman and the Teenagers, Poncho Sandez in a Latin style he called "cubop," and Anita O'Day in one of her prime flights of jazz fancy. The unsung but surehanded pianist Paul Smith has recorded it, and in a version that would either put a smile on Romberg's face or make him long for Vienna, so has blues master Joe Williams in a smashing, medium-jump jazz outing. All this for a song introduced to New Yorkers in the operetta *The New Moon*, and to the rest of America by Lawrence Tibbett and Grace Moore in the 1930 film version. Standards are sometimes made, not born.

"Love Walked In" (Ira Gershwin/George Gershwin, 1938): This beautiful love song was part of George Gershwin's final film score—*The Goldwyn Follies*, introduced by the popular tenor Kenny Baker. The pattern of the song is the fairly commonplace ABAC, with the final section employing a slowly descending scale passage that seems to match perfectly Ira Gershwin's sanguine lyric, which predicts that love, having walked in, will "...find a world completely new..." For a small song it has enjoyed a long reach. It inspired the opera star Jessye Norman to record it with the Boston Pops under John Williams. It's had wide appeal to singers of every persuasion, starting with Dinah Washington's hit record of the song shortly after its introduction. Another hit record came along in 1959 with The Flamingos, and since then "Love Walked In" has become one of the Gershwins' most beloved songs.

"The Man I Love" (Ira Gershwin/George Gershwin, 1924): This Standard is obviously a woman's song, and those who've performed and recorded it form a long and illustrious list: Billie Holiday and June Christy, Etta James and Carmen McRae, and most recently, Cher. Without words, however, the song's descending chord progression has entranced pianists for years, starting with Hazel Scott's on-film version in the Gershwin biography *Rhapsody in Blue* (1945) to a recent Fred Hersch version. The Gershwins struggled to find a place in several Broadway shows for this Standard, starting with *Lady Be Good!* in 1924, but dropped it, and never did find a perfect fit for it on stage. The song made its own way through performance and recording to become a beloved Standard.

"Mean to Me" (Roy Turk/Fred Ahlert, 1929): This tune is run-of-the-mill Tin Pan Alley, but has outlasted others of the same ilk, perhaps because it's become a favorite for female singers. Linda Ronstadt included it on her *Lush Life* album; Mama Cass Elliott recorded it, as did Billie Holiday, Carmen McRae, and Diana Ross. The lyric seems gender neutral to the postmodern eye, with the possible exception of "...I stay home each night when you say you'll phone..." which can evoke memories of songs like the ancient Dillon/von Tilzer hit of 1911 "All Alone (By the Telephone)" in which the victim of loneliness is clearly female. By now, though, at least 50 percent of the sorrowful souls waiting for their cell phones to trill are male.

"Memories of You" (Andy Razaf/Eubie Blake, 1930): The minimalist lyrics of this Standard are not heard often enough, probably because the wide range of the melody (an octave and a fifth) causes many a singer to shun it entirely. Those who have reached for it are rewarded with one of most evocative songs ever written. Ethel Waters was the first to record it, after it was introduced in *Lew Leslie's Blackbird of 1930*. It was perfect for Kate Smith, and then Carole Sloan and Joan Morris. It has had another life as an instrumental Standard, birthed by Sonny Dunham's brilliant trumpet solo with the Glen Gray orchestra in 1938. As a jazz vehicle, where the wide range is painless, it's been covered by Al Hirt, Lionel Hampton, and Butch Thompson on piano as well as dozens more.

"Misty" (Johnny Burke/Errol Garner, 1954): It's rare when the music comes first in the creation of a Standard, but "Misty" was composed, then successfully recorded by pianist Erroll Garner, before it had words. Its life as a Standard, however, didn't begin until a haunting lyric was added by Johnny Burke. The song brought fame to singer Johnny Mathis with his hit recording (1959). It's a sure-enough Standard, recorded by an amazing cross-section of musicians including Led Zeppelin, Astrud Gilberto, Yo-Yo Ma, Fifth Dimension, Etta Jones, Dean Martin, and, in perhaps the definitive version, Ella Fitzgerald.

"Mood Indigo" (Duke Ellington, Irving Mills, and Barney Bigard, 1931): This Ellington Standard started life as "Dreamy Blues" with bland and boring lyrics. It might have fallen through the cracks without tough new lyrics and an evocative title (uncredited) by Mitchell Parish (same guy that set the words to Hoagy Carmichael's "Star Dust"). The Ellington orchestra recorded this version for both Victor and Decca, and it turns up on many of the reissues deployed in 1999, celebrating the Duke's one hundredth birthday. Among the best of the newly recorded tributes that year: Tony Bennett's *Hot and Cool*, live at a Lincoln Center concert, and the funky *Duke Elegant* from New Orleans' Dr. John. Dozens of other recordings through the years include those of Nina Simone, Dinah Shore, Al Hirt, Jimmy Lunceford, and Cab Calloway.

"The More I See You" (Mack Gordon/Harry Warren, 1945): Arthur Fiedler and the Boston Pops included this song in an album some years back and called the package *Popular Favorites*, their way of saying "Popular Standards." Not that this lovely Gordon/Warren song needed their signature by then. It had been a favorite since Dick Haymes and Betty Grable introduced it in the movie *Diamond Horseshoe*. Nat Cole, Johnny Hartman, and Sarah Vaughan recorded it; The Platters had a hit record with it, as did Chris Montez (1966). The song has a long arialike melody and some extra-special chord changes in the second phrase, reasons perhaps that recently attracted Diane Schuur and Doc Severinsen to it.

"My Funny Valentine" (Larry Hart/Richard Rodgers, 1937): *Babes in Arms* was a Broadway show for and about young people. A future star, the sixteen-year-old Mitzi Green, played the lead in show, the granddaddy of all the plays and films built on the cliché "let's turn this barn into a theater and put on a show!" "Funny Valentine" is a superb example of the many Standards that outlived such mildly sappy beginnings—in this case, to become a tender expression of love for all the funny valentines whose "...looks are laughable, unphotographable..." but still a "favorite work of art." It's also one of those Standards that leads a double life. Singers take the simple and touching lyric and make it their own (Betty Buckley and Etta James). Jazz musicians cherish its odd melody and haunting chords that open a phrase in a minor key and close on a hopeful major (Chet Baker, pianist Bill Evans—once with Miles Davis—and again with guitarist Jim Hall.)

"My Romance" (Larry Hart/Richard Rodgers, 1935): The perfect closing line for a love song: "...my romance doesn't need a thing but you..." Lyricist Larry Hart then used his gift for listing the small and the topical to enumerate the things this love affair doesn't need: "...a castle rising in Spain...soft guitars...a moon in the sky..." The song was an immediate hit when introduced by the Paul Whiteman orchestra in the Broadway show *Jumbo*, and was recorded by some big voices of the time including Jan Peerce and Morton Downey. Its credentials as a Standard have been updated constantly through the years—Sammy Davis, Jr., Doris Day, Kenny Rogers—and continue to attract cabaret and jazz performers. Andrea Marcovicci and Rosemary Clooney have sung it; both Carly Simon and Kevin Mahogany have not only sung it but used it as an album title. Keith Jarrett has followed George Shearing and Dave Brubeck in exploring it on the piano without Hart's words. It works both ways, like a Standard should.

"Nice Work If You Can Get It" (Ira Gershwin/George Gershwin, 1937): Fred Astaire first got nice work on this Standard in a 1937 film musical, *A Damsel in Distress*. Jazz pianists immediately dug its opening circle of fifths and its bridge in the relative minor, inviting endless improvisation ever since by the likes of Erroll Garner, Earl Hines, Bud Powell, and Andre Previn. The "nice work," of course, proves to be such things as "...holding hands at midnight..." and "...sighing sigh after sigh...," so it's been a lovesong for Nat "King" Cole, Peggy

Lee, Ann Hampton Callaway, Carmen McRae, and Michael Feinstein, who also used the song in 1995 as the title for his fascinating book about Ira Gershwin, Harry Warren, and others.

"Night and Day" (Cole Porter, 1932): "Star Dust" is undoubtedly the Standard most often recorded, but "Night and Day" is a close second. The variety of style and performance on hundreds of recordings testifies to both the quality and the challenge of the song itself. It has always held a strong position across the board in jazz—Big Bands: Goodman, Charlie Barnet, Claude Thornhill; pianists: Dick Hyman, Art Tatum, Dave Brubeck; saxes: Zoot Sims, Stan Getz; on and on, not to overlook guitarist Django Reinhardt. Vocally, Doris Day and Sammy Davis, Jr. are among the dozens who have recorded "Night and Day," and that great country crossover Willie Nelson mastered it. This is a lengthy Standard—sixty-four measures if you include the verse, which almost everybody does. The chords are excitedly dissonant, and the release moves up a minor third (E to G). Fred Astaire was, again, present at the creation in both the original theater production *Gay Divorce* with Claire Luce, and the 1934 film adaptation (entitled *The Gay Divorcée*) with Ginger Rogers.

"On the Sunny Side of the Street" (Dorothy Fields/Jimmy McHugh, 1930): It works both sides of the street, vocal and instrumental, with equal charm. Dorothy Field's sassy lyrics ("... leave your worries on your doorstep ...") invite singers to go for it—Judy Garland and Tony Bennett and Frankie Laine, who made it a hit record in 1949 after singing it in *Make Believe Ballroom*, one of half-a-dozen movies that have soundtracked it. Jimmy McHugh's chords and AABA format may look conventional, but they just happen to *swing*, and the list of jazz musicians who've kept this Standard company would read "all of the above." Ellington's 1938 rendition is primary, and the short list would also include Lionel Hampton, Sidney Bechet, Roy Eldridge, and Louis Armstrong.

"Over the Rainbow" (E. Y. Harburg/Harold Arlen, 1939): This Standard belonged to Judy Garland throughout her career, her unofficial theme song. It still belongs to the enchanted Kansas teenager named Dorothy that Garland portrayed in *The Wizard of Oz*, winning the Oscar as Best Song of the Year (1939). But unlike some songs that become trapped when too closely associated with one person or one show, "Over the Rainbow" has appealed to a great variety of musicians. Nashville guitarist Chet Atkins and tenor sax master Ben Webster have recorded it, followed later by Kenny G on alto, pianists Dave Brubeck and Keith Jarrett, and flutist James Galway.

"St. Louis Blues" (W. C. Handy, 1914): This epic work defines the blues form itself and at the same time, by its universal popularity both as a song and an instrumental, defines the American Popular Standard. In another sense, it feels almost like a folk song or a Stephen Foster tune, lying deep in our musical subconscious. It has produced a flood of recordings—an open-ended list of singers and bands down through the twentieth century. In every style from every era, the "St. Louis Blues" seems to change its nature to suit each musician who takes it on: Django Reinhardt, Louis Prima, Eartha Kitt, Bob Wills and the Texas Playboys, Etta James, the Boston Pops, Sidney Bechet, Roy Eldridge, Herbie Hancock, Chet Atkins, Bessie Smith, and Glenn Miller, with his WWII goose-bump version in march time. The piece has three melodic themes; the first and third define precisely the twelve-bar blues progression. The central theme, couched in the minor of the standard key (G), is a sixteen-measure statement functioning somewhat like the expository verses essential to most of the routine pop tunes of the time. The three themes are easy to identify from their commonly known opening lines: (I) "I hate to see the evening sun go down..." (II) "St. Louis woman, with her diamond rings..." (III) "Got the St. Louis blues, just as blue as I can be..." By the way, regarding the dangers of depending on labels in popular music, the original sheet music of the "St. Louis Blues" calls it "The Most Widely Known *Ragtime* Composition."

"September Song" (Maxwell Anderson/Kurt Weill, 1938): This true Standard was made famous by the Walter Huston recording on Brunswick, delivered in the same half-spoken technique he used in playing Peter Stuyvesant in the Anderson/Weill musical *Knickerbocker Holiday* (1938). The show enjoyed only moderate success, but the song was an immediate hit. In keeping with Huston's autumnal delivery another classic version was released by Jimmy Durante in 1963. But countless recordings of "September Song" belie any need for it to be only an old man's lament. Its basic AABA form and its first measure intimation of the blues has inspired many a jazz version, including a major hit in 1951 by the Stan Kenton orchestra. Vocally it has crossed over to every style, with versions operatic (Mario Lanza), country (Willie Nelson and Roy Clark), doo-wop (Dion and the Belmonts), and jazz (Sarah Vaughan).

"Skylark" (Johnny Mercer/Hoagy Carmichael, 1942): Johnny Mercer said he preferred for the music to come first, then the lyrics. Plenty of lyric writers would disagree, especially when confronted with the odd but irresistible melody (and elusive chord changes) of this Hoagy Carmichael Standard. But Mercer did it, and singers have praised him ever since for permission to ask the skylark if it has "... seen a valley green with spring ..." or in its lonely flight "... heard music in the night." Mercer's imagery and Carmichael's melody brought the song immediate success, posting three straight months on *Your Hit Parade* driven by the Glenn Miller recording with vocal by Ray Eberle. Dinah Shore also had a hit single at the time, and it's been a winner ever since. Linda Ronstadt included it in her *Lush Life* album and Ann Hampton Callaway has recorded it, along with pianists Keith Jarrett and Marian McPartland.

"Smoke Gets in Your Eyes" (Otto Harbach/Jerome Kern, 1933): For a routine thirty-two-bar AABA Standard, this song is full of surprises—and challenges: for the singer, the octave-and-a-half range, and for the player, a key change at the bridge that is at once surprising but then just right. Harbach's lyrics are elegant. Not many lyricists were using words like "chaffed" and "deride," but he makes them all work toward the final line, where, for the first and only time, we hear the title of this poignant song about the end of a love affair: ". . . when a lovely flame dies, smoke gets in your eyes." It would seem to be only a singer's song, but fine jazz recordings have come from players such as Andre Previn and Gerry Mulligan. Vocally, it brought The Platters a number one record in 1958, and has cut a swath through every style in recordings by Liberace and Eartha Kitt, Dinah Washington, and David Sanborn on alto sax with a Johnny Mandel orchestra. The song originated on Broadway in *Roberta* (1933), then picked up film credits in the 1946 Kern biography, *Till the Clouds Roll By*, and again in the 1952 update of *Roberta*, starring Kathryn Grayson.

"Some of These Days" (Shelton Brooks, 1910): The Tin Pan Alley phase of popular music (c. 1895–1920) produced few Standards, but "Some of These Days" is a valid one, with qualities that foreshadow the great body of Standards to come after 1920. The composer, Chicagoan Shelton Brooks (1886–1975), was well-known as a performer as well as a composer, and in the 1920s took part in major Black musical productions in New York and Europe, including the Lew Leslie *Blackbirds* revues. The song's structure is ABCD, highly unusual for a Tin Pan Alley song. The verse is a throwaway boy/girl setup that in no way prepares singer or listener for the dark minor sequences of the chorus, that somehow combine cantoral echoes of the synagogue with intimations of the blues. The moody lyric of failed love and retribution is equally dark and compelling, but unfortunately vocal recordings were rare for years because the song was effectively trapped by the great star Sophie Tucker, who had originally introduced it, then made it her exclusive trademark. Jazz versions, however, are rife. Musicians love the open spaces and chord changes within the odd melody, inspiring the improvisations of dozens of players across nearly a century, from New Orleans' pioneer Bunk Johnson to New York's young star Scott Hamilton.

"Someone to Watch Over Me" (Ira Gershwin/George Gershwin, 1926): The British star Gertrude Lawrence, in her American debut, introduced this Standard-to-be in the Broadway show *Oh Kay!* A very young Frank Sinatra sang it in the film *Young at Heart* (1942), the first of many screen exposures for this plaintive Gershwin love song, and it has appeared in many a style down through the years, from country (Willie Nelson) to cabaret (Julie Wilson) to pop crossover (Linda Ronstadt, on her *What's New?* album with Nelson Riddle's orchestra). In jazz, the pianists lead the way with Art Tatum and Barbara Carroll and George Gershwin himself on the piano with the Victor Symphony Orchestra on a recent CD reissue.

"Sophisticated Lady" (Mitchell Parish and Irving Mills/Duke Ellington, 1933): Lush chords in descending thickets mark this Ellington Standard. Like so many of his works, it began as a song without words, recorded as such by the Ellington orchestra in 1933. Mitchell Parish, who fit words to Hoagy Carmichael's "Star Dust," retro-fit this arching melody with a lyric of world-weary heartbreak that has appealed primarily to women—Linda Ronstadt, Lena Horne, Della Reese—while Ellington's music without words has cut across every instrumental boundary, with superb piano treatments by Willie "The Lion" Smith, Daniel Barenboim, Chick Corea, and Cedar Walton. "Sophisticated Lady" is a very sophisticated Standard.

"Star Dust" (Mitchell Parish/Hoagy Carmichael, 1929): The artists who *haven't* recorded this song would comprise a very short list. Critics and collectors agree it is surely the most-often recorded song in the history of American popular song, the Standard that defines the meaning of the word. Hoagy Carmichael composed it originally as an up-tempo piano solo in 1927, and copyrighted it as such in 1928. In 1929 the lyric was added by Mitchell Parish, and in 1930 the Isham Jones orchestra wisely slowed the tempo and recorded it as a ballad. Louis Armstrong recorded words and music in 1931, and a pivotal orchestral recording was the 1940 Artie Shaw single, said to have sold over two million copies. The melody, now so familiar, was for its time an odd and angular one, as might be expected of a line originally intended to be played, not sung. The lyric is an equally remarkable departure, matching Carmichael's long phrases with hidden rhymes and a reflective first-person reminiscence that at times approaches stream of consciousness. The endurance of this weathered Standard must therefore be ascribed to lyricist Parish and composer Carmichael in equal measure. Even the prefatory verse of this song is so good, so expressive on its own, that in 1961 Frank Sinatra recorded it without the chorus. Wynton Marsalis recorded it in 1984 without a vocal. Everything about "Star Dust" has stood the test of time—its melodies, its words, its timeless evocation of remembered love. *The* Standard.

"Stormy Weather" (Ted Koehler/Harold Arlen, 1933): This prime Standard was introduced by Ethel Waters in one of Harlem's Cotton Club revues, and while Harold Arlen himself made the first recording (with the Leo Reisman orchestra) a Waters recording followed, and the song was identified with her for years. The "Stormy Weather" mantle then fell onto the shoulders of the star of the 1943 *Stormy Weather* movie, Lena Horne, and she proceeded to make it her own, featured in her 1981 Broadway and touring vehicle *A Lady and Her Music*. None of this has prevented the song from crossing every line in popular music, recorded by country singers Ferlin Husky and Willie Nelson and country pianist Floyd Cramer, and by artists as varied as Fats Domino, Ike and Tina Turner, Art Tatum and Steve Allen on piano, and nearly everybody you can think of in the business of jazz.

"Tea for Two" (Irving Caesar/Vincent Youmans, 1924): One of those most-recorded Standards of all time, a mainstay with singers and even more so with jazz musicians. Charles Mingus and Art Tatum and almost everybody else are on the list. It was a big record for Mantovani and for Bob Wills and The Texas Playboys. Ella Fitzgerald and Bobby Short each sipped its tea. The same song that was introduced in the '20s musical *No, No Nanette*, became the stuff of kid tap-dance recitals for decades, and hit number one for the Warren Covington orchestra in 1958 as the "Tea for Two Cha-Cha." Standards do get around.

"Tenderly" (Jack Lawrence/Walter Gross, 1946): Walter Gross was the Artists and Repertoire man at Musicraft Records in the mid-'40s, when he convinced Sarah Vaughan to record his composition, feeling it might become a jazz Standard. He was right. Rosemary Clooney had a million-seller with it (1952) and from then on it raced into the repertoire of everybody in the business: Willie Nelson, Jose Feliciano, and the young pianist Cyrus Chestnut, Roberta Flack, Bob Wilbur, Liberace; Louis Armstrong, Buddy Greco, and C&W sax man Boots Randolph. This kind of cross-pollination is what makes a good song into a great Standard.

"That Old Black Magic" (Johnny Mercer/Harold Arlen, 1942): The Glenn Miller orchestra with the Modernaires got this Standard off to a flying start with a number one record not long after it was introduced in the film *Star-Spangled Rhythm*. It was then closely associated with the singer Billy Daniels for many years, but has also been explored by practically everybody in popular music, from Judy Garland to Spike Jones, Mark Murphy, Toni Tennille, and Mary Cleere Haran. Its jazz outings include trips with Miles Davis, Benny Carter, and Dizzy Gillespie, and Hollywood kept returning to it in other films, including Marilyn Monroe's *Bus Stop* (1956).

"There Will Never Be Another You" (Mack Gordon/Harry Warren, 1942): At first glance the tune is routine—thirty-two measures,

ABAC—but it unfolds sweeping quarter-note passages that as-
cend and descend through harmonies just odd enough to in-
trigue and challenge every singer, ever since Helen Merrill sang
it with the Sammy Kaye orchestra in the 1942 film *Iceland*,
(which starred ice-skater Sonja Henie). Here a great song tran-
scends a bland beginning to become a Standard of wide interpretation. Sinatra, Nat Cole, Andy Williams, and Connie Francis
have invested those quarter-note passages and odd harmonies
with their own passions. So have Willie Nelson and Little
Jimmy Scott, and pianists Andre Previn and Billy Taylor. A
good song always finds its way.

"These Foolish Things" (Holt Marvell/Jack Strachey and Harry
Link, 1936): "A cigarette that bears a lipstick's traces...," "...
a telephone that rings but who's to answer..." Stunning lyrics
to invoke memories of lost love, doubly so because they are so
simple, listing the everyday things, the "foolish things" we can
never forget. This mighty Standard originated in a 1936 London
revue called *Spread It Abroad*—which indeed occurred for the
song if not the show. The lyric, happily, is set to a comfortable
melody over predictable harmony, so the piece invites the instrumentalist as well as the singer. It seems literally to have
been recorded by everybody in the business, starting with Eddy
Howard, through Sam Cooke, the Platters, and Della Reese, to
players like Harry "Sweets" Edison, Benny Carter, and pianist
Barbara Carroll.

"They Can't Take That Away from Me" (Ira Gershwin/George Gershwin, 1937): It's hard to believe, but this is the only Gershwin
song ever nominated for an Academy Award. It should have
won, but that's hindsight. That it didn't was no fault of Fred
Astaire, who introduced it with Ginger Rogers in *Shall We
Dance* and then recorded it right away and liked it so much he
reprised it in another film, *The Barclays of Broadway* (1949).
It has received unofficial awards ever since, however, by way
of performances and recordings. It was one of the works that

Charlie Parker recorded in his seminal jazz-with-strings album. Singers love the simple touchpoints of remembrance in its lyrics— ". . . the way you hold your knife . . . the way you sing off key . . ." It's a favorite of cabaret master Bobby Short and of Maureen McGovern. Bing Crosby, Pat Boone, and Sarah Vaughan are on the list, as are pianists Art Tatum and John Hicks.

"The Very Thought of You" (Ray Noble, 1934): In the film biography of trumpet legend Bix Beiderbecke, *Young Man with a Horn* (1950), this Ray Noble Standard was sung by Doris Day. It continues to get a lot of vocal attention, recently Steve Tyrell and Natalie Cole, and before them Etta James, Billie Holiday, and Jerry Vale. Noble himself had the first hit record on it with his own orchestra in 1934.

"The Way You Look Tonight" (Dorothy Fields/Jerome Kern, 1936): Steve Tyrell and Neil Diamond have kept this Standard current with vocal recordings, and the movies by using it on the sound-track of the 1997 Julia Roberts film *My Best Friend's Wedding*. It's always gotten good play as jazz, too (John Coltrane, Stanley Turrentine, Ramsey Lewis), no doubt because of Kern's long, open melody and characteristic key change in the release. Dorothy Field's gentle lyric has made the song as singable to a child as to a sweetheart, and the vocal recordings range from Betty Carter's 1955 side, with Ray Bryant on piano, to the Lettermen, Betty Buckley, and Billy Eckstine. First, though, it was Fred Astaire's song in the film *Swing Time* (he sang it to Ginger Rogers while she was shampooing her hair). It won the Academy Award for Best Song of 1936.

"Time on My Hands" (Harold Adamson and Mack Gordon/Vincent Youmans, 1930): Tenor sax players seem especially drawn to this Standard. Ben Webster, Gene Ammons, Coleman Hawkins are among those that have recorded Youmans's soaring, nicely dissonant melody. The big bands of Ellington, Basie, and British leader Ted Heath have also used it well, and though vocal versions are not as frequent, the classic jazz voice of Lee Wiley was perfect for it. It was introduced in the Broadway musical *Smiles* (1930), and featured in two subsequent films, June Haver singing it in *Look for the Silver Lining* (1949) and Kathryn Grayson in *So This Is Love* (1953).

"Too Marvelous for Words" (Johnny Mercer/Richard Whiting, 1937): In a clever turnaround, one of the best lyricists in the business claimed the subject of this lighthearted love song was impossible to describe in words—just "too marvelous"—and then proceeded to describe her/him with some great ones, like "...glorious, glamorous, and that old standby amorous..." Written for the film *Ready, Willing and Able*, the song turned up later on the soundtrack of a 1951 movie, *On the Sunny Side of the Street*, sung by Frankie Laine. There have been dozen of recordings since—music and words, all marvelous: Michael Feinstein, Jackie and Roy, the Norman Luboff Choir, John Pizzarelli, Joe Williams, Gerry Mulligan, and Bobby Short.

"What Is This Thing Called Love?" (Cole Porter, 1930): Plenty of singers have recorded this Porter Standard, but the jazz instrumentalists outnumber them five to one. Porter was equally inventive with words and music, and in this thirty-two-bar AABA composition, the chord progression is the magnet, attracting Clifford Brown and Doc Severinsen on trumpet, Dave Grusin and Fred Hersch on piano, orchestra leaders Artie Shaw and Enoch Light and hundreds more, including jazz violinist Stuff Smith. In the Porter film biography *Night and Day* (1945) it was sung by Ginny Simms.

"What'll I Do?" (Irving Berlin, 1924): This sweet waltz, with its spare, yearning lyric is a Standard that has *not* crossed over into jazz and instrumental performance as most have done. But it's on every singer's honor roll. Mezzo Joan Morris with William Bolcom's piano lovingly frames its verse and chorus like the art song it is; Linda Ronstadt and Cher and Michael Crawford have kept it alive, adding to a catalog of recordings dating back to those of Nat "King" Cole, Ray Charles, Perry Como, and Johnny Mathis, not to mention at least two members of the Sinatra family, Nancy and Francis Albert.

"What's New?" (Johnny Burke/Bob Haggart, 1939): Here's another Standard that was originally wordless. It was played by the Bob Crosby band until Hollywood's Johnny Burke added a lyric and a new title, and Bob's brother Bing recorded it for Decca. But it thrived mainly as an instrumental (Benny Goodman, Stan Getz, John Coltrane, and Milt Jackson) until Linda Ronstadt picked it as the title tune of her grand foray into Standard land with Nelson Riddle's orchestra. Since then it's become a Standard all over again as a *song*, recorded by Rosemary Clooney, Harry Connick, Jr., and Nancy Wilson.

"When Your Lover Has Gone" (EA Swan, 1931): The popular music world might have heard a lot more from Einar Aaron Swan if he hadn't died at age thirty-six (in 1940), in the midst of an active career as an arranger and composer in the radio and concert business. He composed this one great torch song, and the torch has been carried ever since by Ray Charles, the Four Freshmen, the Ray Anthony orchestra, Miles Davis, Billie Holiday, Maxine Sullivan, Carly Simon, pianists Eddie Heywood, and Dave McKenna.

"Willow Weep for Me" (Ann Ronell, 1932): This may be a sad song, but it's lived a happy life. It was introduced by the Paul Whiteman orchestra, Chad and Jeremy had a hit record with it in 1964, it received crossover jazz styling recently on alto sax by David Sanborn, and hard-bop trumpet treatment in 1961 by Howard McGhee. Vocals range from June Christy's classic version with the Stan Kenton orchestra to Frankie Laine's hit single, through Sam Cooke and Etta James to Rosemary Clooney's recent and wonderful reading.

"Without a Song" (William Rose and Edward Eliscu/Vincent You-mans, 1931): Elvis Presley often recited the opening words of this Standard to convey his feelings about music—"Without a song the day would never end..." Introduced on Broadway in the musical *Great Day!* it first became a staple for the big voices of Lawrence Tibbett, Nelson Eddy, and Mario Lanza. But it proved so appealing that it has since cut across all times and styles. Jimmy Durante recorded it, as did Itzhak Perlman, Neil Sedaka, and Willie Nelson. The Carpenters recorded it a cappella, Diana Ross and the Temptations made it their own, and Art Tatum delivered the definitive piano version.

"You Go to My Head" (Haven Gillespie/J. Fred Coots, 1938): Gil-lespie and Coots, a couple of Tin Pan Alley stalwarts who turned out plenty of good songs together or with others, probably paid most of their bills with royalties from their biggest hit, "Santa Claus Is Comin' to Town" (1934). "You Go to My Head" would be close behind, a major hit and a dominant Standard, intro-duced by the Glen Gray orchestra with a Kenny Sargent vocal. Hundreds of recordings since, in every style, unfold its sophis-ticated lyric set to a truly intoxicating melody and challenging harmonies developed in AABA form, with a surprising ten-bar coda. Everybody has recorded this Standard, singers and players. An early highlight is the Sarah Vaughan vocal with a John Kirby combo; Linda Ronstadt picked it *For Sentimental Reasons*, her third album of Standards with Nelson Riddle. Marlene Die-trich recorded it, as did Robert Goulet.

SEVEN

Popular Standards on CD

Building a Popular Standards collection is both a delight and a daunting process. An immense number of recordings are out there, in retail shops and on the Internet. You can lose your way. With an eye toward making the process somewhat less arduous, below is a list of seventy-five CDs and CD sets that should satisfy all but the most particular fan. No such list can be considered definitive, but all the CDs here are excellent and demonstrate the remarkable variety of styles that the Standards invite. Consider them a great jumping-off point, but don't hesitate to explore further on your own.

The list favors the work of singers and musicians from the first generation—partly in recognition of their original dedication to the Popular Standards, but also because they're the best interpretations of these songs on record. Worthy successors to that first generation, however, also appear prominently among the seventy-five. The CDs are listed alphabetically by title, and each entry below offers some basic information on the CD, including the label, year of issue (or latest reissue), the total number of tracks, a few featured songs, and occasionally the years in which the songs were recorded. More information on the major artists can be found in "Performers"; a word or two about the younger artists have been incorporated into the entries.

Building a Popular Standards CD collection can be costly, too, so the selections here are generally limited to single CDs or two-CD sets. Many of the early stars have been the subject of expensive multidisc boxes, which may be worth purchasing, but it is probably best to sample a variety of artists before putting major dollars into these total retrospectives. Remember, too, that most of the reissues were originally analog (old-style) LPs remastered to digital CD. If you can listen before you leap, do so by all means.

Over the past few years, the Smithsonian Institution has issued a line of CDs under the rubric of *The American Popular Song Recordings*. They are another superb point of access to Popular Standards—although they may be a bit tough to find outside libraries, collectors, and the Smithsonian itself. The collections have been selected by experts in each field; the remastering is excellent. Dozens of key artists are included. The *American Songbooks* series consists of twenty-four volumes, each dedicated to a different songwriter, from Arlen to Youmans. Other Smithsonian gems include: *American Musical Theater: Shows, Songs, and Stars; American Popular Song: Six Decades of Songs and Singers; The Classic Hoagy Charmichael; Souvenirs of Hot Chocolates;* and *Star-Spangled Rhythm: Voices of Broadway and Hollywood.* They are all worth a listen.

Am I Blue? Ethel Waters: Nine tracks recorded between 1925 and 1939, including "Am I Blue?" "Sweet Georgia Brown," and "Stormy Weather."

The Best of Chet Baker Sings Chet Baker (Capitol, 1989): Twenty tracks recorded in the mid-1950s, including "My Funny Val-

Where Else to Listen

CDs may be the simplest way to get your ears on some first-rate Popular Standards, but they are not the only way. The Standards no longer occupy the radio waves as they once did, but plenty of stations still serve them up, either as part of everyday fare or in programs dedicated to jazz or to Golden Age popular music. National Public Radio's member stations—which offer such shows as *Jazz from Lincoln Center* and *Marian McPartland's Piano Jazz*—are good places on the dial to find this musical treasury, such as New York's cherished outings with masterful host Jonathan Schwartz (WNYC). For more information, contact your local NPR station directly, or click on www.NPRjazz.org. It can of course be immensely rewarding to hear the Standards performed live in nightclubs, cabarets, and concert halls so keep an eye on the listings.

entine," "But Not for Me," and "Like Someone in Love." Baker, known principally for his innovative trumpet playing, shows off a thin but highly musical vocal style.

Best of Ella Fitzgerald: First Lady of Song (Verve, 1994): Sixteen tracks, including "Don't Be That Way," " 'Deed I Do," and "A Fine Romance." The larger collection from which these tracks are drawn is simply *Ella Fitzgerald: First Lady of Song* (Verve, 1993). Its fifty-one tracks on three CDs—many in collaboration with other greats such as Louis Armstrong, Ben Webster, and Charlie Parker—include "Too Darn Hot," "Bewitched, Bothered, and Bewildered," and "Summertime." Fitzgerald has also recorded songbooks of Rodgers and Hart, Duke Ellington, Irving Berlin, Harold Arlen, Cole Porter, and others.

The Best of George Shearing George Shearing (Capitol, 1995): Eighteen instrumental tracks recorded between 1955 and 1960, including "Cheek to Cheek," "Have You Met Miss Jones?" and "Dancing on the Ceiling."

The Best of Lester Young Lester Young (Pablo, 1987): Eight tracks including "Almost Like Being in Love," "Lullaby of Birdland," and "These Foolish Things."

The Best of the Capitol Years Frank Sinatra (Capitol, 1992): Twenty tracks from Sinatra's midcareer, including "Three Coins in a Fountain," "In the Wee Small Hours of the Morning," and "Come Fly with Me." For a good selection of his earlier work, there's *Portrait of Sinatra: Columbia Classics* (Columbia, 1997). Its thirty-six tracks on two CDs include "All or Nothing at All," "It Never Entered my Mind," and "Where or When." Sinatra's later work can be heard on *From the Reprise Collection* (Reprise, 1991). Its twenty tracks include "Summer Wind," "The Way You Look Tonight," "My Way," and a late-issue standard, "New York, New York." *Duets* (Capitol, 1993) pairs Sinatra with contemporary pop stars; its thirteen tracks include "What Now My Love?" (with Aretha Franklin), "I've Got You Under My Skin" (with Kenny G), and "Come Rain or Come Shine" (with Gloria Estefan).

The Best of the Roost Years Stan Getz (Columbia, 1991): Sixteen instrumental tracks recorded in the early 1950s, including "Autumn Leaves," "Lullaby of Birdland," and "Moonlight in Vermont."

Billy's Best Billy Eckstine (Verve, 1995): Thirteen tracks recorded in 1957, including "Zing! Went the Strings of my Heart," "A Sunday Kind of Love," and "Trust in Me." Another fine Eckstine album is *Everything I Have Is Yours* (Verve, 1985). Its twenty tracks on two CDs include "I Wanna Be Loved," "Body and Soul," and several duets with Sarah Vaughan.

Blue Rose Rosemary Clooney and Duke Ellington (with his Orchestra) (Columbia, 1999): Thirteen tracks from a 1956 collaboration, including Duke's "Sophisticated Lady," "Mood Indigo," and "I Got It Bad and That Ain't Good."

Blue Skies Cassandra Wilson (JMT, 1998): Ten tracks, including "Sweet Lorraine" and "Shall We Dance?" Wilson's repertoire covers a wide range of musical styles, but she really shows off her voice in this collection of Standards.

Blue Skies: The Irving Berlin Songbook Various artists (Verve, 1996): Sixteen tracks, featuring Joe Williams, Dinah Shore, and Ella and Louis. This series includes two more Berlin songbooks: *Cheek to Cheek* (Verve, 1997), whose sixteen tracks feature Bing Crosby, Anita O'Day, and Billie Holiday, and *How Deep Is the Ocean?* (Verve 1997), whose sixteen instrumental tracks feature Lionel Hampton, Teddy Wilson, and Gerry Mulligan. The music of these three CDs has also been gathered into a single package, *The Complete Irving Berlin Songbook* (Verve).

Blues in the Night: The Johnny Mercer Songbook Various artists (Verve, 1997): Sixteen tracks, featuring Bing Crosby, Joe Williams, and Woody Herman. This series includes two more Mercer songbooks: *Trav'lin' Light* (Verve, 1998), whose sixteen tracks feature Sarah Vaughan, Buddy Rich, and Astrud Gilberto, and *Too Marvelous for Words* (Verve, 1998), whose sixteen instrumental tracks feature Johnny Hodges, Bill Evans, and Don Byas. The music of these three CDs has also been gathered into a single package, *The Complete Johnny Mercer Songbook* (Verve).

Body and Soul Coleman Hawkins (1996, BMG): Nineteen instrumental tracks recorded between 1939 and 1956, including "My Blue Heaven," "Say It Isn't So," and the title song.

Body and Soul Errol Garner (Columbia, 1991): Twenty instrumental tracks, including "Honeysuckle Rose," "I Can't Get Started," and the title song. A more extensive offering, *The Complete Master Takes* (Savoy, 1998), features forty-one tracks on two CDs, including "Laura," "All of Me," and "Stormy Weather."

But Beautiful Nancy Wilson (Capitol, 1989): Thirteen tracks recorded in 1969, including "I'll Walk Alone," "Easy Living," and "In a Sentimental Mood." Wilson is a veteran all-around performer and longtime friend of the Standards.

Carmen McRae Sings Great American Songwriters Carmen McRae (Decca, 1993): Twenty tracks recorded in the 1950s, including "Ev'ry Time We Say Good-bye," "Nice Work If You Can Get It," and "My Romance."

The Complete Capitol Hits Margaret Whiting (Capitol, 2000): Forty-five tracks on two CDs including "Old Devil Moon," and "Baby, It's Cold Outside," "Moonlight in Vermont."

The Complete RCA Victor Recordings Dizzy Gillespie (RCA, 1995): Forty-three instrumental tracks on two CDs, including "King Porter Stomp," "That Old Black Magic," and "You Go to My Head."

Confirmation: Best of the Verve Years Charlie Parker (Verve, 1995): Thirty-four instrumental tracks on two CDs, including "Laura," "Embraceable You," and "How High the Moon." Parker has also recorded a fine Cole Porter songbook.

The Decca Years Sammy Davis, Jr., (Decca, 1990): Sixteen tracks recorded in the mid-1950s, including "My Funny Valentine," "That Old Black Magic," and "Easy to Love."

The Dinah Washington Story Dinah Washington (Verve, 1993): Thirty-one tracks on two CDs, recorded between 1944 and the early 1960s, including "Embraceable You," "I've Got You Under My Skin," and "What a Diff'rence a Day Makes."

Easy Living Ann Hampton Callaway (Sin-Drome, 1999): Thirteen tracks including "Come Rain or Come Shine," "All of You," and "In a Sentimental Mood." Callaway is one of the most versatile and successful of the younger Standards performers.

Ella and Louis Ella Fitzgerald and Louis Armstrong (Verve, 2000): Eleven tracks on a 1956 album, including "Moonlight in Vermont," "They Can't Take That Away from Me," and "Under A Blanket of Blue." The two masters collaborate again on *Ella and Louis Again* (Verve, 1987). Its twelve tracks include "Gee Baby Ain't I Good to You," "Let's Call the Whole Thing Off," and "I've Got My Love to Keep Me Warm."

The Essential Count Basie—Vol. 1 Count Basie (Columbia, 1987): Sixteen tracks, including "Oh, Lady Be Good" and "Love Me or Leave Me." Equally fine is *The Essential Count Basie—Vol. 2* (Columbia, 1987). Its sixteen tracks include "Between the Devil and the Deep Blue Sea."

Every Day: The Best of the Verve Years Joe Williams (Verve, 1993): Thirty-one tracks on two CDs, featuring recordings both from the 1950s and from the 1980s, including "Teach Me Tonight," "A Fine Romance," and "Sometimes I'm Happy." Williams, one of the great blues singers of the century, actually preferred singing the Standards.

A Fine Romance: The Jerome Kern Songbook Various artists (Verve, 1994): Sixteen tracks, featuring Margaret Whiting, Billie Holiday, and Ella Fitzgerald. This series includes two more Kern songbooks: *All The Things You Are* (Verve) and *Yesterdays* (Verve, 1997), whose sixteen instrumental tracks feature Bud Powell, Erroll Garner, and Charlie Parker. The music of these three CDs has also been gathered into a single package, *The Complete Jerome Kern Songbook* (Verve).

The Gentle Side of John Coltrane John Coltrane (Impulse, 1974): Thirteen instrumental tracks, including "What's New?," "Lush Life," and "In a Sentimental Mood."

The Great American Songbook Mel Tormé (Telarc, 1993): Fifteen tracks, including "You Make Me Feel So Young," "Autumn in New York," and "Star Dust." Another fine choice is *Mel Tormé in Hollywood* (Decca, 1992). Its twenty tracks include "Blue Moon," "That Old Black Magic," and "Imagination."

The Great Summit: The Master Takes Louis Armstrong and Duke Ellington (Roulette, 2000): Seventeen tracks from a 1961 session, including the Ellington compositions "Mood Indigo," "Azalea," and "Duke's Place."

Greatest Hits Benny Goodman (RCA, 1996): Fifteen tracks recorded between 1935 and 1937, including "Love Me or Leave Me," "Tea for Two," and "You Turned the Tables on Me."

Greatest Hits "Fats" Waller (RCA, 1996): Fourteen tracks recorded between 1929 and 1943, including Waller's own compositions "Honeysuckle Rose" and "The Joint Is Jumpin'."

Greatest Hits Lena Horne (RCA, 2000): Fourteen tracks recorded between 1941 and 1962, including "Stormy Weather," "I Got Rhythm," and "What Is This Thing Called Love?" Some of Horne's fine later work can be found on *Love Songs* (RCA, 2000). Its sixteen tracks include "At Long Last Love," "Someone to Watch Over Me," and "People Will Say We're in Love."

Greatest Hits Rosemary Clooney (RCA, 2000): Fifteen tracks recorded in 1959 and 1960, including "April in Paris," "Bye Bye Blackbird," and "You Took Advantage of Me." Clooney's equally fine later work can be found on *At Long Last* (Concord, 1998). Its sixteen tracks include "Like Someone in Love," "In the Wee Small Hours of the Morning," and "Old Devil Moon."

Clooney has also recorded collections of Cole Porter, Jimmy Van Heusen, Ira Gershwin, and Johnny Mercer, among others.

Hello, Young Lovers: Capitol Sings Rodgers & Hammerstein Various artists (Capitol, 1994): Twenty tracks, featuring Bobby Darin, Nancy Wilson, and Dick Haymes.

Hoagy Sings Carmichael Hoagy Carmichael (Blue Note, 2000): Eleven tracks on a 1956 album, including Hoagy's own "Georgia on my Mind," "Skylark," and "Lazy River."

Hooray for Hollywood Doris Day (Columbia, 1988): Twelve tracks, including "Night and Day," "Over the Rainbow," and "Easy to Love."

The Immortal Bing Crosby (Avid, 1994): Twenty-five tracks recorded in the 1930s, including "The Very Thought of You," "How Deep Is the Ocean?," and "Just a Gigolo." For a more extensive look at Crosby, there's *A Portrait of Bing Crosby* (Gallerie, 1997). Its forty-eight tracks on two CDs include "Don't Be That Way," "Brother Can You Spare a Dime?" and "White Christmas."

Isn't It Romantic Michael Feinstein (Elektra, 1988): Twelve tracks, including "A Fine Romance" and "I Wanna Be Loved." More extensive and just as good is *Romance on Film, Romance on Broadway* (Concord, 2000) Its twenty-two tracks on two CDs include "Taking a Chance on Love," and "Something's Gotta Give." Feinstein is an entertainer extraordinaire as well as one of the foremost authorities on the Standards.

Jazz Tony Bennett (Columbia, 1987): Twenty-two tracks on what was originally a two-record set, including "Just One of Those Things," "Don't Get Around Much Anymore," and "Solitude." A good later album is **MTV Unplugged** (Columbia, 1994). Its twenty tracks include "Body and Soul" and "Steppin' Out with

My Baby." Bennett has also recorded a magnificent Duke Ellington songbook.

Johnny Mathis Johnny Mathis (Columbia, 1996): Thirteen tracks, including "Easy to Love," "Cabin in the Sky," and "In Other Words." This was Mathis's first album. Mathis also has a strong Duke Ellington tribute album.

Lady Day's 25 Greatest Billie Holiday (ASV, 1996): Twenty-five tracks recorded between 1933 and 1944, including "What a Little Moonlight Can Do," "They Can't Take that Away from Me," and "You Go to My Head." Many great later recordings can be found on *Lady in Autumn: The Best of the Verve Years* (Verve, 1991). Its 35 tracks on two CDs, recorded between 1946 and 1959, include "Stars Fell on Alabama," "Strange Fruit," and "God Bless the Child."

Let's Do It: Best of the Verve Years Louis Armstrong (Verve, 1995): Thirty-four tracks on two CDs including "Stars Fell on Alabama," "Stormy Weather," and "Like Someone in Love."

Let's Face the Music Fred Astaire (Avid, 1994): Twenty-five tracks recorded in the 1930s, including "Fascinating Rhythm," "Cheek to Cheek," and "A Foggy Day."

Loch Lomond: Her 24 Greatest Hits Maxine Sullivan (ASV, 1998): Twenty-four tracks recorded between 1937 and 1942, including "The Folks Who Live on the Hill," "It Ain't Necessarily So," and the title song.

Louis Armstrong Meets Oscar Peterson Louis Armstrong with Oscar Peterson (Verve, 1997): Sixteen tracks from a 1957 session, including "What's New?," "Just One of Those Things," and "That Old Feeling."

Midnight in the Garden of Good and Evil Various artists (Warner, 1997): Fourteen tracks, all Johnny Mercer compositions, featuring Alison Kraus, Paula Cole, and Tony Bennett.

Music Is My Life Diane Schuur (Atlantic, 1999): Eleven tracks, including "Over the Rainbow," "You'd Be So Nice to Come Home To," and "Bewitched, Bothered, and Bewildered." Schuur is a superb and somewhat iconoclastic interpreter of the Standards.

Never Never Land Jane Monheit (N-Coded Music, 2000): Ten tracks, including "Never Let Me Go," "More Than You Know," and "I Got It Bad (and That Ain't Good)." Monheit is a talented young singer who has attracted the attention of jazz veterans, many of whom join her on this album.

Night and Day: The Cole Porter Songbook Various artists (Verve, 1990): Seventeen tracks, featuring Blossom Dearie, Mel Tormé, and Sarah Vaughan. This series includes two more Porter songbooks: *I Get a Kick Out of You* (Verve, 1991), whose seventeen tracks feature Billie Holiday, Helen Merrill, and Fred Astaire, and *Anything Goes* (Verve, 1992), whose fourteen instrumental tracks feature Dizzy Gillespie, Max Roach, and Art Tatum. The music of these three CDs has also been gathered into a single package, *The Complete Cole Porter Songbook* (Verve).

Piano Starts Here Art Tatum (Columbia, 1995): Thirteen instrumental takes, nine of them live, recorded in the 1940s, including "The Man I Love," "Willow Weep for Me," and "Someone to Watch over Me."

Portrait in Jazz Bill Evans Trio (Riverside, 1987): Eleven instrumental tracks from a 1959 session, including "When I Fall in Love," and "Witchcraft." Evans can also be heard outside the trio in *The Best of Bill Evans Live* (Verve, 1997). Its twelve tracks, recorded between 1964 and 1968, include "Make Someone Happy," "Spring Is Here," and "How Deep Is the Ocean?"

A Portrait of Dinah Shore Dinah Shore (Gallerie, 2000): Forty-eight tracks of on two CDs, including "Smoke Gets in Your Eyes," "I've Got the World on a String," and "You'd Be So Nice to Come Home To."

A Portrait of Peggy Lee Peggy Lee (Gallerie, 1999): Forty-seven tracks on two CDs, including "How Long Has This Been Going On?," "Summertime," and "Stormy Weather."

A Portrait of Perry Como Perry Como (Gallierie, 2000): Forty-four tracks on two CDs, including "Blue Skies," "Love Me or Leave Me," and "With a Song in my Heart."

Pres and Teddy Lester Young and Teddy Wilson (Verve, 1987): Seven tracks from a 1956 session, including "Love Me or Leave Me," "Taking a Chance on Love," and "Our Love Is Here to Stay."

Relaxin' with Miles Miles Davis Quintet (Prestige, 1987): Six instrumental tracks, including "If I Were a Bell," "I Could Write a Book," and "It Could Happen to You." John Coltrane is on saxophone.

The Rockin' Chair Lady Mildred Bailey (Decca, 1994): Twenty tracks recorded between 1931 and 1950, including "Rockin' Chair," "Willow Tree," and "Georgia on My Mind."

Sarah Vaughan Sings Broadway: Great Songs from Hit Shows Sarah Vaughan (Verve, 1995): Thirty-four tracks on two CDs from a 1956 session, including "Can't We Be Friends?," "It Never Entered My Mind," and "Comes Love." Vaughan has also recorded Irving Berlin and Rodgers and Hart songbooks, among others.

Sleepless in Seattle Various artists (Columbia, 1993): Twelve tracks, featuring Jimmy Durante, Louis Armstrong, and Joe Cocker.

The Song Is You: Best of the Verve Songbooks Oscar Peterson (Verve, 1996): Thirty-two tracks on two CDs recorded in the 1950s, including "I'm in the Mood for Love," "The Lady Is a Tramp," and "It Ain't Necessarily So." Some of Peterson's later work can be found on *My Favorite Instrument* (Verve, 1968). Its nine tracks include "Someone to Watch Over Me," "Little Girl Blue," and "I Should Care."

Sophisticated Lady Duke Ellington (RCA, 1996): Fourteen instrumental tracks recorded by Duke and his orchestra between 1940 and 1946, including "I Got It Bad (and That Ain't Good)," "Take the A Train," and "In a Sentimental Mood." For a more comprehensive picture, there's *The Duke: The Essential Collection, 1927–62* (Columbia, 1999). Its sixty-six tracks on three CDs include "Solitude," "Sophisticated Lady," and "Don't Get Around Much Anymore."

Spotlight on Judy Garland Judy Garland (Capitol, 1995): Eighteen tracks including "Memories of You," "Come Rain or Come Shine," and "Over the Rainbow." Another fine album is *The London Sessions* (Capitol, 1992). Its twenty tracks include "Why Was I Born?," "I Can't Give You Anything but Love," and (of course) "Over the Rainbow."

Standard Time—Vol. 1 (Wynton Marsalis (Columbia, 1987). Twelve tracks. "The Song Is You," "Memories of You," "Autumn Leaves." Marsalis—a master trumpet player and the artistic director of Lincoln Center's jazz program—followed this up with five more *Standard Time* albums.

Standards Ray Charles (Rhino, 1998): Seventeen tracks from the R&B great, including "Ol' Man River," "It Had to Be You," and "Makin' Whoopee."

Sweet and Lovely: Capitol's Great Ladies of Song Various Artists (Capitol, 1992): Twenty-five tracks, featuring Nancy Wilson, Kay Starr, and Peggy Lee. The follow-up album, *Sentimental Journey: Capitol's Great Ladies of Song* (Capitol, 1992), has twenty-six tracks, featuring Dinah Shore, June Christy, and Anita O'Day.

'S Wonderful: The Gershwin Songbook Various artists (Verve, 1992): Sixteen tracks, featuring Bing Crosby, Ella Fitzgerald, and Betty Carter. This series includes two more Gershwin songbooks: *'S Marvelous* (Verve, 1994), whose sixteen tracks feature Antonio Carlos Jobim, Dinah Washington, and Shirley Horn, and *'S Paradise* (Verve, 1995), whose sixteen instrumental tracks feature Coleman Hawkins, Stan Getz, and Art Tatum. The music of these three CDs has also been gathered into a single package, *The Complete Gershwin Songbook* (Verve).

That Old Black Magic: The Harold Arlen Songbook Various artists (Verve, 1997): Sixteen tracks, featuring Mel Tormé, Billy Eckstine, and Margaret Whiting.

That Towering Feeling/On the Swinging Side Vic Damone (Savoy, 2000): Sixteen tracks on one CD containing two old albums, including "Let's Fall in Love," "Deep Purple," and "Cry Me a River."

There's a Small Hotel Mary Cleere Haran (Columbia, 1952): Eighteen tracks recorded live at Manhattan's legendary Algonquin hotel, including "Let's Do It," "A Fine Romance," and "The Way You Look Tonight." Haran is a leading New York Cabaret artist.

25 Harry Connick, Jr. (Columbia, 1992): Thirteen tracks, including "This Time the Dream's on Me," "Star Dust," and "On the Street Where You Live." Singer Connick is also a wonderful pianist, movie actor, and composer in his own right.

Unforgettable Nat "King" Cole (Capitol, 2000): Twenty-five tracks, including "Straighten Up and Fly Right," and "The Very Thought of You," as well as the famous title song.

We'll Have Manhattan: The Rodgers & Hart Songbook Various artists (Verve, 1993). Sixteen tracks, featuring Abbey Lincoln, Nina Simone, and Bing Crosby. This series includes two more Rodgers and Hart songbooks: *My Funny Valentine* (Verve, 1995), whose sixteen tracks feature Tony Bennett, Cassandra Wilson, and Shirley Horn, and *Isn't It Romantic?* (Verve, 1996), whose fifteen mostly instrumental tracks, feature Sonny Rollins, Clifford Brown, and Ben Webster. The music of these three CDs has also been gathered into a single package, *The Complete Rodgers & Hart Songbook* (Verve).

What's New Linda Ronstadt (Asylum, 1983): Nine tracks, including "I've Got a Crush on You," "Guess I'll Hang My Tears Out to Dry," and "Crazy He Calls Me." Pop star Ronstadt followed this album with two more collections of Standards: *Lush Life* (Asylum, 1984)—twelve tracks, including "You Took Advantage of Me," "Sophisticated Lady," and "Can't We Be Friends"—and *For Sentimental Reasons* (Asylum, 1986), with eleven tracks including "Am I Blue?," "Straighten Up and Fly Right," and "Little Girl Blue." The three albums have also been collected into a single volume entitled *Round Midnight* (Asylum, 1986).

When I Look in Your Eyes Diana Krall (Verve, 1999): Twelve tracks on a Grammy-winning album, including "Let's Fall in Love," "East of the Sun (and West of the Moon)," and "Let's Face the Music and Dance." Krall is a fine jazz pianist and singer who has toured with Tony Bennett.

Willow Creek and Other Ballads Marian McPartland (Concord, 1985): Ten tracks, including "The Things We Did Last Summer," "Long Ago and Far Away," and "I've Got a Crush on You." McPartland is the *grande dame* of jazz piano.

The Language of Popular Standards

To talk with precision about the popular music of the Golden Age requires a language unique to the subject. This language borrows some of the words from other arts and professions, but also has an argot all its own. Below is a glossary of some essential words and phrases. While the terms often have multiple meanings in music or in other disciplines, the definitions here are limited to those that apply to popular music in general and the Popular Standards in particular.

Accompaniment: Music supplied by a pianist or ensemble in support of a singer or solo instrument. Musicians often chop the verb form of the word *accompany* down to one syllable: to *comp*.

Alley: Short for "Tin Pan Alley," the name that came to define the popular music publishing business during 1900–1930 or so.

Arranger: One who writes out the parts for the instruments of the band or orchestra or group. The finished product is an *arrangement, orchestration*, or, informally, *chart*. (*See* chart.)

Ballad: An ancient term that has gone through a dozen meanings in music, poetry, and dance. In popular music, it has come to mean a love song. A good percentage of the Popular Standards are ballads, and the word can cross over to cover instrumental versions, too. Pianists and jazz bands can play *ballads*.

Band: Any sort of instrumental grouping, from Sousa to the Rolling Stones; technically, a band contains no string section.

Bar: *See* measure.

Blues: Musically, a tune in duple time twelve measures in length, with a strict chord progression, usually I-IV-I-V-VI-I in the major mode, with certain variations depending on time, locale, and individual approaches. The chords are characterized by "blue" notes—flatted sevenths and thirds on fixed-pitch instruments such as the piano, but bent when delivered by the human voice and most other instruments. The vocal pattern of the blues is composed of three lines, the second line a repeat or near-repeat of the first, and the final line an answer or resolution. Like many other labels applied to popular music, the word *blues* became imprecise and ambiguous, e.g., when used in songs such as the Popular Standard "Limehouse Blues" or Nora Bayes's lament "The Prohibition Blues," which do not adhere to the classic blues pattern. Real blues, clearly of African-American origination, was one of the ingredients in the development of jazz, and remains so today.

Book: The story, the play, the spoken lines in a musical theater production. In the dance band business the *book* is the total of musical selections in the band's repertoire, each piece usually identified by a number.

Bop: Originally *rebop* or *bebop*, a coined word often attributed to saxophonist Charlie Parker, to encompass certain harmonic and rhythmic changes taking place in jazz during the mid-1940s, largely in New York. Players often used the Standards (e.g. "Whispering" and "Cherokee") as a basis for extended and highly technical improvisation. Leading jazz musicians originating the style included Parker, Dizzy Gillespie, the pianists Lennie Tristano and Bud Powell. They were giants of jazz at mid-century who exerted a powerful influence on the future of the genre.

Break: In jazz, an improvised instrumental figure played at open measures in a piece of music.

Bridge: In popular music, the third phrase in the four-phrase pattern AABA, usually totally different from the opening phrases in melody and harmony, often in a different but related key; also known as the *release* or the *middle eight.*

Cadence: The ending of a phrase or strain; the melodic and harmonic elements that occur at the end of a composition; a section or a phrase that signals a temporary or permanent conclusion.

Changes: Short for "chord changes," meaning the harmonic sequence in a given tune; the chord progression.

Chart: Slang for *orchestration*, as in the dictionary definition: a *map* or *guide*. A *head chart* refers to an agreed-upon arrangement with nothing written down. In trade publications such as *Billboard* and *Variety*, *charts* are the tables of song titles and numbers compiled weekly to track sales of current recordings.

Chord: In harmony, any combination of three or more tones, commonly known as a triad; chords in their basic structure are built in intervals of thirds. (*See* interval.)

Chord symbols: In jazz and popular music, capital letters signifying the root of a chord, in use on lead sheets, orchestral/choral parts, or orchestrations. Numbers or small lowercase letters indicate alterations to the basic three-tone chord or triad. Thus the basic C major chord is written as C, C minor as C_m, with added seventh C^7, etc. In the more complex harmonies that mark many popular Standards, especially in modern jazz arrangements, chord symbols can send four or five messages to the musician, e.g., $C_{m7}{}^{+5-9}$.

Chorus: In popular song, the section following the verse. Alternated with verse—brief, more melodic, and easier to recall. Increasingly during the twentieth century, the chorus *became* the song. Also called the *refrain*.

Chromaticism: Technically, the use of the full chromatic (twelve-tone) scale as opposed to the diatontic (seven-tone) scale in harmonic and melodic structures; based on the Greek *chroma*, meaning "color." It's also a good, nontechnical term to describe its function in music; it adds color.

Combo: A small ensemble of musicians (not singers), less in number than an orchestra, more than a trio, their music generally in the jazz vein; (also *group*).

Composer: One who writes music.

Copyright: A service of the federal government to protect the exclusive rights of composers, lyricists, and other creators of intellectual properties; also, as a verb, to use or implement this service.

Cover: For a performer, to record one's own version of a popular new recording. The term also applies to the new version itself. In the heyday of the Standard, it was common for an artist to *cover* a potential hit song on a competing label. Sometimes it was the cover itself that went on to become a hit.

Croon: The technique of singing made possible by the advent of the microphone. A singer no longer needed a "big" voice, but could sing to the mic and be amplified electronically in either the recording studio or live performance. Bing Crosby was the first star to be associated with the word, which for a time implied only the characteristics of his easygoing personal style rather than the wide-ranging innovation in pop singing technique that it first labeled. It's quaint and no longer in use, but a case could be made that every singer since Crosby has "crooned."

Crossover: A performance in a musical style or genre other than that for which the piece is commonly known. An example would be the C&W star Willie Nelson performing Standards, as he has done consistently. The term also refers to a recording that was originally aimed at one market and succeeds in another.

Dissonance: Notes and chords juxtaposed in such a way as to violate the "consonant" harmonies of the major chords and intervals; elements considered dissonant by one generation or school may not be so considered by others. Dissonance is in the ear, and highly subjective.

Double: To perform on more than one instrument. As a verb, reed players are expected to *double* on clarinet and sax; as a noun: euphonium and trombone are a commonplace *double*.

Duple meter: Any rhythm or meter divisible by two: 2/4, 4/4, 4/8, etc. One of two basic meters, the other being triple meter.

Evergreen: A song that is considered a Popular Standard.

Fake: To improvise. To a working musician, *fake it* also means what *wing it* means in other lines of work. The term added another meaning when the so-called fake books appeared in the 1950s. These were mimeographed copies in lead sheet form, with melody, chord symbols, and lyrics for hundreds of popular songs (including most of the Standards) provided to working musicians. They were illegal—bootlegged—as no royalties were paid for reproduction of copyrighted material. The term has now fully matured without any negative connotation, as it is employed by major pop music publishing houses to market their songs in lead sheet format, a great boon to the seeker of Popular Standards who wants to play and sing them.

Four: As in "in four," 4/4 time; the essential duple-time signature: often written in musical notation as a **C.**

Ghost band: A large dance band, usually on tour, which uses the name, style, and many of the actual orchestrations of a famous band from the heyday of the Big Bands.

Gig: A job, originally a booking for a musician, singer, entertainer, now also used in most other professions.

Group: An ensemble, a small band or vocal chorus; in jazz the word was *combo* (for *combination*) for years, a term no longer fashionable.

Harmony: Loosely, any combination of musical sounds in a *chord*; a narrower use is taken to be an "agreeable" chord, pleasant to the ear. Broadly, harmony refers to the the succession of chords in a piece of music, and the relationship between them.

Improvise: To perform music immediately by instinct or ingrained mental processes without written aid; in jazz and popular music, to invent elaborations on a particular piece of music, written or memorized. A sequence played in such a manner is an *improvisation*.

Instrumental: As a noun, with *an*, music that contains no vocal component. Some works are conceived as instrumental only, such as marches. Songs may be rendered without their words, thus *instrumentally*. Many Popular Standards (songs) have attained currency through *instrumental* recordings and performance.

Interval: The difference in pitch between two musical tones; also the number of tones between them, e.g., third, sixth, octave (for eight). (*See* chord.)

Intonation: The proper adjustment of voice or instrument to the musical tone or pitch specified in a song or orchestration; singers and musicians without proper *intonation* are said to have "a bad ear," the nth degree of which is to be "tone deaf."

Jazz: The name originally attached to improvised music probably derived from marches, ragtime, blues and gospel, and performed in ensemble by five or six players (cornet, clarinet, trombone, piano, drums, and banjo or tuba), initially by African-Americans, in New Orleans in the period c. 1915–1918. Any quick definition of this word must be considered suspect, inadequate, oversimplified, subjective, and probably unhelpful. Like the rest of the terms in American music, *jazz* quickly came into careless and often invidious usage. Then like *ragtime, blues, swing,* and *rock,* it lost any precise musical meaning that it may originally have possessed. That said, *jazz* is an American form of music of immense scope and cultural importance. Nonetheless, it challenges verbal definition. Or in the words of Louis Armstrong: "If you have to *ask* what it is, you'll never know."

Jump/Jump time: Bright, up-tempo jazz, usually associated with the hard-driving swing bands of Cab Calloway, Jay McShann, and Count Basie in the early '40s, and leading to the R&B bands a decade or so later.

Key: (1) Tonality; the root of the scale upon which a musical selection is based, e.g., the key of F, the key of A-flat minor; (2) various levers, valves, and other devices on musical instruments: piano *keys*, clarinet *keys*; (3) relating to proper attention to a given pitch or intonation, as in singing or playing out of key.

Lead: The melody in a musical ensemble. In a vocal group, the singer with the melody is said to be singing lead. In traditional jazz, the trumpet is the lead instrument. A simple one-staff music score is referred to as a lead sheet, meaning it contains only the melody and words (if any), and sometimes the chord symbols.

Legit: Short for "legitimate" theater, originally drama of literary value as opposed to farce and melodrama; later, any play or musical with dialog, plot, and action. By late nineteenth century legit meant any shows in theater that were *not* vaudeville, burlesque, and the like.

Libretto: The text of an opera or choral work; also used with operetta and musical theater to indicate the author of the dialog as opposed to the *lyrics* of the songs. In American musical theater, *book* is the preferred term.

Lick: A jazz musician's brief improvisational figure, often a repeated one that can become characteristic of the particular player. An especially catchy invention is a *hot lick*. The term is antiquated but still in use.

Lyrics: The words of a song. The entire set of lyrics can also be called *the lyric*.

Measure: The smallest musical unit, which is a complete particle or cell of the time or meter in which the piece is written; measures are separated by vertical lines called *bars* and in modern usage, bar is often used to mean *measure*.

Medley: Several songs or portions of songs sung or played in a single continuous arrangement, usually connected or related by style, composer, content, or period.

Melisma: Improvised or intuitive vocal expression imposed upon one syllable; the "bending" of sustained notes.

Melody: A succession of musical tones, as opposed to harmony, in which the tones are sounded together. The melody is the tune itself, sometimes called the *air* or the *strain*.

Meter: The beat or rhythm of a composition.

Mode: The selection of tones arranged in a scale that dictate the tonal nature of a piece of music. In most popular music (and Standards) no *mode* except the major and minor are in common use.

Modulation: To pass from one key or tonality to another, usually by way of a chord sequence.

Octave: The eighth tone of a diatonic (eight-note) scale; also the interval formed by two notes an octave apart.

Orchestra: A large ensemble of instruments divided into four principal groups: strings, brass, woodwinds, and percussion. In popular music, the word is applied more loosely, and *band* and *orchestra* are often used interchangeably, although a band has no string section. Most of the major dance bands of the swing era had no strings, but it was common to employ either term: the Benny Goodman *Band* or Glenn Miller and his *Orchestra*.

Orchestrate: To write out the parts for the various instruments in the orchestra; also any band or ensemble; the completed work is an *orchestration*. (*See* chart.)

Phrase: A natural division of a song's harmonic and melodic line, like a stanza in poetry. The exact length of the phrases varies; in much of popular music, a phrase is eight measures long.

Pitch: The location of a musical sound in the tonal scale, familiar names of which are found in do-re-mi-fa-sol-la-ti-do, or in the C scale C-D-E-F-G-A-B-C; pitch is governed by the number of sound wave vibrations per second. "Standard" pitch in the U.S. is a' = 440; in Europe 435. The term is often used to mean *key* or *tonality* as well.

Ragtime: Originally a new style of music for piano originated by African-American composers c. 1895–1900, consisting of three or four related themes in duple (2/4) time, the left hand supplying a steady beat, the right hand working against the beat with syncopated figures. Ragtime was "a craze" during the first fifteen years or so of the twentieth century, and was a deep influence on American popular song, dance styles, language, and culture in general. Like other names that mark the changing styles in popular music, *ragtime* soon lost precise musical meaning, and referred to all sorts of popular tunes of its day.

Range: Referring both to the human voice and to musical instruments, the reach or spread or extent of variation in pitch for which that voice or instrument is capable. Trained voices normally achieve a range of approximately two octaves. Popular Standards generally ask less than that of the singer, generally a maximum of a tenth (octave plus two more notes).

Release: Another term for the "B" section in the AABA pop song format. (*See* bridge.)

Refrain: See *chorus*.

Scat: A vocal technique that parallels the instrumental impro-visations characteristic of jazz; the singer ad-libs syllables and vowel sounds, attached to free-ranging melody and rhythmic figures based on the song at hand, the scat chorus usually de-livered after the singer has first sung the song "straight." Louis Armstrong is generally credited with originating the style, mas-tered by others, including Mel Tormé and Anita O'Day, and especially Ella Fitzgerald, who once made an all-scat recording, "Lullabies of Birdland."

Score: The original and entire draft of all the components of a musical work, including the parts for all orchestral instruments and the vocal line (if any) with lyrics; the musical sound track of a film; also, as a verb, to write or prepare such a work.

Sideman: A member of an orchestra or group, subordinate to the leader.

Song: A short composition for voice, usually accompanied, but composed and arranged in such a way that the accompaniment supports but does not compete with the voice. Unfortunately this ancient term has recently been corrupted, mainly by radio and recording people, to mean *any* short musical selection, words or not, as in "...that song was Count Basie's 'One O'Clock Jump.'" Admittedly, other choices of terms are limited: *piece, selection, tune.* But a *song* must have *words*!

Songwriter: Formerly two words, a writer of songs. It first referred primarily to the author, the writer of lyrics, with the music provided by the composer; now, simply, somebody who writes songs for a living.

Stride: A piano style prominent in jazz through mid-century, characterized by a solidly rhythmic left hand keeping the beat, often using tenths as well as octaves, and the right hand weaving melodic and counter-rhythmic figures over it. A descendant of ragtime, which is a simpler, easier form. Pioneer practitioners included James P. Johnson, his student "Fats" Waller, and Art Tatum.

Swing: A jazz style coming out of the 1920s, gaining currency in the mid-'30s through the popularity of the Big Bands, especially that of Benny Goodman, who became known as "The King of Swing." *Swing* is another of those facile terms in popular music that indicates a time and a social climate with much more accuracy than it does a musical form. The arranging talent and band leaders of the 1920s, mainly Black musicians such as Fletcher and Horace Henderson, Chick Webb, Don Redman, Luis Russell, and others, were responsible for innovative jazz band arrangements of tremendous drive and impetus. The word itself may have been established by the 1932 Duke Ellington record of "It Don't Mean a Thing If It Ain't Got That Swing."

Syncopation: A displacement of the regular metrical accent in music, upsetting the normal pulse; temporary syncopations have been used in music for ages, and have been called "disturbing" or "contradictory." In American popular music *constant* syncopation was first exhibited in ragtime, provided an impelling new zest to piano, band, and vocal music, and led to further complex subdivisions of meter (or beat) in jazz and popular music that are now intrinsic and taken for granted.

Tempo: The rate of speed at which a piece of music is played or sung, from the slowest to the quickest. Traditional Italian labels (still used to some extent in popular music) include *adagio* (comfortably slow), *presto* (fast), and the commonly used *moderato*.

Three: As in *in three*, 3/4 time, waltz time.

Time: A catchall synonym for meter, rhythm, the signature of a piece of music; also, more loosely with a type of music, as in rag*time*, waltz *time*

Tonality: The basic scale or key in which a song is sung or written. The single note or root position of a tonality is known as the *tonic*.

Torch song: A type of love song, the name of which obviously came from "carrying the torch"; therefore a song of lost love and memory.

Trad: Short for *traditional*, referring to various early forms of jazz, mainly the New Orleans and Chicago styles, often to the style known as Dixieland.

Triple meter: Any rhythm or meter divisible by three: 3/4, 6/8, etc. One of two basic meters, the other being duple meter.

Two: As in *in two*, 2/4 or 2/2 time. Marches are generally in two.

Vaudeville: A form of theatrical entertainment that flourished from the late nineteenth century into the mid-1930s, consisting of variety acts unconnected by plot or theme.

Verse: The section preceding the chorus. In folk songs and even Tin Pan Alley songs, the verse functioned as the exposition or preface to the chorus, and was of equal importance—though usually longer and less melodic.

Vocal: As an adjective, vocal music is music to be sung; the vocal, a noun, is that portion or entry by the singer in a given selection.

Waltz: Music in 3/4 time, and the dance commonly done in that meter.

Resources for Curious Listeners

The best resource is still the music itself, but there are other resources available to the curious listener eager to learn more on the subject of Popular Standards.

Books

Hundreds of books have been devoted to the study and celebration of American popular music of the Golden Age, its creators, the culture in which it arose, and its relationships to business and technology. Histories, biographies, and anthologies abound, so the problem is not so much the finding of these materials, but deciding which ones to beg, borrow, or buy. There are, however, two truly indispensible titles: *American Popular Song: The Great Innovators, 1900–1950*, by Alec Wilder (with James T. Maher), and *Lissauer's Encyclopedia of Popular Music in America*, by Robert Lissauer. Wilder is a renowned composer himself; in his book, originally published in 1972, he analyzes hundreds of Popular Standards from his own point of view, reporting his likes and dislikes with candor and charm. The Lissauer book lists alphabetically thousands of popular songs from 1890 to the present, with extra attention to the Popular Standards, and cross-lists the same songs by year and by composer. It's invaluable. Below are a few further suggestions.

American Musical Comedy: From Adonis to Dreamgirls, Gerald Bordman: A first-class survey.

The American Musical Theater, David Ewen: Published over forty years ago, but still one of the best coverages of musicals important to the Popular Standard canon; includes biographical material.

American Singers: 27 Portraits in Song, Whitney Balliett: Essays, many originally in *The New Yorker*, by one of the best-known jazz critics; these are the singers of the Standards, and he honors them.

As Thousands Cheer: The Life of Irving Berlin, Larry S. Bergreen: One of the first biographies of America's greatest songwriter.

Benny Goodman and the Swing Era, James Lincoln Collier: The life and work of the master clarinetist and bandleader; insights into the musical world he inhabited.

Beyond Category: The Life and Genius of Duke Ellington, John Edward Hasse: One of the best of the many books appearing on Ellington as composer, pianist, and bandleader.

The Big Broadcast, Bill Owen and William Hugh Owen: Updated from an earlier 1970s version; everything (and more) you'd want to know about the big hits of network radio, including the musical shows and their use of the Popular Standards.

Big Band Jazz, Albert McCarthy: Hard to find, but a great place to start on the story of the great jazz bands; goes back to the earliest roots, continues in great detail.

Bing Crosby: Pocketful of Dreams—The Early Years, 1903–1940, Gary Giddens: the first volume of a monumental work that is finally bringing renewed attention to the performer who set many standards of performance and *sang* so many Standards.

Broadway Musical Show by Show, Stanley Green: Organized by year, provides a brief synopsis of each show; photographs.

Broadway to Hollywood: The Musical and the Cinema, Robert Matthew-Walker: The crucial crossover of theater to film, vital to the Popular Standard story; well told.

Complete Lyrics of Lorenz Hart, Dorothy Hart and Robert Kimball: That's Larry Hart of course, and in this beautifully made volume his lyrics shine like poetry (no music is included); it's clear why he was, and is, so revered.

Discovering the Great Singers of Classic Pop, Roy Hemming and David Hadju: Biographical sketches with considerable detail, candidly but gently revealed; excellent.

Easy to Remember: The Great American Songwriters and Their Songs for Broadway Shows and Hollywood Musicals, William Zinsser: Delightful personal reminiscences of growing up with the Popular Standards.

Ella Fitzgerald: The First Lady of Song, Katherine S. Krohn: A good biography of a great lady; information on her vast legacy of recorded songs, including *The Song Book* of Popular Standards for which she is so admired.

The Encyclopedia of Jazz, Leonard Feather: *The* reference book on the great players; lots of detail in this classic, originally published in 1960 and updated several times since.

The Gershwin Years, Edward Jablonski with Lawrence D. Stewart: Good material on Gershwin and his times.

The Gershwins, Robert Kimball: George and Ira, in a big book with pictures and artwork, but built on solid research with plenty of lists and dates.

The Great American Broadcast: A Celebration of Radio's Golden Age, Leonard Maltin: The renowned movie authority turns his attention to another business; text and lists.

Harold Arlen: Rhythm, Rainbow, and Blues, Edward Jablonski: A prominent biographer examines one of America's most unusual songwriting masters.

The Hollywood Musical, Jane Feuer: Plenty of background on the films that produced hundreds of Popular Standards.

Irving Berlin: American Troubadour, Edward Jablonski: One of several biographies of Berlin, by a veteran of the trade, who has also written bios of Gershwin and Arlen.

Jerome Kern: His Life in Music, Gerald Martin Bordman: A critical biography of one of the first master composers, creator of dozens of Popular Standards, and a model and mentor for many other composers.

Lady Day: The Many Faces of Billie Holiday, Robert G. O'Mealy: A tribute to Holiday, her art, and her influence on generations of singers to come.

Lena: A Biography of Lena Horne, James S. Hoskins and Katherine Benson: A tribute and a well-researched biography of this great and courageous performer.

Louis Armstrong, Michel Boujut: A foreword by jazz performer and authority Wynton Marsalis; excellent look at the master of jazz trumpet and singing.

Nice Work if You Can Get It, Michael Feinstein: Singer/pianist/author/archivist, Feinstein was Ira Gershwin's secretary for seven years, and an assistant to songwriter Harry Warren in his late years; informal biographical data, combined with the author's personal insights into American music and its Popular Standards. Excellent.

Our Huckleberry Friend: The Life, Times, and Lyrics of Johnny Mercer, Bob Bach, ed. Ginger Mercer: The happy story of one of our greatest wordsmiths; without Mercer the list of Popular Standards would shrink considerably.

The Oxford Companion to Jazz, Bill Kirchner, ed.: A collection of essays on aspects of jazz, also popular music and jazz singers who worked with the Popular Standards.

Pennies from Heaven: The American Popular Music Business in the Twentieth Century, David S. Sanjek: A thorough study of popular music's interplay with radio, recording, unions, business, and government; heavy going but worth it.

The Poets of Tin Pan Alley, Philip Furia: Does for the lyrics of the Popular Standards what Alec Wilder's *American Popular Song* does for the music—a subjective analysis.

Reading Lyrics, Robert Gottlieb and Robert Kimball: The lyrics only of hundreds of songs, mostly Popular Standards, printed like poetry, accompanied by capsule biographies of authors.

Show Tunes, Steven Suskin: Informally written, but with accurate, highly detailed summaries of Broadway show scores.

Spreadin' Rhythm Around, Gene Jones and David A. Jasen: Biographies of talented African-American composers and lyricists of Broadway and Tin Pan Alley; a groundbreaker.

They're Playing Our Song, Max Wilk: Background and off-the-cuff reminiscences as told in personal interviews with the author; great stuff.

Varity Music Cavalcade, Julius Mattfeld: An excellent 1962 compendium (if you can find a copy); major songs listed by year, published by *Variety*, the "bible" of show business.

Why Sinatra Matters, Pete Hamill: The celebrated New York newspaperman writes his take on the life and music of the man who was perhaps America's greatest friend of the Popular Standard canon.

Websites

There are also countless Web sites with detailed information about popular music, jazz, theater, and recordings. Four of the most complete and accessible are listed below, and more are coming on-line every day. There is no shortage of sites set up by technologically sophisticated fans of particular songwriters or performers, as any quick search of "Cole Porter" or "Billie Holiday" will reveal. So look around.

The All Movie Guide (www.allmovie.com): A film database helpful in tracking down all kinds of information on the movie musicals that spawned so many Popular Standards.

The All Music Guide (www.allmusic.com): A continuously updated music database with biographies, album listings, reviews, im-

ages, and more—including plenty on the creaters and interpreters of the Popular Standards.

The Internet Movie Database (www.imdb.com)

Musicals.Net (www.musicals.net): A great site to dig into the history of the Broadway musical, the principal source of the Popular Standards.

Index